WHERE LOSERS LIVE, HEROES DIE

Gary Helzer

Copyright © 2025 **Gary Helzer**

All rights reserved. No part of this publication may be reproduced, distributed, or transmitted in any form or by any means, including photocopying, recording, or other electronic or mechanical methods, without the prior written permission of the publisher, except in the case of brief quotations embodied in critical reviews and certain other noncommercial uses permitted by copyright law. For permission requests, write to the publisher, addressed "Attention: Book Rights and Permission," at the address below.

Published in the United States of America

ISBN 978-1-958518-15-1 (SC)
ISBN 978-1-958518-16-8 (Ebook)

Library of Congress Control Number: 2025904037

Gary Helzer
1645 Trainer Way,
Reno, NV 89512
www.stellarliterary.com

Ordering Information and Rights Permission:

Quantity sales. Special discounts might be available on quantity purchases by corporations, associations, and others. For details, contact the publisher at the address above.

For Book Rights Adaptation and other Rights Permission. Call us at toll-free 1-888-945-8513 or send us an email at admin@stellarliterary.com.

Contents

Chapter 1: Last Big Viet Cong Battle 1
Chapter 2: Getting out of the Army and coming Home 12
Chapter 3: Grasshoppers, gophers, and bribery to go to the Bahamas 20
Chapter 4: Hans tells his parents he's going to the Bahamas. 31
Chapter 5: Miami: The Good, Beautiful, Bad, and Ugly 38
Chapter 6: Gambling Fever 45
Chapter 7: The Lady Hans Can't Have. 53
Chapter 8: A Flashback to Vietnam 62
Chapter 9: Ship Sinks 72
Chapter 10: U.S. National Guard Armory Rip-Off 78
Chapter 11: Hans Gets Thrown in Jail 89
Chapter 12: Hans breaks out of the Jail 97
Chapter 13: Stealing Another Car and Van 106
Chapter 14: Hans Boards the Ship 115
Chapter 15: Sneaking Pete and the Guys onto the Pier 123
Chapter 16: Getting Pete and the Guys out of the Boxes 132
Chapter 17: The Hijack 139
Chapter 18: Tying up Loose Ends 149
Chapter 19: Mr. Bacco Learns That Pete's Dead 160
Chapter 20: Hans Meets Joannie 167
Chapter 21: Hans and Mrs. Bacco get together 175
Chapter 22: Blind Date 193
Chapter 23: Car Bomb 210
Chapter 24: Car Chase, Explosions at the Building site. 220
Chapter 25: Lagno put's a hit out on Hans. 235
Chapter 26: Trashing Lagno's Casino with the Car 241

Chapter 1

Last Big Viet Cong Battle

    VIETNAM WAR: Around the year 1969, two hours before dawn, Sarge and Hans are carefully walking along a path through the jungle, looking all around. The moon is full, and the sky is clear and full of stars. They can see everything. No breeze; the jungle is humid. They keep slapping their faces and necks; the mosquitoes are eating them for breakfast. Sarge complains in a low voice, "Damn these mosquitoes. I kill more of them than I do the V.C."

    Sergeant Pete Saran is a big man, over six feet tall, with husky, broad shoulders. He has short dark hair that's slowly turning gray. He's somewhere in his late forties. He's a full-blooded Greek and looks it, too, especially when he is mad. He can be an asshole at times. He's the man who can keep soldiers tough and wanting to push onward. Hans doesn't know what they would do without Sarge.

    Hans is twenty-four years old, five feet six inches tall and heavyset, with broad shoulders, a light complexion, blue eyes, and light blond hair that has been sun-bleached almost white. He's half German and half Norwegian. His name is Hans Metzger, nicknamed Cowboy.

    They get to an enemy ammunition depot inside a manmade cave in the hills, just north of an enemy village. There's an open space about fifty feet long and forty feet wide right in front of the cave's entrance and a gravel road that leads toward the village. Sarge and Hans are just inside the jungle near the clearing and staying quiet. The cave entrance is open and dark. Two V.C. guards, fully armed with rifles and ammunition and engaged in conversation, are pacing back and forth just outside the cave entrance.

Sarge and Hans are waiting for U.S. troops to raid the V.C. village as a distraction for them to get into the cave and blow it up. The silence is suddenly shattered by the crack of gunfire from the village, and explosions shake the trees and light up the night sky.

One of the V.C. guards is on a radio, and the other runs into the cave and starts yelling. He comes back out, and he and the other guard race down the road toward the village. More V.C. soldiers pour out of the cave, armed with rifles and ammunition, and set off toward the village.

Hans gets on the radio and calls, "Alfa two to alfa one. Over."

A voice says, "Alfa one. Over."

"You're getting about fifty V.C. from the cave coming your way. Over."

"Thanks, cowboy. We'll be watching for them. Out."

Sarge and Hans slowly make their way into the cave. Turning on their flashlights, they creep in, scanning the shadows for any booby traps or anyone who might have been left behind.

The cave is about a hundred feet wide, a hundred and fifty feet long, and eight feet high. Vertical bamboo beams run up to the ceiling, connected by horizontal beams on top, and it is a sauna in there.

Sarge goes left. Hans goes right. They creep down rows of C-4 plastic explosives, handguns, rifles, ammunition, grenades, and bombs.

Hans gets to the end of a row and hears a groan and a thud behind him. He turns around; a V.C.'s body is lying face down on the dirt floor with a knife in his back. Sarge is standing over him with a grin on his face. He reaches down and pulls the knife out of the dead man's back. Hans grins back at him, but before he can say anything, Sarge puts his finger in front of his mouth and goes, "Shh." Then he puts his right hand up to his ear as if to listen and points toward the back of the cave. Sarge and Hans hear voices coming from the back. Sarge motions for Hans to go up the end of the rows to the back. Hans nods and silently pads forward. Sarge goes up the other side.

There are five V.C. sitting at a table, playing a game. Candles provide the only light. There are no explosives against the back wall of the cave. There's an entrance to a tunnel just to the left, by the table.

Hans looks over at Sarge, and he gives Hans a thumbs up. They come out from behind the boxes of C-4 and start shooting. They get four of them.

Sarge blurts out, "One went into the tunnel. I'll get him." Hans yells, "Let him go! There might be booby traps in there. I'll get a couple of grenades and throw them into the tunnel."

Instead of using his own grenades, he pries open one of the boxes with his knife blade, grabs two of them, runs over to the tunnel entrance, pulls the pins, and throws them in.

Hans yells, "Let's get the hell out of here." They race out of the cave. The grenades explode.

When the dust settles, they head back in, flashing the flashlights around, and go all the way to the back. The entrance to the tunnel is now completely blocked.

There's some detonator cord, a plunger box, blasting caps, and tape at the end of the table.

"Let's get this done." Sarge demands." Using candles for light, they tape some of the C-4 at the bases of the vertical beams and stick blasting caps and cords into them, moving some of the boxes around to make sure the whole cave blows up. Then they stick caps and cords into the plastic explosives that are still in the boxes. Hans unrolls the cords out of the cave and to a safe place in the jungle. Then he hooks the cords to the detonator box and pushes the plunger down.

The cave explodes with an earth-shattering rumble and collapses within seconds. Nothing is left of the ammunition depot.

Hans gets on the radio and calls, "Alfa two to alfa one."

A voice says, "Alfa one, over."

"The ammunition depot mission is complete. Get the hell out of there now. Over."

"Thanks, Cowboy. Out."

Sarge and Hans are heading east. The rest of the troops, and some choppers, should be waiting about two miles from here. They walk about a mile and a half. The sun is just coming up, and the jungle's hot. It's now too hot for the mosquitoes. They've stopped biting.

They head up a hill that runs in a north-south direction. As they get to the top, Sarge demands, "Let's turn south instead of crossing on down to the other side because, in the end, it drops down to a gravel road that leads us to the choppers."

Hans looks to the left, down the side of the hill.

He comments, "Hey, Sarge, look down at the bottom of the hill and to the east. The land is flat and clear, with no jungle for about half a mile wide and two miles long. It looks like it had been farmed at one time because it's full of dried rice paddies that have been left unattended. Looks like there's been nobody there for a long time because in amongst the paddies are some abandoned huts and ruins."

Sarge asks, "What's that in the field?

Hans replies, "It looks like a bunch of rocks and large boulders. They farmed around them instead of trying to move them."

Sarge nods, "Makes sense to me."

Hans's looking to the right and down the hillside. The jungle isn't very thick. The road winds around the base of the hill, and some men are walking. It's the troops.

Pointing to them, Hans quickly says, "There are our guys down there on the road."

Sarge says seriously, "It looks like they got hit hard. Something must have gone wrong. Seventeen are walking, and four are on stretchers. Colonel James and Lieutenant Simpson aren't among those who are walking. They must be either wounded or dead."

Sarge commands, "Let's get down the road and join them. They could use a little help carrying those stretchers." Sarge and Hans start down the south end of the hill to meet the rest of the troops as they come around the bend.

Suddenly Sarge stops. He doesn't say a thing but points straight ahead, down toward the road.

Just inside the jungle, on both sides of the road, enemy soldiers are crouching low in the bushes. The Troops below don't know they're waiting for them, but from up here, Sarge and Hans can make out the tops of their helmets and the barrels of their rifles when they move around.

Sarge bluntly says, "Shit! The troops are going to walk right into an ambush!" He demands, "Get on the radio and warn them."

Hans calls, "Alfa two to alfa one." No answer.

He calls again, "Alfa two to alfa one." Still no answer.

"I can't get through to them. Are we close enough to hit some of them? The noise alone will be enough to warn the troops. It doesn't look like too big of a force down there, and they don't know we're up here. We can catch them totally by surprise. There's a good chance of getting all of them before they know what hit them."

Sarge replies, "We're close enough. Cowboy, you're a better shot than I am with long-range. You get the ones on the other side of the road! I'll get the ones on this side. Let's give them hell." "Okay, let's get them."

They aim and start shooting. Hans empty's his magazine and quickly pulls it out of his rifle. He reloads and starts shooting again. V.C. soldiers are falling all over the place.

Hans blurts, "Damn it, a twenty-round magazine doesn't last long." He reloads again. Sarge does the same.

Hans is ready to start shooting when Sarge quickly says, "Wait a minute. I think we got them all. No one's moving around anymore, and I don't hear anything." They look down at where they have been shooting. There are bodies lying all over the place.

Sighing with relief, Sarge says, "We did it, Cowboy, we got every damn one of them." Then he asks, "Are the troops still on the road?" Looking down the hill to the right, Hans replies, "No, not anybody. They must have heard us shooting and hiding in the jungle." They stand there for a minute, watching and listening. They want to make sure it's safe to move on.

Suddenly a bullet grazes Hans's helmet. They duck down low in the bushes. Bullets slam into the earth all around them.

Hans carefully looks and quickly indicates, "It looks like the whole V.C. army is on top of the hill on the other side of the road. They're shooting at us and running down the hill toward us."

Hans ducks low again and blurts out, "They must think we're the whole damn division up here."

Sarge demands, "Let's get the hell out of here and make a run for that bunch of boulders!"

They turn to the left and race down the hill through the dry rice paddies. Even though it's dry, the rice crop's high. They crouch low and run as fast as they can. Sarge can run a lot faster than Hans. He makes it into the boulders first. Just before Hans gets there, he stumbles forward into the boulders.

He shouts, "I'm hit. He feels pain in his left leg. A bullet grazed it just below the knee." He leans his rifle against a boulder, takes his knife, and cuts the pant leg open down to the boot. It's not bad, but it took a chunk of skin off, and it sure is bleeding. He gets a handkerchief out of his left back pocket and wraps it around the wound to stop the bleeding.

Looking at Hans's leg, Sarge asks, "Are you okay? Can you walk?"

Hans gets to his feet and stays low behind the boulder. Putting some weight on his leg to test it, he replies, "It hurts a little, but I'll be all right."

He picks up his rifle and climbs farther up between the boulders, limping as he goes. They slowly look over the top of one of the boulders, back in the direction they just came from. The enemy soldiers are moving toward them. They're crouching low as they make their way through the rice paddies.

Sarge says, "They're still far enough away from us that we can head out of here. Once we get to the jungle, we'll have a damn good chance of making it to where those choppers are waiting for us. Can you run with that bum leg?"

"You're damn right I can. Let's go."

They start out from the boulder, and shots and bullets immediately hit all around them.

Sarge and Hans duck back behind the boulders and get low. They peek over the top of one. More V.C. soldiers are pouring out of the jungle from the east and into the rice paddies.

Hans yells, "We're surrounded. There is no way out."

They raise their rifles, aim, and start shooting. They hit several of them, but they keep coming. Hans turns and leans against another boulder.

The enemy soldiers from behind them are moving in fast.

Hans starts shooting again. Then, from out of nowhere, a couple of huge explosions blow open the rice paddies, making massive craters and tossing V.C. soldiers up in the air and into pieces.

Then the explosions go off again behind them. Then there's a loud roar. Looking up into the sky, a U.S. Navy A-4 jet's climbing straight up just as fast as he can go. Over into the sky to the right, another jet's diving straight down over the paddies. He's firing his twenty-millimeter guns. He levels off and drops two bombs. Then he turns straight up and hauls ass. As the bombs explode, more planes swoop down. They bomb some of the huts, which explode in massive fireballs. There must have been some ammunition hidden in them, which is probably why the jets are bombing this place.

Sarge and Hans look at each other, not saying anything, and smile.

Then some F-8s shoot off some missiles. They keep on coming.

They damn near have all the rice paddies on fire.

One of them flies over low, close enough that Hans can read the name of the aircraft carrier he's from, the USS Bonhomme Richard.

The planes streak away.

Hans blurts out, "I'll be damned. Miracles do happen. Thank God for the U.S. Navy."

The fire is almost all around them. There's a gap big enough to get past, but the flames are closing in fast. They don't have much time.

Hans shouts, "Sarge, let's get the hell out of here!"

Sarge and Hans start running, Hans, with a slight limp, across the field, heading east toward the jungle.

Hans groans because he can feel the flames nipping at his heels; he's close that the heat alone seems like it could burn him to a crisp. If they run as fast as they can, they might make it in time.

The gap closes behind them just as they get to the jungle, and they keep running. They're not in the clear yet, though; the wind is pushing the fire their way. Hans is feeling the heat from the fire blowing down his neck and back, and the smell of the smoke is getting stronger. Breathing hard, growing tired, and slowing down, they push themselves to keep going.

They hear something besides the fire popping: a motor running. Ahead, the trees thin out a little. There are the choppers!

Sarge and Hans pick up the pace and run straight out of the jungle and into the clearing. Suddenly Hans yells, "Snake." He stops.

About five feet in front of him is a big King Cobra about eighteen feet long, ready to strike him. Trying not to move too fast, Hans slowly points the rifle and shoots it.

Sarge yells, "More snakes." He starts shooting them. The crew in the chopper starts shooting the snakes. They are waving and yelling at them. "Come on, you guys." As the crew shoots the snakes, they run up to the chopper. Two crewmen reach down and help Sarge and Hans in because they're so exhausted from running that they can't climb in by themselves.

After they're in and sitting down. Sarge remarks, The snakes are trying to get away from the fire just like us, and that's why there's so damn many of them.

The pilot yells, "The fire is getting too close. Better get this thing out of here." He lifts the chopper up off the ground.

Sarge looks out; the rest of the troops are running up from the road.

"Sit this thing back down," he yells. "There's the rest of the troops,"

One of the crewmen says, "There are four more choppers down there. Don't worry, they'll get them."

The chopper turns, and they lose sight of the troops. The chopper stays up in the air and hovers over the area, waiting for the others to load up. Three more choppers get into the air.

As the last one starts to rise, a gust of wind blows a burning tree branch onto it. It catches fire, and just like that, it explodes. No one gets out alive.

The pilot yells, "Dammit, all to hell! Let's get out of here." He turns and heads up and out. One of the crewmen starts cleaning Han's wound.

The chopper lands at the base. It's built out of sandbags. The pilot turns off the engine.

Sarge and Hans climb down and look around for the other choppers.

As the troops climb out of the choppers. They all come over to Sarge and Hans.

One of them states, "Colonel James and Lieutenant Simpson are dead. We lost five men altogether."

Sarge asks, "What about the chopper that exploded?"

"Just the crew got killed. We put the dead bodies in that one."

Sarge quietly says, "Thanks, you all did a good job. You're all dismissed." The troops all leave.

Hans suggests, "Let's go have a beer."

"That sounds good. Let's go."

They walk into the barracks with the others. They have their own little bar.

Sarge and Hans each get a beer and take a big sip. Some of the other troops are getting a poker game going. Some sit on their beds and write letters.

Over the voices of the troops talking, Sarge and Hans hear someone yell, "Corporal Metzger and Sergeant Saran." The corporal from the office comes over to them and hands them each a large brown envelope.

He explains, "Your orders came in. you're both going home. Get your bags packed. You have ten minutes before the chopper leaves."

They yell, "Yea!"

They get their bags packed and are on their way.

About an hour later, they land in Da Nang and take their bags to the barracks.

Sarge and Hans walk into the Enlisted Men's Club. It's a big place and looks very hazy. They can smell cigarette smoke. There is a bar in the back. The room has a lot of tables with a few other soldiers sitting at them.

Sarge points to an empty table to their right and commands, "Take that one, Cowboy, and I will get us some beer."

Hans sits down and gets to thinking that it's about to be over. He's finally getting out of the army. He starts feeling a little sad about some of the friends he lost over the past three years. Sarge comes with a pitcher of beer and two mugs and sets them down on the table. Hans takes the pitcher and pours beer into the mugs.

Sarge notices the sad look on Hans's face and asks, "Is something wrong, Cowboy?"

Hans sighs, "Oh, I'm glad to be getting out of the army. But I keep thinking about some of the friends we made in the past three years, and they're not here. They're all dead; I feel guilty for being alive. I should be dead. They're more of a hero than I am. What good did all this do me? He stops feeling sad and starts getting mad."

"I joined the army, and they put an M-Sixteen rifle in my hands and shipped me off to Vietnam. I learned how to shoot people and get shot at. The schools I put in for all got turned down. As a matter of fact, the more I sit here talking about it, the madder I get. I'm no better off now than before I joined the army."

Sarge takes a puff from his cigarette and a drink from his beer and replies, "I miss those guys also. They were good friends and soldiers. We'll have to go on living without them. You'd better suck it up, move on, and stop feeling sorry for yourself."

"You're right, Sarge, Hans sighs, "I'll suck it up and move on." They changed the subject and had one more pitcher with something to eat.

Hans asks Sarge, "Why are you getting out of the army? You've been in over ten years. You over halfway to retirement."

Sarge replies, "Because all we are here are hired killers. They put a uniform on us and a gun in our hands. Then, they tell us to go fight for the cause. They just forgot to tell us what the cause is. Because big companies can get rich from us, that's why,"

Hans takes a nice hot shower in the barracks and goes straight to bed. He can't fall right to sleep thinking about getting home and helping his Dad on the farm or going off some place on his own.

Sarge and Hans are back in the states at Fort Ord, California.

It takes eight mostly cloudy and a few sunny days to get through separations, and they make it through seven of those days without incident.

On the evening of the seventh day, Hans is getting his uniform ready for the next day when Sarge comes up to him and suggests, "Cowboy, let's go over to the E. M. Club and have a few beers, and I have something I want to talk over with you."

"Okay. Let me get this stuff put away, and I'll be right with you."

Chapter 2

Getting out of the Army and coming Home

The sun's setting. They walk over to the EM Club and sit down at a table. The bartender comes over and takes their order. Sarge pulls out a cigarette and lights it.

He asks, "Well, do you have any definite plans for the future now that you're getting out of the army?"

Hans replies. "You're damn right, I do. I'm going to do what I should have done before joining this thing. I'm going back home to Idaho and helping Dad run the farm."

The bartender brings them a pitcher of beer and two ice-cold mugs, and Sarge pays for them.

Taking a puff from his cigarette, Sarge remarks, "I didn't think you liked farming all that well because the schools you put in for didn't have anything to do with farming."

Taking a drink of his beer, Hans explains, "My dad has worked his ass off most of his adult life just to pay for that farm and make a living for mom and me. Dad has been talking about building a new house for mom ever since I can remember. Well, he's still talking about it, but he hasn't been able to do anything about it. I don't mind farming if you can do something with it instead of just existing. So, I listened to all the bullshit that comes on television and radio about joining the army, learning a trade, getting a skill, and having a future. I wouldn't take back my experience in the army, but what a waste."

Sarge can sense that he's starting to get mad.

"Okay, cool down now, Cowboy," says Sarge. "Don't go getting all bent out of shape again. I know just how you feel. But it's not the end of the world. Now, you don't have to go back to farming if you don't want to. You can come and work with me. You will make much more money with me than you will ever make farming."

Sarge takes a puff from his cigarette, and they both take a drink of beer.

"Sarge Continues. "A good friend of mine will be here in a short while. His name is Tony Bacco. We served together in Vietnam. His father is building a casino in the Bahamas. Tony will be a casino manager, and I will be his assistant manager."

There's a gleam in Sarge's eyes. Hans had never seen him this excited before. It's a surprise that he would even think of anything like this because he doesn't gamble. At least Hans has never seen him gambling. Every time some of the guys got a poker game going, Sarge would refuse to play. Then Hans gets tense about something.

He asks, "Does the syndicate run those gambling casinos? You're not getting mixed up in anything like that, are you?"

Sarge starts to say something but stops. He looks over at the door.

"Here's Tony now." He waves him over.

The man coming towards them is a little shorter than Sarge. He has short dark brown, almost black hair. He looks around thirty-five years old and is thin with solid-looking shoulders. He's wearing a light brown suit.

Smiling, he says, "Pete, it's damn good to see you again." He reaches out to shake Sarge's hand.

Sarge gets up from the table, shakes his hand, and replies with a big grin, "It's about time you got here."

Hans, get up from the table.

Tony looks over at him and says, "You must be Cowboy. I sure have heard a lot about you."

Hans just smiles and shakes hands with him.

Tony goes to the bar, comes back with another pitcher of beer with a mug, and sits down.

Sounding more excited than ever, Sarge says to Tony, "I have been explaining to Cowboy a little bit about the casino."

"Good," replies Tony. "From what I hear about you, Cowboy, we can sure use you. What do you think about it, anyway?"

"Well, this is all coming at me kind of fast. I really don't know what to think. Just where do I fit into all of this?"

Sarge explains, "Cowboy, you will be the head of the security department, and you will be Tony's and my personal bodyguard."

He asks, "Is the security something like the police?"

Sarge replies, "Yes, but the police come in after the crime. Before the crime, security comes in and stops it."

Feeling a little disgusted with the idea, Hans asks, "You mean I might have to shoot people? Dammit, Sarge, I quit shooting at people over in Vietnam."

"Don't worry about that," Tony quickly replies. "People come to the casino to have fun and try to win some money. With security around, they feel safe. There's a ninety-nine percent chance that you or your men will never have to use a gun. They're a lot like traffic directors, directing people to the restaurant, restrooms, and so on. They'll check young people's identification to ensure they are at least twenty-one years old. Throwing a few loudmouth drunks out and be watching for slot and card cheats."

Hans doesn't say anything. Finishing his beer, he pulls some money out of his pocket and sets it on the table.

Getting up out of his chair, he suggests, "Here! One of you guys! Go and get us another pitcher while I take a piss and think about this more."

Hans goes to the restroom. While in there, he starts thinking. This doesn't sound all that bad. A lot of the neighbors up in Idaho talked to Dad about going to places like Las Vegas or Reno. They all acted like they had a good time. Whenever somebody went to Nevada, Dad always wished them good luck.

He never says anything bad about those places.

Hans has heard that casinos are terrible places to go to, although the only person who told him that was his mom. I guess because she is so religious. Then, of course, Dad always sides with Mom when she talks about things like that.

Well, he'll just tell those guys that he needs more time to think about it and that he had better go back to Idaho first. Hans returns to the table, sits down, and tells them his decision.

Leaning back in his chair, Tony looks over at him and replies, "That's fine. Take all the time you want because it will be several months before the casino will be built and ready to open."

Sarge agrees. "You go ahead and go back to your home. I have your home address and phone number. I'll keep in touch.

After that, Sarge and Tony change the subject and start talking about their army days together. Listening to them is beginning to bore Hans, so he finishes his beer and says, "I'm getting tired. I'm going to turn in for the night."

The next day's sunny, with some clouds and no breeze. Sarge gets his discharge papers, and Hans gets his separation papers.

They return to the barracks, get their gear, and walk about a block to a taxicab zone, where they set their gear down on the sidewalk while waiting for a taxi.

Sarge lights up a cigarette and asks, "Cowboy, are you going to fly home?"

He replies, "Yes, I am."

About this time, a taxicab pulls up. Hans helps Sarge put his gear in the cab, and they shake hands.

Sarge smiles at him and states, "Cowboy, be careful going home, and good luck. I will keep in touch with you now and then."

"Okay, Sarge. Good luck to you also, and be careful down there."

As the cab pulls away, a lump comes into Hans's throat. Sarge and he have gone through a lot together over the last three years.

Now it is all over, just like that. They're both going their separate ways.

A taxi pulls up. The cab driver helps Hans with his gear.

He happily says, "Take me to the airport. I just got out of the army today.

The cab driver replies, "That's good."

When he gets to the airport, Hans goes in and gets his plane ticket, and checks in his gear.

At the gate, Hans gets on the plane. From here, he flies to Lewiston, Idaho.

When the plane lands in Lewiston, the sky's clear and sunny. He gets a taxicab and goes downtown to catch a bus.

The cab stops at the bus station, and there's a group of hippies. The men all have long hair. They're all walking around holding signs and protesting the Vietnam war.

The cab driver states, "Just ignore them. They have nothing better to do.

Hans laughs and replies, "People will do anything for some attention."

He pays the cab driver and heads for the bus station door.

One of the protesters, a man, the whites of his eyes red, acts like he is high on something and shouts, "Hey, man. Army guy. Watch this, man; I'm burning my draft card. Hey man, that's what I think about Vietnam. Do you like killing and getting shot at? Is that why you wear that uniform?" He laughs. "Hey, man. Did I piss you off?"

Hans completely ignores him and keeps going.

He runs up behind Hans, grabs his arm, and blurts out, "Hey man, you answer me when I talk to you. You son of a bitch man."

Hans stops, drops his gear on the ground, and faces him, still not saying anything. He just glares at him.

The protester glares back at Hans, makes a fist with his right hand, and takes a swing at him. Hans ducks and hits him three times in the stomach, then Hans hits him in the face. He falls to his knees.

Hans broke his nose, and it's bleeding.

He looks over at the others and asks, "Any others that are too chicken shit to fight for your country want to fight this tough army guy?" Most of them are women. They and the men just stand there glaring, and some of the men are flipping Hans the bird.

Hans picks up his gear and goes to the bus station, and no one follows him.

The next thing he knows, he's on the bus and going through seventy-three miles of beautiful pine tree-covered Idaho mountains. Hans can smell the pine trees as the bus goes to Grangeville, Idaho. Just before he gets to Grangeville, the mountains end, and a big farming valley comes into view. He's almost home. In town, he takes his gear and puts them in a locker.

Hans has time. He looks around in some of the car lots. He saved up some money. He going to find him a nice car or pickup and buy it.

Hans goes through two lots.

On the third lot, a car salesman comes up to him and asks, "May I help with something, Soldier?"

Hans replies, "I kind of like this blue ford pickup over here. If it doesn't cost too much, that is."

He gives him a quote.

Hans remarks, "If you lower the price by four hundred dollars, I can pay you cash for it. I can't pay any more than that."

The salesman doesn't say anything for a bit.

He asks, "Do you have the cash money on you now?"

Hans replies, "Yes, I have the money."

He says, "Okay, it's a deal."

He pays for the pickup. They shake hands.

He drives to the bus station, gets his gear out of the locker, and drives home.

Around 6:50 p.m., Hans pulls into the driveway and sighs. He is finally home.

Hans stops the pickup, gets out, and walks up onto the porch. He is looking through the window in the kitchen door. Mom and Dad are eating supper.

They both still look about the same as when he left.

Mom's about as tall as he is, with blond hair turning grey. She's heavy set and wearing a house dress as always. She's Norwegian.

Dad's a little taller than Mom, with dark brown hair with a bald spot on the top of his head. He's wearing a gray shirt with denim overalls, as always. He's German.

Not making a sound, Hans opens the door, walks in, and sets his gear down on the floor.

Dad looks up. His eyes get big, and a huge grin comes over his face,

He kind of stammers with surprise, "Ah, ah, h-hello there."

When Mom sees Hans. She leaps up, shrieking, "Hans!" She gives him a big hug and a kiss.

Dad gets up and comes over. He shakes his hand and says, "Welcome home, Son."

"Thanks, Dad. It's sure good to be home."

Mom asks, "Have you eaten supper?"

He looks at the steaks, boiled potatoes, and gravy on the table. "No, I haven't."

Mom reaches up in the cupboard and gets down a plate and a glass. As she puts them on the table, she says, "If there's not enough food here on the table, I will find something more around here to eat."

"Oh, don't go to any trouble, Mom."

While they're eating, Dad asks, "How did you get home, Hans?

Hans replies, "I flew To Lewiston and took a bus to Grangeville. In town, I bought a pickup truck. It's two years old.

After supper, Hans takes them out and shows them the pickup. Then he takes them for a ride. They get back home, and Dad suggests parking it in the empty part of the implement shed. He pulls it into the shed, and they go back into the house.

Hans picks up his gear and takes it into his room.

The next morning, Hans gets up and looks through his closet and dresser drawers for some of his civilian clothes. He finds his Levi's, a black T-shirt, and roughout Western boots. As he dresses, he can hear Mom in the kitchen, getting breakfast ready.

While they're eating breakfast, Dad asks, "Well, son, are you ready to go back to work?"

Hans grins and says, "I'd rather farm than be sitting in a foxhole getting shot at.

After breakfast, Dad puts his straw hat on, and then he goes out, gets in the pickup, and drives off to irrigate. Hans puts his western straw hat on and goes outside. It's sunny and hot, with a breeze this morning. The first cutting of hay is already raked and ready to bale. Hans gets the International Harvester Model M Farmall tractor and hooks up the hay baler.

Hans bales just about all the hay and has about three more rows to do when suddenly the field gets muddy and soft. The tractor's right rear tire starts spinning and digs deep into the mud.

"Damn!" Han is stuck. This field is supposed to be dry. He shuts off the tractor, climbs down, shuts the baler down, and walks over to the edge of the field, through the mud to the irrigation ditch. Then he follows the ditch bank road to the south. The bank is high and dry until he gets to the end. He sees just what happened.

Chapter 3

Grasshoppers, gophers, and bribery to go to the Bahamas

The gophers dug through the ditch bank so much that when Dad turned on the water in the ditch this morning, some of the banks washed out into the field. A dead gopher is lying in the mud where it drowned when the water washed through. Hans looks in the ditch; the water is low and not running anymore. He turns around and looks back up the ditch bank to the other end of the field. There's Dad at the head gate. He's just shut the water off.

Hans waves and yells, "Dad!" He doesn't hear or look his way, so he starts running up the ditch bank to catch him before he drives off. While running, there are several fresh gopher mounds along the ditch bank road. About halfway up, Hans yells again. This time, he is getting his dad's attention and waving to him to come here.

Hans stops and waits for him. Dad looks over to where the tractor and baler are sitting. He notices that the tractor's leaning on one side.

When he gets close enough to hear him, he says, "Looks like you have a flat tire."

"Flat tire, hell! I'm stuck!"

Looking puzzled, his dad asks, "Stuck?'

Hans explains as they walk toward the tractor, "The gophers are raising hell with the ditch bank road."

When Dad looks at what's happening, he snaps, "Damn it all to hell! First, the grasshoppers take over, and now the gophers. What's going to happen next?"

Hans looks over at Dad but says nothing. Something must really be bothering him. Before, he always had the attitude that things like this happen, and a person just needs to stop what he is doing and go fix them.

What does he mean, "the grasshoppers take over"? He's so upset that Hans probably better not ask him about them now. Disgusted and upset, Dad and Hans turn and head back to the pickup.

Dad suggests, "Hans, you better leave the tractor and baler there until the ground gets dry, or you will tear things up worse."

"Okay," Hans replies." Then he asks, "Do you want me to go to the shop and get some gopher traps to set out here?"

"That's a good idea. I will drive you back to the shop to get the traps."

In the shop, Hans finds some traps lying around. He throws them and a shovel in the back of his pickup and goes back out to set gopher traps for the rest of the day.

During supper that evening, Dad's still a little uneasy. Nobody talks much, not even Mom.

The next day after breakfast, Hans walks outside to another sunny, hot, windless day.

Hans gets in his pickup and goes to reset the gopher traps farther up on the ditch bank. He drives over to check if the ground is dry enough to drive the tractor out. It's not quite dry enough yet.

Hans looks at the bald back tires. He unhooks the baler and backs the pickup to the tractor, as close as he can get where it's dry. Taking a chain hanging on the tractor, he hooks one end up to the front of the tractor and hooks the other end to the back of the pickup. He puts the tractor gear in neutral. He then gets in the pickup, puts it in low gear, and pulls the tractor out of the hole and onto dry ground. He unhooks the chain from the pickup and tractor and hangs it back on the tractor. He drives the pickup to the implement shed, walks back to the field, and drives the tractor to the shop.

Hans jacks up the rear axles, place wooden blocks under them, takes the tires off, loads them in the bed of his pickup, and heads for town.

He drives up in front of the tire shop, stops, and goes in.

Slim Nielsen is still running the place. Hans walks over to him and says, "Hi, Slim," interrupting him as he changes a tire.

Slim looks up, grins, and replies, "Hello there, hero. Welcome home."

He's tall and very slim. He's also unshaven and dirty from working.

He reaches out and shakes hands with Hans. "What cha up to, Hans?"

"I need some tractor tires for Dad's tractor." He takes him out and shows him the tires.

Slim says, "Okay, I can get them for you for three hundred dollars. They will be ready for you late tomorrow afternoon."

"Okay, Slim. You can put that on Dad's charge account."

Looking almost embarrassed, Slim asks, "Did your dad send you here to get the tires?"

Kind of puzzled, Hans replies, "No, why?"

"I can't charge anything to your dad anymore. He owes me over one thousand dollars that he hasn't been able to pay for the last two years."

Getting a little mad, Hans blurts out, "Bullshit. Dad has always been able to pay his bills."

"Didn't you know about the grasshoppers getting most of the farmers' crops the last two years? The grasshoppers almost wiped your dad out."

So that's why Dad's so mad about the ditch bank washing out and mentioning the word "grasshoppers."

Mom never wrote a word about it in her letters when Hans was overseas. Guess they didn't want him to worry.

Slim looks at Hans sadly and politely say, "Hans, I am sorry, but I have a business to run, too."

Hans reaches into his hip pocket and takes out his wallet. He has six hundred dollars of his mustering-out pay left. Pulling out three hundred dollars and handing it to Slim and politely says, "Here, go ahead and get the tires."

They pulled the tires off the bed of the pickup and put them in his shop.

Hans gets home and parks the pickup in the implement shed. He goes into the shop and gets a beer out of the refrigerator; Dad has it there. He opens it and takes a drink.

Dad walks into the shop and comments, "You took the tires off the tractor."

Hans replies, "I took them into Slims Nielsen Tire shop and bought new ones. They'll be ready tomorrow afternoon."

"Want a beer?"

"Okay, I can take a break."

Hans gets him a beer, and they sit down on a couple of stools, Dad made from old tractor seats.

"I know about the grasshoppers, and I know you owe Slim money."

He just looks at Hans, not saying anything.

Hans blurts out, "I'm home now. Tell me what's going on around here. I'll do the best I can to help."

Dad coughs a little and then starts to explain. "Son, we owe the company that sprayed the grasshoppers. We owe hired help. We owe implement dealers for machinery and parts, and there's more. We're fifteen thousand dollars in debt."

"Can you sell some of the lands? That will help some."

"I have forty acres up for sale now. There are a lot of people who want to buy but don't have any money and can't get a loan.

"Mrs. Blake. That fat bitch wants to buy my whole place, and she has lots of money. But she doesn't want to pay what the farm's worth. She buys a lot of the farmers' mortgages in the valley. The grasshoppers put most people so far in debt that they can't make their mortgage payments. Mrs. Blake has foreclosed on their farms. I don't think she could have set this grasshopper thing up, but it wouldn't surprise me if she did. It just worked out in her favor.

"Thank God I got the farm paid off before she could buy my mortgage.

"Stay the hell away from her. She's a crooked son-of-a-bitch, Hans. She wants to own and control the whole valley."

Damn. That's the first time Hans heard Dad swear the way he did.

"What about taxes?"

"All the taxes are paid,"

Dad didn't say anymore.

Hans remarks, "I had to be over in Vietnam getting chased out of rice patties by the V.C. instead of being here to help."

Dad replies, "It wouldn't matter if you were here or not. You couldn't have stopped the grasshoppers any more than I could. Don't blame yourself for not being here to help, Hans. I'll tell Mom you know about the grasshoppers and the money we owe."

Dad gets up, goes out, gets in his pickup, and leaves. Hans sits there for a while, thinking. That's a lot of money. What in the hell is Dad going to do?

Hans goes into the house and cleans up.

Just before supper's ready, Dad comes in the driveway with the neighbor's tractor. He comes into the house for supper.

After breakfast, Dad and Hans start hauling the hay the next morning.

About the middle of the afternoon, they quit hauling hay. Hans takes his pickup back to town to get the tires.

After supper, it's still light outside. Dad and Hans go out and mount the tires on the tractor.

While they're mounting the tires, Hans interrupts the silence by stating, "I almost didn't come home, Dad."

"Why were you planning on staying in the army?"

"No, Sarge offered me a job working with him and his friend Tony in a gambling casino in the Bahamas. I would be head of the security department."

"Sounds like you would be policing the casino."

"Sort of, but there's a lot more to it than that. I think it would be a good job, but I would have to carry a gun, so I turned it down. I guess with what's happening around here, it's good I didn't take it and came home."

Dad doesn't say anything for a while, then he comments, "You're old enough to go and do what you want to. I can't stop you. But yes, I'm glad you're home and didn't take that job."

Dad laughs a little and remarks, "Your Mom is so religious; if she knew you were working in a casino, she would disown you." He laughs again.

"Do you like this farm?"

"Yes. Why do you ask?"

"Your Mom and I aren't getting any younger and won't be here forever. Hans, you may have to take over this place someday. You know this farm, and I know that you can run it. You have no siblings. This place is automatically yours when we die if you want it."

Wow, what a surprise. Hans doesn't say anything for a while. He finishes tightening the bolts on the tractor wheel. He replies, "Yes, I'll take the farm. But don't get in any rush to die. I'm not ready to take it over yet."

The tractor looks a hell of a lot better with those new tires on it. Dad takes the neighbor's tractor back.

Hans goes into the house, shaves, and takes a shower.

Dad gets home, and they all watch T.V.

Around nine thirty p.m. that night, the phone rang.

Mom picks up the receiver and quickly says, "Hello, "Yes, he's right here." She looks over at Hans and states, "Someone wants to talk to you."

She hands him the receiver.

Hans takes it and calmly says, "Hello."

He hears Sarge's voice remark, "Hey, Cowboy. How are you doing? I just got into town. I'm staying at the Lucky Motel in room sixty-nine. Meet me there tomorrow morning, and I will buy you breakfast. Around nine-thirty a.m. Is that okay with you, Cowboy?"

Hans replies, "That sounds good, Sarge. I'll see you tomorrow."

He hangs up the phone.

Mom and Dad look at Hans with a blank looks on their faces.

"My old army sergeant's here in town. I'm going to meet him tomorrow morning, and he will buy me breakfast. So, you don't have to fix me breakfast for me in the morning, Mom."

It's getting late. Dad turns the TV off, and they all go to bed.

It's hard to fall asleep because Hans thinks Sarge's here to try to get him to go back to the Bahamas with him.

The next morning, Hans shaves and takes a shower. He puts on a clean pair of blue jeans, a clean western shirt, and boots.

Hans comes out of the bedroom and heads for the kitchen door. Mom and Dad are sitting at the kitchen table, finishing their breakfast and drinking coffee.

Hans quickly says, "Good morning, and goodbye."

They both reply, "Good morning at the same time."

Hans gets his western hat off a hanger on the wall to the right of the kitchen door. He opens the door, goes out, and closes the door. He puts his hat on, gets in his pickup, and heads for town.

Hans stops in the motel parking lot, walks to room sixty-nine, and knocks on the door. The door opens, and standing just inside is Sarge with a big grin on his face.

Sarge quickly says, "Hi, Cowboy; it's good to see you again. Come in."

As Hans stepped in the doorway, he calmly said, "It's good to see you too, Sarge."

They shake hands.

Sarge states, "You can call me Pete. We're not in the army anymore."

Hans replies, "Okay, Pete."

Hans looks over to his right. Two other men sitting in the room looking at him and smiling. They both standup.

Pete introduces Hans to them, "Cowboy, this is Sam, and this is Carlos. Men, this is Hans, better known as Cowboy.' They all say hi and shake hands.

Sam is a little shorter and thinner than Pete. He has reddish hair covering his ears and a thick red mustache. He's Irish.

Carlos 's built like a bull. He's a little taller than Hans, with curly black hair slightly shorter than Sam's. He's Mexican.

Pete asks, "Is that café across the street any good?"

Hans replies with a grin, "That place has the biggest and best rib steak, three eggs and hash brown potatoes, and any kind of toast you want in the hole world, and I'm hungry."

Pete remarks, "Wow, that sounds great. Let's go."

They leave the motel room, walk across the street, and into the café. They sit down in a booth. Hans sits in the booth first. Pete sits next to him, and Sam and Carlos sit across the table.

The waitress comes over. They all ordered coffee and rib steak, and eggs.

Pete looks around and remarks, "I can sure tell we're in the country and out west. A lot of people are wearing hats. Including the women and kids."

Hans explains. "This is rodeo week. A lot of the people go along with the program and dress in western clothes a lot more than they would normally, Especially the businesses and their employees. The waitresses here normally wear a uniform."

It didn't take long to get their meals.

After breakfast, they get up from the booth, go out the door, and walk back to Pete's motel room.

They all go into the room. Hans waits until they're all inside.

Hans bluntly says, "Well, Pete, you didn't come all the way up here with your two musclemen just to pay me a visit. Let's hear it. What the hell do you want? Let's get it over with, and the answer's still no."

"Wait a minute, Cowboy," says Pete. "Don't get all bent out of shape until you hear what I have to say. We're having some problems, and I need you badly."

"Pete, I just can't go. My parents are in big trouble here. They're about to lose the farm. I couldn't leave them now even if I wanted to."

Pete sighs. "Yes, son, I know all about the grasshoppers and everything."

Wow! What a big surprise hearing that. All I can do is stare at him.

Pete continues. "Cowboy, I need you so badly that I started checking up on you to find out how you are doing these days. With a little money, a person can buy a lot of information. I need your help, and you need mine."

Hans still doesn't say anything. Pete reaches under the bed and pulls out a small briefcase. He lays it on the bed and opens it. Hans gasped when he looked inside the open briefcase. It is full of money; twenties, fifties, and hundred-dollar bills.

Hans has always seen this kind of stuff on television, but he never thought he would ever see it for real.

Hans blurts out, "What the hell did you do, Pete? Rob a bank?"

Pete laughs. "Not quite, buddy. Not quite."

"How much money is in there, anyway?"

Pete doesn't answer Hans's question. Instead, he says, "Cowboy, this is what I will do. First, tell me how much money you need to save your dad's farm."

"About fifteen thousand dollars."

"If you come to the Bahamas with me and help me out down there, this might help you. It might just take a few months or maybe a year. Then you can quit and come back home or do whatever you want to.

"I can't find anybody else to do this. You're the best when it comes to explosives, riflemen, and snipers. Besides, you're the only one I trust.

"I'll give you twenty thousand dollars right here and now to take care of your parents' farm and a little extra to get them going again. Plus, I will give you two thousand dollars in advance salary and a plane ticket to the Grand Bahama. You don't have to pay any of it back.

"Cowboy, there's a lot of competition with a mob boss named Lagno. It's turning into a war down there.

This is how badly I need you.

For a minute, Hans doesn't say anything.

A little voice in the back of Hans's mind says, "I don't really want to do this. I was hoping that my shooting days were over with. But it's the only way to save the farm. I better do it. Pete's always been square with me."

Hans nods. "Okay, Pete, I will do it."

Pete sighs with relief. He counts the money, puts it in a paper sack, and gives it to Hans. Then Hans remembers something he told him when they were still in the army; that everybody has a price and can be bought one way or another. Hans didn't believe it until now. For the first time, Hans has been bought.

Hans just sighs. Well, here he goes again.

Pete closes the briefcase, picks it up, and states, "That takes care of that. So, let's go. I'll follow you home, Cowboy. You always talk about your mom and dad. Now, finally, I'll get to meet them."

Pete puts the briefcase in the trunk of his Rent-A-Car, a black Ford sedan.

Pete explains, "Cowboy, I need these two musclemen. That way, nobody can rip off all the money I brought with me." Hans nods.

Sam and Carlos stay in town, and Pete gets in his car and follows Han's home.

They get home, and Hans parks his pickup in the implement shed. Pete stops in front of the shed. They get out of the vehicles.

Pete looks at Hans's pickup and remarks, "That's a good-looking truck you have."

Hans replies, "Thank you, Pete. I bought it the day I got home."

Hans has the sack with the money in his hand.

Chapter 4

Hans tells his parents he's going to the Bahamas.

They go to the house and go in and walk into the living room. Mom and Dad are sitting in their overstuffed chairs, reading magazines. They both look up at Hans and smile. He smiles back at them.

Hans politely says, "I have someone I would like you to meet. This is Pete Saran, my ex-army sergeant."

"This's Mom, and this's dad."

Dad gets out of his chair, shakes Pete's hand, and states, "It's good to meet you. We've heard a lot about you, Pete."

Pete shakes his hand with Mom.

Mom politely says, "Pete, it's nice to meet you. Please sit down."

She points to the couch. They both sit down.

Hans explains, "Pete didn't come here just for a visit. It's a business trip, and it involves all of us. I have some not-so-good news and some super-good news. The not-so-good news is that I'm going to go to the Bahamas with Pete and work with him. The super good news is that Pete's boss will pay off your debt."

Mom and Dad just sit there with puzzled looks on their face.

Hans gets up from the couch, walks over to Dad, hands him the sack of money, and suggests, "Here, take a look in the sack."

Dad looks in the sack. His eyes get big, and he pulls out all those hundred-dollar bills.

Mom shrieks, "Wow."

Dad counts it all out. He sighs and leans back in the chair, not saying anything.

He gets up, walks over to Mom, hands her the money, returns to his chair, and sits back down.

Hans asks. "Is that all you need? Is there anything else that needs to be paid?"

Mom states, "No."

Dad looks at Pete and indicates, "I don't know when I can pay you back."

Pete states, "I need Hans to go with me to the Bahamas. This money is yours. You don't have to pay it back.

Mom asks, "What will you do down in the Bahamas? Why's Pete willing to pay us all this money for Hans?"

Hans replies, "It's Pete's boss and soon-to-be my boss who is paying for all of this. He's rich. Who cares why? Take the money. Miracles do happen."

Mom softly says, "Thank you, Pete. You are a life saver. Will you stay and have supper with us?"

Pete replies, "Your welcome, and yes, I will stay and have supper with you. Thank you."

Mom looks at the money in her hands and starts to cry.

Hans looks over at Dad. Even he's fighting back the tears. He gets up, walks back over to mom, and takes her in his arms; they both are crying.

That's the first time Hans has ever seen Dad cry.

Hans gets up from the couch and looks over at Pete, and motions for him to come with him. He gets up and follows Hans out of the house.

Walking towards the shop, Hans remarks, "I think that went over better than I thought it would."

Walking into the shop, Pete replies, "You handled the whole thing well, Cowboy. I couldn't have done that well myself."

Hans opens the refrigerator, reaches in, gets a couple of beers, and hands one to Pete.

One beer later, Dad comes out of the house with the paper sack in his hand.

He smiles at them and states, "I'm going to take this money to the bank right now."

Pete suggests, "It would be a good ideal if Hans and I go with you, with all that money you have, Mr. Metzger. Just in case someone thinks there might be more cash in that sack."

Dad replies, "Okay, let's go."

They all get in Dad's pickup and head for town.

Dad pulls into the bank parking lot and parks the pickup. They get out. Dad walks just ahead of Hans toward the bank.

Suddenly they hear a click that sounds like a bolt action shotgun and a man's voice; "Hold it right there, or I'll blow your head off, and hand me that paper sack."

Dad and Hans turn around. There's a man about Dad's age, dressed like a farmer and unshaven, with a dirty wide-brim straw hat on. He's pointing a shot gun at them.

What that man didn't notice was Pete getting out of the pickup. Pete pulls a pistol out from under his coat, sneaks up behind him, sticks the pistol in his back, and demands, "Drop your gun now, or I'll blow you in half."

The man drops his gun.

Hans shouts, "Pete, behind you. He has a hammer."

Pete turns around and shoots the man's teenage son in the shoulder. He falls to the ground.

Hans shouts, "Dad. Get into the bank now." As he runs over and pushes the man away from the shotgun before he can pick it up. Hans picks up the gun and points it at the man.

Hans tells the man as he takes the shells out of the gun. "You get in your truck and get your son to the hospital now. Don't come back until we're gone."

Pete helps the man's son into the pickup. Then he points his gun at the man.

Hans gives the man his empty shotgun back, and they drive away.

Pete remarks, "I think it was a spur-of-the-moment thing when he saw the sack."

Pete puts his gun away, and he and Hans run into the bank.

Dad's standing in line. His hands are shaking as he holds onto the sack very tightly.

Pete and Hans walk up and stand beside him.

There are about six people ahead of them. Hans looks to his right. A security guard is sitting at a desk. He's looking at the sack Dad's holding and at Dad. Hans bets he thinks that Dad is going to hold up the bank and put money in the sack instead of taking money out of it.

Dad steps up to the bank window. He grins and politely says, "Hi. I'm making a small deposit." He hands the sack over to the bank teller. She looks inside the sack. Her eyes get big when she sees all the money in it. She turns around and looks for her supervisor. She motions to him with her hand to come over. He comes to her. She points at the sack, not saying anything. He looks into the sack, and his eyes get big. He looks at Dad. He's still grinning and trying to keep his hands from shaking.

Hans looks over at the security guard. He's standing up and has his hand on his pistol, with it still in the holster. He's watching Dad and the teller closely.

The supervisor looks at the teller and politely says, "Okay, start counting." He turns and walks away. It takes about twenty minutes. She counts it twice.

Hans looks over at the security guard as they start walking toward the door. He's sitting back down but still watching them.

Hans waves at him politely, saying, "Thank you for watching us so closely."

He smiles, not saying anything.

They get outside of the bank.

Dad sighs with relief and remarks, "That's too much excitement for me. Thank you for coming with me."

His hands still shaking. He demands, "Hans! You better drive us home. I'm too shaken up. I'll tell Mom about all about this some other time." He hands Hans the keys.

They get home, park the pickup in the shop, stay there, and have some beer.

Dad gets up off the stool and asks, "When will you leave for the Bahamas?"

"We better get out of here by tomorrow, if possible," replies Pete.

Dad looks at Hans and comments, "I wish you didn't have to leave so soon, Son. You just got home. I'll be okay now. I have the money now. I can get help when I need it."

Hans states, "Just as soon we get the casino built, I can come home. It may not take long. At the most, a year, maybe."

Mom yells from the house, "Supper's ready, you guys."

They finish their beers, throw the empty cans in a barrel, and walk into the house.

They all sit down at the kitchen table.

Mom says grace.

The supper looks good. Home fried chicken, potatoes, chicken gravy, and corn on the cob. Hans's favorite meal.

After supper Pete remarks, "Mrs. Metzger. Wow. This meal was excellent. It's been a long time since I had a meal this good. My mom was a good cook also. But I hate to admit it. This is better."

Mom's eyes light up. She smiles and replies, "Thank you, Pete. I'm glad you liked it.

"Where does your mom live?"

Pete answers, "Both Mom and Dad have passed away. I think I have a couple of aunts and one uncle somewhere. I lost contact with them years ago. They might all be dead now, also. It's just me by myself."

As he gets up from the table, he politely says, "I better go back to town to my motel. I'll be back here tomorrow morning around ten-thirty a.m. Thank you for supper. I enjoyed it."

Dad asks, "Have you ever been to a rodeo, Pete? They put on a good show. You might like it. And it would give you something to do tonight."

Pete replies, "No, I haven't been to one. I might just do that. I have two friends with me. I'll see if they want to go.

Hans gets up from the table and walks Pete out to his car. Pete leaves, and Hans goes back in and helps Mom with the dishes.

After doing the dishes, Hans returns to his room, packs his clothes and things he needs to take, watches TV, and goes to bed around ten p.m.

The next morning, Hans gets up, shaves, and takes a shower. He gets dressed, hears Mom in the kitchen, and can smell and hear bacon frying.

Hans walks into the kitchen and calmly says, "Good morning."

Mom looks over at him and smiles, "Good morning. Breakfast will be ready as soon as Dad brings in some fresh eggs from the chicken coop."

He comes in with the eggs. Dad and Hans both say good morning.

After breakfast, Hans gives Dad his pickup keys and suggests, "Go ahead and drive it if you want. It's not good to just leave it set. If you don't, that's okay too. Just start it up every once in a while to keep the battery charged."

Dad replies, "I may drive it sometimes. Don't worry, I'll take care of it, Son."

Pete gets here right on time.

Hans gives Mom a hug and kiss and softly says, "Goodbye, Mom. I'll call you as soon as I get a phone."

Mom's fighting back the tears and replies, "Goodbye, Hans, and be careful down there. I wish you didn't have to go."

Dad and Hans shake hands, and Dad gives Hans a hug and commands, "You keep in touch with us now. Keep us updated on what's going on."

He looks over at Pete and commands, "You take care of my son, Pete."

Pete replies, "I sure will, sir." They shake hands, and they leave.

Pete and Hans pick up Sam and Carlos and start for Lewiston.

Chapter 5

Miami: The Good, Beautiful, Bad, and Ugly

Pete remarks, "Damn Cowboy, your mom and dad live in this big valley, and in just a matter of minutes, we're in the pine tree-covered mountains. No wonder you wanted to come back home. This country is just beautiful up here."

Hans replies, "There's a lot of places to go fishing around here, and the hunting season is open in the autumn. There's lots of deer, elk, ducks, geese, and pheasants."

Carlos remarks in the back seat on the left side, "speak of the devil, there's a herd of elk just up ahead of us, to the left side of the road, on the hill side."

They all look to the left side of the road; about twenty elk are standing there looking at them. Pete slows down, so they can get a good look at them as we drive by.

Seated to Carlo's right side, Sam says, "Wow, that's neat. I have never seen anything like that before, and that rodeo kind of takes you back about a hundred and fifty years in time. This trip's exciting and fun."

Carlos laughs, "It's about time I got you out of the city, Sam. The only wildlife there are pigeons, mice, stray dogs, and cats."

Pete returns the car at the airport. The next thing Hans knows, they're in an airplane heading for Miami.

It's the beginning of a whole new world for Hans, knowing that things at home are going to be all right.

About five hours later, they landed in Miami. The sun's shining, and it's about eighty degrees, and too humid for Hans anyway. He's more used to the drier climate in Idaho.

They're staying in a charming hotel. It has a big swimming pool. Pete and Hans get a room together. It has two king-size beds and a TV. Sam and Carlos get the same.

After they all get checked in and are in Pete and Hans's room. Pete states, "The Bahamas are British Islands. You'll need to get yourself a passport, Cowboy."

Pete takes Hans over to the post office. Hans fills out the paperwork there, and the postman takes his picture and states, "It will take about ten days."

Pete replies, "That's okay; we can relax for a few days."

What makes things great is that Pete is footing all the bills, so Hans not really thinking about how much things cost. Pete's taking them all over Miami and Miami Beach. There are more beautiful girls in bikinis around here than Hans has ever seen before in his life.

It sure is nice to be off on another adventure with Pete again, just like in the army days. Hans's feeling really relaxed, thinking there's hope yet for a good life in this world for him.

Tuesday is another sunny eighty-degree day. Pete and Hans go to the post office and get his passport.

When they are back in the room, Pete lights a cigarette and explains, "For the next few days, Cowboy, you're going to be on your own. Sam, Carlos, and I need to meet Tony Bacco and his dad in Jamaica on business. You don't have to go with us. We will need you more over on Grand Bahama."

"So, have a good time. You can do whatever you want to. Stay here a few more days or go over to the island. Just be at the Rio Lobo hotel in Freeport by Friday. I will meet you there. Be careful and stay out of trouble."

Grinning, Hans replies, "Okay, I will try."

"We will be leaving in about an hour. I better go get Sam and Carlos."

Pete leaves, and Hans gets a kind of cold, empty feeling washing over him, being here in the big city all by himself, and not knowing his way around. Hans doesn't know what to do. He walks over to the big picture window and looks out over Miami from twelve stories up. Hans is a country boy who doesn't care much for the big city.

Hans has taken Pete a lot for granted without thinking about it; he's been using him as a crutch to lean on, knowing he would always be there in case something went wrong. Well, he is not here, so Hans, you better quit acting like a wet-nosed kid.

Hans goes down to the bar to think about whether he should stay in Miami for a few days or head to the island. It's a very fancy place. There's a room off by itself from the hotel lobby called The Lounge Bar.

It's early in the afternoon, so Hans thinks a nice, cold beer will be good. He orders it, and it costs him one dollars and twenty-five cents. That is kind of high for a beer, but when you're in a fancy hotel, you pay for the atmosphere.

Hans starts noticing the people around him a little more. When Pete was here, they moved around so much that Hans didn't pay much attention to anyone else. Then he starts feeling lonely and out of place again, realizing that he's now in the east and not in the west.

Here Hans's, dressed in a brown Western shirt and brown Levi's with Western boots and a hat. All the people out west don't dress in Western clothes, but it's still very common. Here he stands out like a sore thumb. That's why most everyone looks at him as kind of funny; the hell with it. He wouldn't feel comfortable in these people's clothes, anyway. If they don't like it, that's tough. He will just have another beer.

The bartender brings Hans another beer, and he gets to thinking. The people here act too sophisticated, especially the women, a bit too rich for what he's used to.

In a cab, Hans notices a change before he gets all the way downtown.

Hans gets out of the cab.

There are a lot of people everywhere, and they all seem to be in a big hurry. There's a difference, alright. The people are in such a big hurry they don't even notice Hans, let alone look at him funny.

There are a lot of tall buildings here in this big concrete jungle. Most of the buildings look old. The whole city's kind of dirty.

Spotting a sign that reads "BAR," Hans decides it is time for another beer, so he goes in. It's a dive, but it doesn't look too bad. There are a few customers, mostly older people.

For about ten minutes, Hans drinks a beer and just sits and listens to the half-drunk old-timers' talk. Suddenly a woman's soft voice from behind him says, "Hi, Tex. Mind if I sit down and talk to you?"

Hans bets everybody here thinks anybody that comes to town wearing western boots and hat is from Texas. Hans has never been to Texas.

Hans turns to his right. She's a nice-looking, blonde-haired, blue-eyed woman, nicely built, maybe in her thirties.

Instantly Hans can tell that her blonde hair is a wig. He kind of laughs to himself because she looks kind of like a hooker. That's one thing that never seems to change much, whether you're on the East or West Coast or any place in the world. If you have any kind of brain, you can spot a hooker a mile away.

Hans thinks, what the hell. If nothing else, he'll have someone to talk to for a while. And if the price is right, he might go with her. She's not all that bad looking. So, Hans let her sit down. She introduces herself, "My name is Suzy."

"I'm Hans." He buys her a drink.

They talk for a while. Then she gets a cigarette out of her purse and asks Hans, "Want to go to a room with me?"

Picking up some matches from the bar, Hans lights her cigarette and asks, "How much will it cost?"

"We will talk about that when we get in the room."

Hans asks, "Do you have a room, or do I have to rent one?"

She replies, "You'll have to rent it. But it's only twenty-five dollars for the first three hours. After that, it's fifteen dollars an hour."

Hans laughs a little and thinks to himself. It's not going to take three hours to have sex with her.

Hans agrees, "Okay, let's go."

They go into the hotel (t's a dive). At the hotel desk, Hans pays the clerk. He's fat, filthy, dirty, and drunk. They go into a room on the second floor.

She bluntly says, "That will be forty dollars."

Hans thinks that's not as bad as he thought it would be.

She smiles, takes his money, and suggests, "Go ahead and take your clothes off while I go to the bathroom. I'll be right back."

She goes into the bathroom and closes the door.

Hans takes off his coat. When suddenly, the closet door opens and scares the hell out of Hans.

A man dressed like a cop comes out of the closet with a pistol in his hand.

He demands, "Get your hands up. You're under arrest for illegal sexual activity."

Hans puts his hands up.

Hans looks down. He has white tennis shoes on, not regulation black shoes. It's a set up to rob Hans. He's not a real cop. Probably Suzy's boyfriend or husband.

Hans quickly hits his gun hand so hard he drops the gun. He hits Hans on the head. Hans falls back against the wall. The fake cop bends down to pick up the gun. Hans runs at him and kicks him in the head. He falls against the closet door.

Suzy comes out of the bathroom with all her cloths still on. She bends down to pick up the gun off the floor. Hans quickly grabs the fake cop, hits him in the chest and the chin, and knocks him out. He falls against Suzy. She screams and drops the gun. The fake cop pushes her to the floor with him on top of her. Hans kicks the gun out of her reach. He's too heavy for her to try to get out from under him. Hans checks to make sure she is breathing under him. She's okay and leaves him on top of her. She glares at Hans and blurts out, "You son of a bitch. Get him off me."

Hans laughs and remarks, "You forgot to get undressed, Bitch."

Hans gets his coat and hat and gets the hell out of there. He gets down to the hotel desk. The clerk's passed out drunk. Hans runs out of the hotel and down the street as fast as he can. Hans starts to cool down from the excitement he just had.

Realizing the sun has gone down and feeling hungry, Hans starts looking for someplace to eat.

Walking about two blocks, Hans comes up to a big drugstore. He investigates through the window. There's a counter restaurant.

Hans goes in and sits down. It isn't very busy there. An elderly woman comes over with a glass of water, smiling, and softly says, "Good evening. May I help you?"

"Yes, ma'am," Hans replies with a smile. "I'm hungry."

The food here is good.

When Hans finishes eating, he decides he's had enough excitement for one day. He goes into a liquor store and buys a sixpack of beer. Then he gets in a cab and goes back to his hotel room.

Hans is thinking. Miami's just like all the other cities and towns he has seen. There are beautiful and good parts, and there are also bad parts. He managed to find a little of both here.

Hans drinks the beer while watching TV and decides to head over to the island tomorrow.

At about nine o'clock in the morning the next day, Hans looks out of the big picture window. It's a partly cloudy but mostly sunny day. Hans calls the airport to find out when the next plane to Freeport leaves.

The lady at the airport states, "Your flight leaves at twelve p. m. this afternoon."

That's enough time to take a shower, get packed, and get some breakfast.

Hans gets to the airport a little before eleven a.m. and checks in his bags. To kill some time, he finds a café in the airport and has some coffee.

"Well, the next thing Hans knows, he's boarding the plane. Twenty minutes later, he's in Freeport Bahama. It's a sunny, clear day, about eighty degrees and humid.

Hans goes through customs and shows them his passport.

Chapter 6

Gambling Fever

The customs officer asks: "What is the purpose of your visit to the Bahamas?"

Hans replies, "I have a job."

"What kind of a job?"

"I'm going to help build a casino."

The officer gives him a dirty look, stamps his passport, hands it back, and says, "Okay, you can go."

Hans asks, "Where do I go to change my American money for local currency?"

He answers, "American money is good here. You don't have to change it."

From the terminal, Hans gets in a cab. On the way to the hotel where Hans is supposed to meet Pete, he gets to do some sightseeing. The country's very green. There are a lot of palm trees along the narrow freeway. Almost the entire way, across the countryside, short bushes and small, skinny pine trees fill the landscape, kind of like a jungle. He can smell the pine. Every now and then, they would pass a nice-looking hotel. Most are big and have swimming pools. Hans is so busy looking at the countryside that he almost misses the fact that the cab driver is driving on the left side of the road.

If Hans does any driving over here, he'll have to learn how to drive like that. he hopes he doesn't need to do that.

The cab driver pulls up at the hotel.

The lobby's large and round, with wings connecting the cocktail lounges and restaurant to a big seating lounge in the lobby itself. Boy, what a fancy place this is!

Hans walks over to the hotel desk to get a room. A well-dressed black man stands behind the counter.

He asks, "May I help you?"

"Yes, sir. I would like a room, please."

"How long will you be staying?"

Today is Wednesday. Pete will be here Friday. Better say until Sunday to be on the safe side. Hans tells him, "Four days."

"Okay, sir. Will you please sign the register? That will be one hundred and sixty dollars, please."

That's forty dollars a day for a place to sleep. It's hard to believe that people will pay that much for something like that. An Idaho farmer wouldn't pay that much. Huh, he can't! But this is where Pete told Hans to stay, so this Idaho farmer will pay for the room.

A bellboy picks up Hans's bags and politely says, "Come with me, sir."

They exit the building onto the patio and go around the swimming pool and past several two-story buildings that look a lot like the motels in the States. They're all spread out around the pool. The hotel's a lot different than any he's ever seen.

Hans tips the bellboy a buck and goes in. It's a nice room, but it's not as lovely as the room in Miami. It sure is not worth forty dollars a day.

Hans takes his hat off, unpacks a few things, and freshens up. He takes all the money out of one of the bags and counts it. He has about seventeen hundred dollars. He puts four hundred dollars in his wallet and the rest back in the bag. Hans thinks he might as well check things out and go live it up a little. He puts his hat back on.

The late-afternoon sun shines as Hans walks the hotel grounds, looking them over. They must cover at least twenty acres. Besides the unit buildings, swimming pool, and golf course, the hotel has a big parking lot and a great lawn with palm trees. There's a small clump of pine and palm trees with flowers altogether, like a flower garden, with a path leading into it. Hans follows the path through the trees and bushes and comes across a little pond with a footbridge. He crosses and continues through the path and out the other side of the trees. Then there's more lawn. The whole place is just beautiful.

The sun has just gone down, so Hans decides to go to one of the lounges and have a drink before getting something to eat. He goes into the bar and sits down. The bartender comes over. Hans gets a bourbon and water, and he charges Hans two dollars for the drink. Damn, this is really an expensive place.

Hans's having trouble getting it into his thick head that this is a tourist trap and a high-class place for wealthy people who can afford to throw money away and think nothing of it.

The more Hans thinks about it, he decides what the hell. He has over seventeen hundred dollars. The two thousand dollars is about the most money he's ever gotten in his life. His parents are okay now, so Hans doesn't have to worry about them. When Pete gets back, he will be making good money. For the next few days, until Pete gets here, Hans thinks he might as well go along with the rest of the people around here. And just go and have himself one hell of a good time and stop worrying about money and how much things cost.

Hans has another drink, and after that, he goes and has a nice dinner with a small jug of white wine.

Stepping outside to get some air, Hans notices it's dark out and the air's cooling down. He goes to his room and puts on a drawstring tie and sweater. Then he goes back to the lobby. There's another lounge here, and this one has live music. Hans goes in and has a drink, and watches the band. A real nice-looking lady comes out and does a belly dance. She's good, not just an old go-go dancer like they have in Monterey, California. She balances a long sword on her shoulder and hips while she goes through the motions. It's a real work of art.

When the show ends. Hans decides to go check out some other places and do a little barhopping. Outside, he's wondering if he ought to get a cab or just walk. A few small groups of people walk across a four-lane street. Then they turn to the left and walk up the street. Hans decides to follow them.

Turning left, Hans looks to the right. There's a long, wide, single-story building with white stucco and gold trim. It looks a lot like an old Egyptian building from the days of the Bible. Hans walks over to an archway entrance and goes in.

Hans thinks, well, I'll be damned. This is a casino. Is this why Pete wants Hans to stay at that hotel?

The electricity of the crowd inside gets Hans excited. He starts looking around. There are slot machines all over the place. A sign hangs from the ceiling to his right: "ROULETTE." The room's filled with roulette tables, about ten in all, and a row of slot machines separated the roulette room from the rest of the casino.

At the sight of the slot machines, Hans decides to try the few nickels that he has in his pocket, but as he makes his way through the casino, Hans doesn't find any nickel machines. He can't believe it! They are all quarter, half-dollar, or one-dollar machines. They don't have any nickel or dime machines at all, let alone any penny machines. Boy, this place is only for the high rollers and the wealthy.

Several card tables sit in the center of the casino. Hans walks over to one of them and recognizes the game they're playing: blackjack. At one end are four tables shaped differently than the blackjack tables. Hans goes over to it. There are a lot of different markings, and numbers on the green felt covering the table. A man throws a pair of dice.

Hans asks the person beside him, "What do they call this game?"

He replies, "Craps."

The tables cover a large area of the casino that's full of people. Hans has never seen anything like this before in his life.

In about four different places among the slot machines stand small, yet tall, booths with a lady sitting in each one of them and a sign that reads "CHANGE." The booths have lots of rolled coins in them.

Uniformed men patrol the area, some are white, and some are black. They have "CASINO SECURITY GUARD" patches on their sleeves and guns at their sides. Huh, is that the kind of work Hans will be doing? This job may not be as bad as he thought.

There's only one man behind each table. Think they call them dealers. They all wear black suits with white shirts and black bow ties. They are all white men, and most of them speak with a British accent.

Several cocktail hostesses are making the rounds. Some are black, and some are white, but all are good-looking. They're wearing such sexy outfits! They're a lot like Barbara Eden's outfit on that television show *I Dream of Jeannie*.

There's only one bar in the whole place, crowded with people. Hans has a hard time getting in close enough to get a drink, but he finally manages to push his way up to it. The bartenders are all men and dressed about the same as the dealers, with red vests. After getting a bourbon and water, Hans pushes his way back to the center of the room.

As Hans sips his drink, he decides to try his luck at a slot machine. He goes over to one of the change booths and buys twenty dollars' worth of quarters. Then Hans walks through the rows of machines until he finally finds one that no one's playing with. He hits a few cherries and bells a couple of times but he puts everything that drops back in the machine.

Before losing his first roll of quarters, a cocktail hostess asks people if they want a drink. His's almost gone when she comes by Hans., He orders another one. While waiting for his drink, Hans keeps on playing. He almost lost all the quarters when a bell rang: Hans hits the jackpot, three stars. The machine pays out twenty-five dollars in quarters. Hans feels better now, having won his money back plus five dollars more. He starts playing again, and the cocktail hostess comes up the row with the drinks.

People give her money when she hands them their drink, so when she brings him his, Hans asks her, "How much does this drink cost?"

She replies with a smile, "Nothing, sir. If you play at the slot machines or tables, the drinks are on the house."

That surprises the hell out of Hans.

"If they are free, why do people give you money?"

She gives him a funny look. "That's a tip they give me."

Hans suddenly feels stupid and embarrassed. He thinks nothing about tipping waitresses in a restaurant but never realizes that casino cocktail waitresses work for tips, also. Hans reaches over, gives her fifty cents, and tells her, "I'm sorry."

She softly says, "That's okay, sir, and thank you." She goes on her way.

Hans goes back to playing his machine and gets a few more pays. About two drinks later, Hans puts all the money back in the machine.

Looking over at the bar, he saw that the crowd had thinned out, and a few seats were now open. Hans goes over to the bar and sits down. Two drinks later. He is feeling a little lightheaded and loose.

Getting up, Hans goes over to the roulette tables. After watching the game for a little while, he buys twenty dollars in quarter chips. One drink later, having lost all of that, he goes over to the craps table. Looking in his wallet, Hans doesn't have any small bills. All there's left are three one-hundred-dollar bills.

What the hell. Hans might get lucky. He takes one hundred dollars, buys five-dollar chips, and starts playing craps. He starts playing five dollars at a time and then goes up to ten dollars. Hans wins about fifty dollars. The game's getting more interesting with every throw of the dice. He really doesn't know much about playing craps. It's a lot more complicated than how he played it in the army, but his learning.

The drinks keep right on coming, and Hans keeps right on drinking and gambling.

His luck runs up and down, but mostly down.

In Hans's drunkenness, he grows more frustrated, having lost all but thirty dollars out of that one hundred.

Hans pulls out of the game and goes to the restroom. When he comes back, he sits down at a blackjack table. Hans should have played blackjack in the first place. He was quite lucky at that in the army.

Hans bets ten dollars a hand and loses the first two hands. On the third hand, he draws a seven and a four. That's eleven, so to double down, he reaches into his wallet and pulls out another hundred, once again buying five-dollar chips. He almost wins his money back, then loses the last hundred, and has just enough left to go have a drink. After losing all that money, he needs another drink.

But that isn't enough. Hans has caught the fever and caught it bad. He wants to go win his money back. He gulps the drink down, walks out of the casino, goes straight to his room, pulls six hundred dollars out of his bag, and then heads straight back to the casino. Hans plays blackjack for a long time and keeps right on drinking.

Hans keeps on playing until he finally loses the six hundred dollars. He's so drunk that he gets an "I don't give a damn" attitude about losing. Ready to get some more money, Hans staggers out the casino door and damn near blinds himself when the sun hits him right in the face.

Oh shit. Hans has been up all night long, drinking and gambling. Hans, you better quit.

He returns to the hotel room, and when his head hits that pillow, he passes out cold. The next thing Hans knows, it's eight o clock that night. He wakes up with the biggest hangover he thinks he has ever had in his life.

He gets up, counts his money, and finds seven hundred dollars left. Hans lost a thousand dollars last night.

After realizing what he did, he feels like a real ass and almost gets sick.

Boy, Hans will sure be glad when Pete gets here, and he can start doing something right for a change.

Oh shit! Hans's not going to tell Pete what happened. He'll never hear the end of it if he does.

After going out and eating something, Hans still feels like shit with that hangover. So, he goes back to his room and decides to quit worrying about the money he lost. It's gone, and there's nothing that can be done about it. Hans watches television for a while, then goes to bed and sleeps off the rest of the hangover.

Hans wakes up Friday morning around ten a.m. with a clear head. It sure feels good. Hans looks out the window. It's cloudy and raining. He opens the window and feels the humid air. It's more humid when it rains. He closes the window, shaves, showers, gets dressed, and puts on his hat. He goes and gets some breakfast. Hans feels even better after having breakfast. But as the day progresses, while he sits in his room and waits for Pete to arrive, he can't get his mind off his night of gambling. The more he thinks about it, the sicker he gets. He can just kick himself square in the ass for doing such a dumb thing. To think he was bitching about paying forty dollars a day for a room and two dollars for a drink, and then go out and willingly throw one thousand dollars away without even thinking. Guess without realizing it, people are all a little greedy. Most people can control it, but when they get to drinking, they start to get braver and start gambling, unable to quit.

Oh shit. Hans wishes he was drunk. Then he could get an "I don't give a damn" attitude and quit feeling sorry for himself.

Finally, at about 3:30 o'clock p.m., there is a knock at Hans's door.

Chapter 7

The Lady Hans Can't Have.

Hans opens it, and there, with a big grin on his face, stands Pete. Right behind him is Tony. As Pete steps into the room, he remarks, "Well, Cowboy, you made it in one piece. You aren't even in jail. Things are looking up. There's hope for you yet,"

Tony walks over and shakes Hans's hand. Hans just smiles at him, not saying anything but thinking about what Pete just remarked and his night of gambling. Hans is starting to get a complex mentality. It seems like when Pete isn't around, everything Hans touches or tries to do turns to shit.

Pete reaches into a paper sack that he has in his hand and pulls out a six-pack of beer. He opens three cans and gives Tony and Hans each one.

Hans sighs and politely says, "Thanks, Pete. This is just what I need. A good, cold beer."

Pete and Tony both sit down and light up a cigarette. Hans goes over and sits on the bed. Their expressions turn from smiles to serious looks.

Pete takes a drink of his beer and says, "Cowboy, tomorrow your vacation ends. You will start working, and it will not be much fun. It's going to be tough. Maybe tougher than Vietnam and just as dangerous.

Hans replies, "Oh really?"

"Tony here will tell you why and what they're up against."

Hans doesn't say anything. he just takes a drink of beer and waits to hear what Tony has to say.

Tony takes a drag from his cigarette and seriously says, "Deano Lagno owns the casino here on the island. He owns the oil refinery here and a cargo ship line.

Lagno is a dangerous mob boss. He's so rich he has almost the whole island police force in his hip pocket, including the chief and the only criminal judge here on the island. Anybody that gets in his way gets killed. Everybody is scared to death of him. He's that corrupt and more.

"When anybody goes to work for Lagno, and when they find out what he's like and try to quit, Lagno has them killed.

"My Dad isn't scared of him. He worked for Lagno for many years. He was his head accountant and head of security. He took care of the legal end of the business. Lagno promised Dad a partnership when he first started working for him. He never gave it to him.

"Dad decided to build a casino of his own. He bought some land on the other side of the island. It wouldn't hurt Lagno's business a bit. But Lagno is very greedy. He told Dad that he would imprison him for embezzling or killing him if he tried to build a casino on this island.

"Dad had signed a contract to work for Lagno for twenty years, and he'd worked seven years of that contract. He told Lagno to go ahead and try to put him in prison or kill him. Lagno's bodyguards went to work for Dad. Dad isn't worried about getting killed. Dad told Lagno he would sue him for failure to fulfill the contract. That really made Lagno mad."

"Lagno is going to try anything and everything in his power to stop Dad from building the casino. If he can't get Dad thrown in prison, we are afraid he might try and kill him."

"Lagno's a real crook. But Dad can't prove it yet, which could take years, so we will go ahead and build Dad's casino. We are not going to let anyone get in our way, no matter what. We don't know just what we're going to do yet. This is the reason why Pete went up to Idaho to get you. You will be paid well for your work, and your job will be done when Dad gets Lagno legally put away. Then you can go back home or stay and keep working for us in the casino.

With our army training, we should make it through somehow. Tomorrow there will be a meeting with my dad, and you will be there with us."

Pete bluntly says, "Cowboy, don't chicken out on me now. Tony's dad spent a lot of money to get you over here. Besides, it may not be all that bad. You go ahead and have the rest of the beer. Clean up and put on your suit. I will be back about seven o'clock tonight to pick you up. We will go over to Tony's dad's and have dinner with them. After dinner, we'll go to some nightclubs around here and have a few drinks."

"Okay," Hans replies. "I will be ready."

After they leave. Hans just sits there on the bed for a few minutes, not doing anything except thinking about all the things Tony told him. Huh, this is nothing like Hans thought it would be here. Bet Pete didn't know it was this bad either when he joined Tony.

Boy, that Lagno must really be a bad guy if he is going through all the trouble to stop Tony and his dad from building their casino, even if it means killing Tony's dad.

The more Hans thinks about it, the more he doesn't like the whole thing. They can get their asses killed over this. It's not worth it. But then again, it must be worth it because Pete's helping them. Hans knows Pete too well. If he doesn't think it's worth taking the chance of getting killed for, he would have bailed out of this himself. And he wouldn't have come all the way up to Idaho to get Hans.

Besides, that casino of Lagno's got Hans for one thousand dollars. Piss on him. This way, he can get back at him.

Suddenly all of Hans's fears leave him. Instead, he feels challenged. Why not? There's really nothing else to do. The army was hell, but on the other hand, it was quite an adventure. Guess this will be like that also.

Hans gets up from the bed, finishes his beer, and opens another one. Then he starts getting ready for dinner. He polishes up his black Western boots, then shaves and showers, puts on his blue Western suit, a white Western shirt with a blue print, and a light blue regular businessman's tie. His pants bell out a little from the knees down. Boot cut, they call it.

Hans is drinking his last beer when Pete comes to get him.

It stopped raining, but it's still cloudy and humid. They walk out to the parking lot. Pete stops beside a green four-door Chrysler sedan. He unlocks the door and opens it for Hans. Wow! This is neat!

Once they are both seated, Hans asks, "Is this your car?"

"Yes. I bought it back in California the day we left the army. I drove it to Miami and shipped it over here. I really like it. It's the first brand-new car I've ever had. I paid cash for it with the money I saved and my mustering-out pay,"

"This is really a nice car."

While driving, they pass several hotels. Many of them are all different shapes and sizes, but most generally look the same.

Then they drive up to a big hotel right by the ocean. It has its own private beach. They stop right at the front door and get out of the car, and then a parking attendant comes out to park the car for them.

They walk into the lobby, and Pete tells Hans, "Wait here, and I will be right back."

He goes into a banquet room.

Hans glances to his left and sees a man standing all by himself. He is dressed in a black suit, is clean-shaven, and has short blond hair.

What stands out about him is that he has his right arm in front of him with a newspaper draped over his right hand. A strange way to hold a newspaper. He keeps looking into the banquet room. Hans thinks he might be one of Lagno's men and has a gun under that newspaper.

Pete returns. "Let's go into the lounge and have a drink. They aren't down yet."

Hans doesn't say anything to Pete about the man and the newspaper because it might not be anything. But he'll try to keep an eye on him.

They've just about finished with their drinks when Sam and Carlos enter the lounge and walk over to them.

They both smile at Hans and politely say, "HI, Cowboy." They shake his hand.

Sam explains, "Mr. Bacco and his four bodyguards are in the banquet room. Come on, let's go in."

Pete and Hans get up and follow Sam and Carlos out of the lounge, and Hans looks over at the man he is suspicious of. He still has the newspaper draped over his hand and slowly walks toward the banquet room.

Hans quickly and quietly runs up behind him. He's to his right but still a little behind him. Hans reaches around him and grabs the newspaper out from over his hand. He has a gun.

Hans shouts, "Gun." He grabs his gun hand, trying to take the gun away from him.

Hans hits him in the stomach. He falls to his knees. The gun fires into the ceiling.

Hans breaks his arm and hits him in the face. That knocked him out. He falls to the floor.

Hans gets the gun away from him. It drops on the floor, and Hans kicks it away from him.

Bacco's four gorillas come running out of the banquet room.

Hans looks at them and bluntly says, "He's all yours."

Sam, Carlos, and Pete are just standing there watching Hans with surprised looks on their faces!

The four of them go into the banquet room. It's a big, partitioned room, kind of off by itself. Tony is standing there, talking to an older man. Pete and Hans walk over to them, and Tony introduces Hans to Mr. Bacco. "Dad, this is Hans, otherwise known as Cowboy. Cowboy, this is my dad." They exchange greetings and shake hands.

Mr. Bacco remarks, "Sounds like you had a problem out there. You saved my life before you even met me. Thank you, Cowboy."

Hans laughs a little and replies, "Just a little one, sir, and you're welcome."

Mr. Bacco's shorter than Tony, closer to Hans's height. He has on a dark gray suit and vest. His hair is light gray, almost white. He has a kind of rugged-looking face, and when he speaks, his voice is deep and slow. He must be in his late fifties or early sixties.

He's smoking a big black cigar. Hans gets the impression that this man doesn't take any shit from anybody. Even Pete seems to act a little uneasy around him.

Mr. Bacco glances over at the doorway. His eyes kind of light up, and a smile comes over his face.

Hans hears a soft woman's voice say, "Here I am, dear. Sorry, I'm a little late."

Hans turns. A woman who doesn't look like she is over twenty-five years old walks right past him. She takes Mr. Bacco's arm, reaches up, and gives him a kiss on the cheek.

Wow, what a beautiful daughter he has. She has shoulder-length coal-black hair, all neatly curled. She's short, wearing a long red dress, and has a shape that does her small body justice. Her eyes are a very dark, beautiful brown. They are out of this world. It's like he can see them, but they aren't there. Don't know if that makes sense or not, but that's the only way Hans can explain it.

Mr. Bacco brings her over to Hans and introduces them. "Hans, this is my wife, Mrs. Bacco. Dear, this is Cowboy Hans."

Hans gets the surprise of his life when he hears him say "wife." She flutters those eyes at Hans and says in a soft, cool voice, "Is this what a real cowboy looks like?"

A big lump gets in Hans's throat. His mind goes blank, and he can't find anything to say. He just kind of shrugs and smiles.

Then Hans stammers, "Y-yes, I g-guess it is."

Mr. Bacco says, "I think you know everyone else, Dear. We're all here now."

Hans hasn't felt this bashful since he was a freshman in high school. He thought he'd outgrown that kind of stuff. He's starting to feel a little embarrassed.

Mr. Bacco sits at the head of the table, with Mrs. Bacco just to his left. Sam and Carlos sit on the same side that she's on. Tony sits across from her. Hans sits in between Tony and Pete.

While they're all eating, Mr. Bacco says, "I don't talk business in front of my wife during dinner. That we'll do tomorrow,"

The dinner is good, a little spicy for Hans,

The conversation is just small talk, mostly about when Tony and Pete were in the army together. Hans doesn't say much. He just quietly eats his dinner.

Every once and a while, Hans can't help it. He would glance over at Mrs. Bacco and catch her looking at him. Each time, she quickly glances away, trying not to make Hans think she's staring at him.

She must have married him for his money. He's old enough to be her father. Dammit, she's driving Him crazy; he thinks she knows it too. She is over there, loving every minute of it.

Dammit, all to hell. She's married. It's better for me to forget her.

Shit! If he tries and make it with her and that old man finds out, he'll kill Hans.

The more he thinks about it, the more he wishes for this dinner to be over soon. Then he can get the hell out there.

Huh, He'll probably just be seeing the old man over the business and will never see her again.

Finally, everyone is done eating.

Lighting up a cigar, Mr. Bacco says, "We'll see you all tomorrow. I think it is time Mrs. Bacco and I call it a day,"

They all get up and go into the lobby.

Mrs. Bacco flutters those eyes at Hans again and softly says, "It's nice to meet you, Cowboy." She smiles.

Hans stammers, "I-it's nice meeting you, too, M-ma'am."

Hans watches them walk to the elevator. Just after they step in, she looks back at him and smiles as the door closes.

The rest of them go into the lounge and have an after-dinner drink. Then Pete and Hans go barhopping on their own.

They stop at another hotel. It's not as fancy as the one they had dinner at.

They get out of the car. The night sky is clear and full of stars, and the air is cooler. It's a good thing Hans has his suit coat on,

They walk into the bar from the outside without going through the hotel lobby first.

The bar has softly dimmed lights, is a little smoky and smells like it. There are quite a few people in here.

Pete finds a small round table with two chairs. They sit down, and a cocktail hostess comes over to them and asks, "What are you gentlemen having to drink?"

Hans states, "I'll have a bourbon and water."

Pete replies, "I'll have the same as him."

The hostess takes their order and walks away.

Hans starts thinking about Mrs. Bacco and remarks, "Old man Bacco's so rich that it must be easy for him to find a beautiful woman young enough to be his daughter."

Pete laughs a little and replies, "When I first got here, there was nothing for me to do, so I became her bodyguard. I thought okay, I'll stay close to her and act tough. Well, that didn't quite work that way. I would drive her little red corvette, take her shopping, and push the shopping cart for her. I really didn't mind doing that; it kept me from getting bored and gave me something to do."

The cocktail hostess brings their drinks. Pete pays for them. She walks away.

Pete continues, "But when she has guests over, she bosses me around like a slave. I had to serve coffee, tea, and so on. She has some tall dumb, muscle man to be her slave now. She can be a bitch sometimes. Forget all about her and stay away from her. She's not what you think she is, Cowboy."

Hans just sits here thinking about what Pete told him about her and says nothing.

It's late. Pete takes Hans back to his hotel and then leaves for wherever he's staying.

Hans gets to thinking. He must have kept his cool. Nobody seemed to notice how he was acting at dinner because of her.

Hans goes to bed and doesn't fall asleep right away. He starts thinking about Mrs. Bacco and what Pete says about her. It's not scaring him about her. It's making him more interested in just what kind of a bitch she could be. Hans finally falls asleep.

At about 8:30 a.m. the next day, Hans gets up, goes to the restaurant, and has breakfast. Then he goes back to his room and waits for Pete.

At ten a.m., Pete arrives. He tells Hans, "Pack your things and check out of the room because I found you an apartment to move into."

While Hans is packing, Pete says, "We will get you moved into your apartment after we have that meeting with Tony and his dad."

Hans checks out of his room, and then they drive off for the meeting. They don't go to the hotel that they went to last night. Instead, he drives to the ocean and alongside it for a while.

They come to a big marina full of boats, mostly yachts, cabin cruisers, and fishing boats. They stop the car in a parking lot overlooking the marina.

Chapter 8

A Flashback to Vietnam

Pete and Hans walk to one of the docks, past boats of all shapes and sizes on both sides. They walk quite a long way out on the dock. Carlos's standing on the bow of a big cabin cruiser. It's white with gold trim and has a brass rail all around it. On both sides of the bow are the words "THE LADY JENNIFER" written in big, fancy gold letters. Hans asks Pete about the name, and he remarks, "Jennifer's Mrs. Bacco's first name."

They go aboard and meet Carlos, who comes over and is standing by a ladder leading below deck. They follow him down through the passageway Past two cabins, one on each side. Right past the cabin on the left is a galley, and inside, sitting at the end of a long table, is an old Chinese man. He glances up at them as they pass, but he doesn't speak.

At the end of the passageway is a large room, tastefully furnished with a masculine touch of the sea. Against the far wall are two comfortable-looking brown leather chairs. Sam's seated in one, and Carlos sits down in the other one. Between them is an oak table, and on it's a lamp with a base shaped like a sailboat. The shade sits on top of the mast. To the right is a couch matching the chairs, and Mr. Bacco and Tony are sitting there. All of them are drinking coffee and smoking. On each end of the couch are tables matching the one between the chairs, and on each table are large, unique ashtrays made of small, multicolored seashells. To the left is an expensive-looking bar with oak posts and a mirror draped with sea netting. The bar is stocked with the best liquor and wine. The oak panel walls are decorated with stuffed fish. The floor is covered with an expensive-looking dark brown carpet.

As they enter the room, Mr. Bacco gets up and goes to the far end of the bar, where there's a pot of coffee and some cups. He pours Pete and Hans some coffee, refills his own cup, and then turns and faces everybody. He leans on the bar and speaks in his slow deep voice, "Lagno and I go way back. We were good friends. One day I found out just how greedy he is. I've seen Lagno himself smuggle and deal drugs. I also saw Lagno himself doing human trafficking of young teenage girls and gun smuggling. I've also seen Lagno's bodyguards murder one of Lagno's employees instead of having them fired. Owning a shipping line and a casino makes it easy for him to do all of this. Lagno doesn't know I know anything about what he's doing, and I'm not going to tell him. I don't have any pictures of it. It's my word against his. Lagno would have me killed if I tried to testify in court to any of those things.

"Lagno just went crazy, and his getting worse. His wife got murdered.

"I like it here on this island, and I have a right to live here like anyone else and run my own business, even if it's a casino. I'm not going to let that corrupt shithead run me off.

"I'm getting everyone here this morning to get things going and build my casino. This means we are going to have one hell of a fight with Lagno. People are probably going to get killed before this is over with.

"From here on, you will be taking orders from Tony. He will be calling the shots. You all will be working together. If anyone has an idea, tell Tony. He might like it. I don't care how you build that casino; just get it built. Pull out all the stops and do whatever it takes to keep Lagno and his bunch out of the way.

"That is all I have to say. You won't be seeing me much after this meeting is over. Lagno wants me dead. If I stay on this island, he just might get the job done. He almost got it done last night. But thanks to you, Cowboy, that didn't happen. Tony's going to give all of you guys a thousand dollars right now.

"Pete, you get Cowboy moved into his apartment today. I also want you to have a telephone in your apartment, Cowboy. Now, unless there are any questions, you gentlemen can go."

Hans asks, "Sir, do you think maybe Lagno could have murdered his wife himself?"

Mr. Bacco replies, "I have thought about that. Yes, that's possible. He's that crazy. She found out all the bad things he was doing and tried to leave him. Lagno would never let her go. Even back in the early days. When we were still friends, and right after he started all these bad things, they would get in a fight, and he hit her."

Hans asks, "Does Lagno have any kids?"

Mr. Bacco remarks, "Yes, he has a daughter. Her name is Lisa. She was about ten years old or so when I left Lagno. Lisa is probably all grown up by now.

Nobody says anything. Tony pays them the money, which they're all glad to take. Pete and Hans leave. He drives straight over to the apartment. When they get there, Hans follows Pete into a small, light-brown building. This's the office. The manager is a heavyset elderly black woman. She remembers Pete from before.

Pete tells her, "This is Hans. He'll be the one taking the apartment."

The woman gets the key, and they follow her out the back door and over to the apartment building.

The whole place is just beautiful. There are two apartment buildings. They're brown like the office, and they're both two stories high and quite long. There are ten apartments in each building, five downstairs and five upstairs. The two buildings face each other, with a big swimming pool right between them. There's a big lawn and lots of palm trees all around.

They walk on the sidewalk to the apartment building to the left of the office. Of course, it's an upstairs apartment. The manager unlocks the door, and they all go in. It's lovely inside, a lot better than the hotel room. It's completely furnished. It even has a color television set. It has one bedroom with a bathroom, a kitchen, a living room, and a small countertop between the kitchen and the living room.

Hans likes it. He tells the manager, "I'll take it."

He almost shits when she tells Hans, "That will be three hundred dollars, plus a seventy-five-dollar cleaning deposit. All the utilities will be paid by the management."

Hans doesn't say anything; He just looks at Pete.

Pete just shrugs and makes a smart-ass remark: "Why the dog-face look, Cowboy? Just pay her. What the hell? You can afford it."

Grinning, Hans replies, "Yes, I guess I can."

After paying her, Hans asks her, "Can you get a phone put in for me?"

She politely says, "I will take care of that. It might take a couple of days to get it in, though." She leaves.

Pete and Hans sit down in the living room. They just sit there for a couple of minutes, neither saying anything.

Hans thinks about what Mr. Bacco told them back on the boat.

When Tony told Hans what was happening here, he thought this was bad. But that's nothing compared to what the old man says. Shit, this is very bad!

Hans bluntly says, "Pete, what the hell are we doing here? Old man Bacco sounds just like Colonel James over in Vietnam. It's too bad James got killed. He should be here working for Bacco. They both have something in common. They like killing. Pete, this guy's crazy. I feel like I am right back in Vietnam. That's the main reason I got out of the army, so I could quit this bullshit.

Pete just looks at Hans. They sit in silence for a few minutes.

Finally, Pete says, "Cowboy, there was a time I was so proud to wear that uniform. I loved the United States. I still love it. I love what it stands for: freedom. But in Vietnam, we are not fighting for freedom. We are fighting, killing, and being killed so that the United States, politicians, airplanes, ammunition, bombs, and gun factories can get fat. All other kinds of business got fat and are getting fatter.

I didn't vote for Nixon. He's not making things any better. Vietnam is a rich man's war. We should have stopped it when it first got started. We had no business being over there in the first place.

"What did you get out of all that besides a pat on the back and a few worthless medals? We didn't make much money out of the deal. None of those politicians or companies offered to help your mom and dad out of the problems they had. They should have for what you did for them. Now, I'm not cutting down the armed forces. The United States has the best-armed forces in the world. It's those assholes that are telling the armed forces what to do that I don't like.

"The army was my life. I was going to put up to thirty years in before I retired. I turned him down when Tony offered me this deal, just like you did initially.

"But as time went on, the more I got to thinking about it, if I had stayed in, I would more than likely still be in Vietnam, getting myself killed or still fighting and killing people. Then I come out with a small pension. Here I can get killed just as easily. That's the chance I take, anyway. But I will be a rich man if I don't get killed. Richer than I can get from any pension. This way, I can get rich also, instead of just the politicians and big companies.

"Well, Cowboy, does that make you feel better now?"

Hans doesn't say anything. He just sits there, thinking about what Pete stated.

Leaning forward in his chair, Pete continues. "You're talking about killing and liking it. Think back to the day you made corporal. Remember? You killed the V.C. that was in that radio hut. You didn't cry over them. You were happy about that. You think about that for a while, Cowboy, while I use your bathroom."

Yes, Hans remembers. Thinking back, the whole event flashes through his mind as though his there again.

———◆———

He's still a private. They all advance through the jungle. The rain has stopped. The air's humid and hot. They come up to a small hill covered in jungle. Hans looks up to the top, and there's a metal rod sticking above the trees. He points the rod out to Sarge. He says, "That must be the V.C. radio hut we're looking for." He goes over to Colonel James and points it out to him.

Colonel James commands, "We're going up the hill to destroy that radio hut."

They start up the hill. A little over halfway up, the jungle thins out a little. There's the hut. It's built out of bamboo poles, and the roof looks like straw. It's not really big, about fifteen feet wide and twenty feet long. From where they are, there's no door, so it must be on the other side. About halfway up the side of the hut are four little holes and machine gun barrels sticking out of them. Just to the left of the hut and behind it is a foxhole with a machine gun barrel sticking out of it.

The troops are all very well spread out, just inside the thicker part of the jungle.

Suddenly from the hut, the V.C. start shooting. Even the guy in the foxhole's shooting. The troops all hit the ground and stayed low. Hans's getting scared.

Hearing a cry, Hans looks over to his right, and one of the guys has blood all over him. He's dead.

The only thing Hans can do is stare at him. The fear in him starts to change. Hans starts getting mad. He looks back up at the hut and says in a low voice, "I will get you for that, you son of a bitch!"

Not knowing what He's going to do just yet, Hans turns and starts crawling back into the jungle. While crawling, he looks around for Sarge or Colonel James. They must be a lot farther over.

An idea pops into Hans's head. Maybe he can work his way around behind them. One person may have a better chance of getting up that hill and taking the enemy by surprise.

If this doesn't work, Hans will either be dead or in a hell of a lot of trouble with the Colonel for not talking it over with him first.

Hans turns to the left, which puts the hut to his right. He creeps forward, looking carefully up in the trees for snipers and watching for booby traps.

When he finally makes it around to the opposite side of the hill, there's the hut door. There are no holes with rifles sticking out of them. The only one that can give Hans any trouble is the guy in the foxhole, but so far, he's too busy watching and shooting at the other side of the hill. His back is to Hans, but he's so low in the foxhole that he can't get a shot at him.

Hans gets down and crawls to the edge of the thick jungle. The rest of the jungle's a lot thinner on this side of the hill. There's not much cover from here to the hut, which is about thirty-five yards from here. About ten yards back is a large bunch of bushes and trees. The slope isn't very steep from here to the hut. Hans can make it to those trees if the troops keep the V.C. firing in that direction. He will at least get that guy in the foxhole.

Here goes! Hans comes out of the thick jungle and runs up the hill as fast as he can.

The troops must know it's Hans because they start firing back at the hut faster than before. At the top of the hill, he gets to the bushes and makes his way through them to the other side. He stays just inside and behind the trees. There's a giant boulder about ten feet up ahead. It's big enough to hide behind. Hans runs over to it, but just before getting there, he trips over a smaller rock and falls to the ground with a thud. The guy in the foxhole hears him fall and turns his machine gun toward Hans. He jumps straight behind the boulder as fast as Hans can, making it just as the guy starts shooting. Leaning flat against it, he doesn't dare try to look over.

Hans pulls a grenade from his belt, pulls the pin, and throws it over the boulder and toward the foxhole. It explodes, and the shooting stops. Hans slowly looks around the huge rock. The guy's sprawled near the top of the hole, and the machine gun has been blown clear out of the foxhole and is lying upside down.

Crouching low, Hans runs up to the foxhole and jumps in. He's just a few feet from the hut.

He climbs out of the foxhole and runs to the hut. Pressing his back against the wall next to the door, Hans quickly looks at his M-sixteen rifle to ensure it's okay. He looks at the door. It's unlocked.

He Jumps in front of it and swings it wide open. Pointing his rifle into the hut, he starts shooting wildly in all different directions, emptying the magazine. Reloading it before realizing that there are only three V.C. in there. He kills them all.

He looks at all the radio equipment and empties another magazine into the radio, destroying it. He goes inside and looks down at the bodies on the floor.

Shit, they're just kids. This is the first time Hans gets a good look at any of the V.C. he killed. They don't look over sixteen or seventeen years old. Why does there have to be so much hate in this world? But they were shooting at the troops. They had to shoot back.

Colonel James and Sarge are standing at the door, grinning at Hans.

Colonel James walks into the hut and asks, "What are you trying to do, Corporal? Get yourself killed?"

Hans, stammer, "S-sir, I am just a p-private."

Colonel James just grins even wider. "Now, son, you are a corporal."

Suddenly Hans hears something like a toilet flushing, and a door opens. Walking back into the living room, Pete asks, "Cowboy, did you think about that?"

Just like that, he comes back into today's time and finds himself sitting in his apartment living room.

Looking up at him, Hans replies, "Yes, I did. I do feel a little better about the whole thing. I just wish I didn't have to kill anyone. I don't think of myself being a killer. But it's a good thing I did. That was a good day. Not because I made corporal. Because I saved the lives of our troops and destroyed the radio hut."

Pete sighs with relief and says, "Good. I am sure glad to hear that."

Hans gets up, and they both walk outside into the sun.

Pete says, "There is a market within walking distance from your apartment. I'm going to go over to Tony's to find out if he has made any plans."

He leaves.

Hans goes back inside and starts unpacking his bags. He moves the furniture and things around to suit his taste. After getting that all done, He walks to the market that Pete pointed out. It's not just a market. It's a shopping center. So, Hans gets some pillows, linens, a blanket, and bathroom supplies. There's also a little café and bar in the shopping center. Since Hans is by himself and doesn't have anything to cook with, so he'll just come over and eat.

At the market, he only gets the things that he really needs, like ice cube trays, drinking glasses, beer, wine, and bourbon. With all that to carry, he hails a cab to take him back to the apartment.

Once back, Hans makes the bed up, fills the ice cube trays with water and puts them into the freezer, and puts the rest of the things away.

About three beers later, Hans puts on his swim trunks and goes down to the pool for a dip. So far, this's not bad at all. He feels like he's still on vacation. This's too good to be true. Something is going to happen sooner or later, and there's no sense in worrying about it. Let's just enjoy all of this while we can.

After dinner that evening, Hans stays home and has a few drinks while watching television. He goes to bed around eleven p.m. The next day, a knock on the door wakes Hans up. He quickly gets dressed and goes to answer it. A man's standing there with a tool belt full of tools and a telephone in his hand. He asks, "Do you need a telephone put in your place?"

Hans replies, "Yes, come on in."

"Where would you like me to put the phone?"

Hans looks around. "Set it on the countertop."

He looks under the countertop and remarks, "That will work. There's a phone jack already in the wall under here."

While he's hooking up the phone, Pete walks in. Hans remarks, "Since you're here, Pete, I will go ahead and shave, take a shower, and get ready for the day."

The telephone man's done and gone by the time Hans comes out of the bathroom.

He tells Pete, "There's a little café at the shopping center that you told me about yesterday." So, they go there and have breakfast.

The day is cloudy, with no rain, but humid.

While eating, Pete explains, "Cowboy, we have a lot of work ahead of us the way it looks. We are going to have to build the casino ourselves.

Chapter 9

Ship Sinks

"The contractor that Mr. Bacco hired has quit. Lagno's muscleman went over and beat the hell out of him. Then they threatened to hurt his family. If Bacco hires another contractor, Lagno will do the same to him. So, when the time comes, we are going to have to put our work clothes on, lay a few cement blocks, and pound some nails."

After taking a sip from his coffee, Hans replies, "That sounds okay to me. I'm pretty good with a hammer. I'm sorry about the contractor, but we will be able to build the entire casino ourselves. Besides, the work will do me good and get me back in shape."

"Tony's out getting some good, strong men to help us. They'll all be single men like us, with no family for them to worry about Lagno hurting, men who are not afraid to get knocked around a little and are willing to fight back.

"As soon as we get done eating, we're going to some of the supply houses that don't belong to Lagno and find out what kind of deal we can get on building materials.

Pete and Hans finish their breakfast and leave. They go straight from there to the nearest building supply and lumber yard.

When they walk inside, they are surprised and puzzled at what has happened in the store. The whole place's a shamble. It looks like a hurricane hit it. Bins of nails have been tipped over, and tools lie scattered all over the place. They step over the mess to the counter, and behind it are two black men. Their clothes are torn, and both are bruised up bad. One is lying back in a chair with a bleeding shoulder. The other one stands over him, holding a cloth rag on the wound.

Pete blurts out, "What the hell happened?"

The man who is standing over the other one turns around. He looks scared to death. He doesn't answer Pete's question. Instead, he comes back with another question, asking, "Are you Bacco's boys? If you are, you get the hell out of here and leave us alone. If I get caught talking to you, Lagno will burn this place down with me in it. He means it. He'll kill me if I do business with you boys. So, get out of here!"

Pete and Hans don't move. They really don't know what to do.

Suddenly the man moves over to a drawer and opens it. He reaches in and quickly pulls out a pistol. He points it at them and repeats, "Get out of here, or I'll shoot both of you."

At the sight of that gun pointing at them, Pete stammers, "Y-yes, sir. We're going."

They both back up to the door and quickly leave. They get back in the car and drive away.

As Pete drives, Hans asks, "What are we going to do now?"

"I don't know, Cowboy. There are two more building supply houses on the island. I bet Lagno's men have been over to them and beaten them up. There's no sense in going over to talk to them. Let's go find Tony and tell him what's happening."

That Lagno! Hans has never met or even seen the man, but he hates him. He never thought he could hate somebody he didn't know. But come to think of it, he hated the V.C. without knowing any of them. That Lagno's a bastard. Hope Mr. Bacco can get him to put in prison. That way, he can put a stop to all the innocent people who are getting hurt. Bacco just wants to put Lagno in prison. He'll get out later and start all over again. Bacco should just up and shoot Lagno himself. Hans asks Pete about that.

He listens to what Hans has to say and replies, "If Lagno shows up dead or disappears. Bacco will automatically look guilty of what Lagno is accusing him of. Bacco is trying to clear his name and get

Lagno convicted. Lagno's smart. He can rough up people like the ones at the building supply house and get them too scared to call the cops for help. If they call the law, Lagno will have them killed before they can testify in court. If Lagno does have the cops in his hip pocket, it won't do any good to call the cops anyway."

As soon as they get to Hans's place, Pete calls Tony and tells him, "There's something important to talk about. You should come over here rather than talk about it on the phone."

He hangs up, lights a cigarette, and says, "Tony will be here in about an hour. Do you have a coffee pot? I'm ready for some."

Hans hands Pete an ashtray out of a kitchen drawer. "Yea, I have a coffee pot. I'll make some."

After the coffee is made, Hans pours them each a cup.

Hans teases Pete by saying, "Only pussies put cream and sugar in their coffee. A man drinks it black. What the hell is the matter with you? Getting soft in your old age?"

Pete just grins and replies, "Piss on you, smart-ass. I just happen to like cream and sugar in my coffee."

Finally, Tony, Sam, and Carlos get here. Hans tells them, "Help yourselves to the coffee."

They all get some. Pete gives Hans a shit-eating grin because they all put cream and sugar in their coffee. Hans just shrugs and grins back.

After they all sit down in the living room, Tony asks, "What's up, Pete?"

Pete tells them what happened. No one says anything for a bit.

Finally, Tony interrupts the silence by saying, "We're going to have to ship the stuff over from the States. There are a lot of places there that have never heard of Lagno. We shouldn't have any problems."

Sam suggests, "I know of a building supply house in Jacksonville, Florida, that can get us anything we need."

Tony thinks a little and then agrees. "Okay, Sam. You and Carlos get on the first plane to the States. Get to Jacksonville and set everything up. You guys go ahead right now."

"Okay, we are on our way," replies Sam.

He and Carlos leave, and Tony says, "Pete, Cowboy, you guys come with me. We're going to some of the shipping lines here that Lagno doesn't own and find out if they can get a ship to go to Jacksonville, get the supplies, and bring them over here."

They go to two different lines. They're all booked up for months. They go to one more. That representative says, "We'll be able to ship your supplies over, and we have a shipping route through Jacksonville. The supplies will be here the day after tomorrow. We'll even furnish trucks to haul the supplies to the casino site."

Tony makes a deal with them.

On the way back to Hans's place, he says, "You guys meet me at the pier the day after tomorrow with work clothes on. I'll have some men there to help us. We will start breaking ground as soon as we get the supplies to the site."

They drop Hans off at his place, and Tony tells him, "We'll see you in a couple of days."

Hans nods and goes up to his apartment.

That afternoon Hans gets a beer, and around two p.m., he calls home. Mom answers the phone, "Hello." Hans replies, "Hi, Mom. I finally got a phone. I'm doing fine down here. I'm still on vacation. I start working the day after tomorrow. The weather down here's in the eighties, humid and more humid when it rains. How are things going there?"

Mom softly says, "Hi, Hans. We have all our debts paid off. That sure is a big relief. Dad is making sure that the combine is ready and is going to start harvesting the wheat tomorrow. He has hired two men to help him. It's sure good to finally hear from you, Hans."

Hans replies, "Sure, good to talk to you, Mom. Have you got some paper and a pen? I'll give you my phone number and address."

Mom softly says, "Yes, I'm ready."

Hans gives her his phone number and address and politely says, "Please keep in touch, and I'll talk to you again. Goodbye for now."

She replies, "Goodbye! They both hang up the phone.

Hans gets to thinking. After being in the army and coming here, being away from home so much, he's forgotten all about getting homesick. Maybe Idaho isn't the place for him after all. Maybe he's a man of the world rather than settling down and having a family.

Hans's up and gets his levies roughout boots and black T-shirt on.

Pete arrives. Hans suggests, "Let's stop at the shopping center to get a pair of leather gloves." Pete decides to get a pair, also.

They drive over to the pier, where they meet Tony and some of the men.

The ship hasn't arrived yet.

Hans starts looking around. At the pier's east end are stacks of large wooden boxes about six and a half square feet. They have Lagno's name on them. Hans walks over to them; one box is open a little. Inside it looks like something that would be used at an oil refinery. He walks back to where Tony and the rest of the men are.

In about fifteen minutes, looking out on the ocean, there's a ship on the horizon. It looks like a small freighter, and it's getting closer and closer.

One of the men who work for the shipping line comes up and tells Tony, "This's the one you're looking for."

It's close enough now to see that the ship's color is black.

Looking out at the vessel and smiling, Tony says, "Well, it won't be long before we get started on the casino."

Just as he gets the words out of his mouth, there's a giant explosion on the ship's deck, and a massive ball of fire billows into the sky. This is followed by a chain of explosions and fires onboard. The crew members are inflating rubber rafts and tossing them overboard. Right after that, the crew jumps overboard; they swim to the rafts and get on them. Before it can make its way into the harbor, it sinks entirely out of sight. Most of the crew made it off the ship alive.

Tony, Pete, and Hans stare at each other with their mouths hanging open.

Then Tony blurts out angrily, "That dirty son-of-a-bitch, Lagno, I would like to kill him. How in the hell did he know what we were going to do? You can't tell me that was an accident, either. Bullshit! No way.

"Pete, I'm going to get Sam and Carlos. They should be back over here by now. We'll meet you two over at your place, Cowboy. That's a good meeting place. Nobody knows about it. At least, I don't think so, anyway. Dammit, let's get some guns or something and start fighting back. I have tried everything else.

"A lot of innocent people were killed on that ship. I'm not going to be a good guy anymore. You guys think of a way that we can get that son-of-a-bitch. I'll see you later."

Pete and Hans return to the apartment, and Hans makes coffee while they wait for Tony.

Chapter 10

U.S. National Guard Armory Rip-Off

About thirty minutes after Pete and Cowboy get to the apartment, Tony, Sam, and Carlos get there.

Tony has calmed down, but he's serious when he asks, "Has anybody got any ideas? If nobody does, let's sit right here until we do."

Hans waits a minute to see if anyone else has anything to say. No one does, so he states, "Tony, I got to thinking and came up with something that just might work."

"Okay, Cowboy, what do you have on your mind?"

"We can get the supplies here right under Lagno's nose without him knowing it by using one of his own ships."

"Cowboy, you're crazy." blurts out Pete.

"Wait a minute, Pete," says Tony. "Let's hear him out. Cowboy, just how do you plan to pull this crazy thing off?"

"Tony, you have hired more men now. Do any of them know how to run a ship? I mean enginemen, navigators, regular deckhands, and so on. If not, can you get some? Men who are also willing to fight like the men you have now. With them, we can take full control of one of Lagno's ships. But keep the real captain, radioman, or any other bosses or department heads they have on board so that if there's any radio contact with Lagno or whatever, he will think everything is all right."

"The idea is to hijack one of his ships, get the supplies on it, and get it over here on the island before he knows what's going on. This's the only way we can get the supplies shipped in. After what happened today, we'll be unable to get any other shipping lines to get the supplies here. Lagno may not own everything on this island, but he definitely controls it."

Tony says, "You're right about that. I really don't like your idea, Cowboy. But I think that might be the only way we can do it. Have you any ideas on how we should hijack the ship?"

"Yes, I do. Don't know about Sam and Carlos, but the rest of us were in Vietnam. You all say this could be just like that. Well, with that ship sinking today, I say this's like Vietnam. This's turning into a war. Every time we make a move, Lagno hits us a little harder. Now, this time, he has gotten people killed."

"We need weapons. I mean military weapons like M-sixteen rifles and grenades. Maybe you guys might know how we can get some. When we get the weapons, this is what we can do. Lagno doesn't know me. Somehow, get me a job on the ship we plan to take. This morning, at the pier's east end, I saw stacks of wooden boxes about six and a half feet square with Lagno's name. One box is open. It looks like it has oil refinery stuff in it.

"We'll have to find out which ship is bringing the refinery stuff in or where they're loading them up in the States. Get me a job on one of those ships. Then, at night, on the pier, just before they load the boxes on the ship, we'll sneak onto the pier and pry some of the boxes open. There's enough room in the boxes for a man and some weapons to fit in without taking anything out of them.

"After you're all in the boxes, I'll nail them shut again. Then, when they get all of you aboard the ship and get out to sea, I'll sneak down, pry open the boxes, and get all of you out. That's when we take over the ship. It won't be easy, but we were in tougher spots before over in Vietnam and got through them.

"Well, what do you all think about that?"

Nobody says a word. They just sit there for a while.

Finally, Tony says, "There's only one way we can get the weapons. We can't buy them, so we'll have to steal them from somewhere."

Pete blurts out, "You mean you're going through that crazy idea?"

Tony nods. "Why not, Pete?" he asks with a slight grin.

Pete thinks for a minute, and then a big smile comes over his face. "Why not? Let's do it."

"I remember when Sam and I were in Jacksonville, we rented a car," says Carlos. "While driving to the building supply houses, we passed Lagno's pier and saw some of those same boxes Cowboy's talking about with Lagno's name on them. We can get into them there.

"When we were in a bar in Jacksonville, some guys were there who are in the National Guard. They were saying that they're going to have combat drills this next weekend. The drills are to be held at the National Guard Armory just outside a small town about twenty-five miles past the Georgia state line. I don't remember the town's name, but only about five deputies are in the whole sheriff's department there. I have been in that armory more than once. We should be able to rip it off without too much trouble."

"The man we got the supplies from in Jacksonville has another supply house in Daytona Beach," says Sam. "After we take over the ship, we can port there and have the rest of our men waiting. We can load our supplies there."

"It's all set," says Tony. "First, we get the weapons and then the ship."

"Carlos, how many men will we need to take the armory?" asks Pete.

"The five of us can do it," replies Carlos. "If we use any more, somebody might suspect and get wise to us. We'll have to do it right before the weekend. The armory doesn't supply the ammunition. We'll have to get it right after the ammunition supply gets into the armory. Plus, the bolts for the rifles are locked in a safe in the sheriff's office downtown. When I was in the guard and stationed at that armory, I found out that's where they keep them. We'll have to hit that place also."

Looking at everybody, the anger they all had left them. Everyone's excited and can feel the challenge. They're acting like they can't wait to get going.

Wound up tight and excited, Tony demands, "You guys pack your work clothes and bring them with you. That's all I want you to take. I'll set things up and be on our way tomorrow. I want to think about this some more. You guys all take the rest of the day off but don't drink too much tonight. I want clear heads from all of you when we pull this off."

They all get up and leave. Boy, Hans sure started something. To think they'll have to rip off the National Guard Armory just to hijack a ship. But they sure can't get any M-sixteen rifles out of a Sears Roebuck and Co. catalog!

That night, even after a few drinks, it's hard to fall asleep because of the things that are going to be happening in the next few days. Hans doesn't know whether he is more scared or just excited about the whole thing, probably both. His stomach feels like it's full of butterflies.

The next day, they're on their way. Sam and Carlos had already left the night before. They land in Jacksonville. There they meet Sam and Carlos.

They put their gear in lockers at the terminal, except for Tony's binoculars. Then Tony rents a car and takes them across the state line into Georgia and to the small town to look over the armory. They also look over at the sheriff's department as they drive by. It's a tiny place.

The guard grounds take up about ten acres. There's a high chain-link fence with rolled razor wire on top of it all the way around.

In the center is a building, tan in color and shaped rectangular. It looks a lot like a big basketball gym or a small airplane hangar with a long, dome-shaped roof.

A few feet from the front of the building are a big cannon and a flagpole. The flag is up. Right in line with that are two big wooden doors, and just above the doors is the name "Georgia National

Guard."

They drive past the place, go down the street, turn right onto a side road, drive down it, and then turn around and come back. Just before they get to the corner, Tony pulls over and stops to watch what's happening inside the guard grounds.

Behind the building are two other fences, just like the one in front. They reach from two ends of the building to the main fence in a straight line. Inside are army trucks, pickups, and tanks. One of the fence gates stands open. Men in fatigues are driving the tanks and trucks to the front of the flagpole. They're lining them up, pointing them toward the road.

Then four army trucks drive up from behind them. They go around them, turn left at the corner, and go up a quarter mile to the main entrance. The gate's open. They drive in and back the trucks in front of the big wooden doors. Men come out of the building and start unloading boxes from the trucks.

Tony looks at them through his binoculars. "Here's our ammunition. We'll hit them tonight."

He starts the car and goes back into Jacksonville.

At the airport, they get their gear out of the lockers and then go to the men's room, clean up, and change into their work clothes. Tony turns the car in at the car rental.

When they're all gathered in the terminal, Tony asks Sam, "Can you and Carlos get everything taken care of?"

With a sly grin on his face, Sam replies, "Yes, everything will be ready."

"Good. You two guys get something to eat someplace, then get the equipment ready and meet Pete, Cowboy, and me by the theater we passed on the north end of town coming back in. In about two hours."

Sam and Carlos get in a cab and leave.

As they walk out of the terminal, Tony suggests, "Let's go eat something also."

So, they get in a cab, head north, and find a place to eat close to the theater.

Tony doesn't say what Sam and Carlos are to take care of. There must be a reason he won't tell Hans, so he doesn't ask.

The sun has gone down, with a clear sky by the time they finish dinner. It's close to the time they're supposed to meet Sam and Carlos. They walked to the theater and were only there about five minutes when they heard a horn. They turn, and Carlos is in a green Ford van, waving for them to get in.

Heading for the van, Tony demands, "Come on, you guys, let's go."

After they're in the van, Carlos drives out of town. He states, "Everything we need for tonight is in that box on the floor."

Tony reaches down and picks up the box, and looks inside. He pulls out a bolt cutter, a hacksaw, and a couple of flashlights. Then he pulls out a pistol and some bullets and hands them to Pete. He also gets one for Hans and one for himself. They're all thirty-eight specials.

While driving, Carlos states, "Sam and I already have ours."

"Okay, we're all set, then," replies Tony.

Carlos pulls up behind a brand-new dark red Buick with a white top. Sam's in the car waiting for them. He gets out, comes over, and gets in the van with them.

Tony looks over at Sam and asks, "Did you have much trouble stealing all of this?"

"Not at all. It's like taking candy from a baby."

"Pete," Tony orders, "you and Cowboy, come with me."

They leave the van, walk, and get into the car. Carlos and Sam drive ahead of them as they head for the armory. Hans has a feeling that they stole all of this, even the van and car. He really doesn't know just how Tony plans to do this, but in some cases, you're better off not knowing.

As they drive to the armory, Tony explains, "Remember something, you guys. If anything goes wrong, and there's a lot of heat, and we all can't get out of there, you may be on your own for a while. Don't go getting yourself killed. If you get caught, we may not be able to help you right then, but we'll help you as soon as we can."

They get to the armory, and nobody's around. There's a big light on a power pole that lights up the whole yard. The gates are closed and locked with a chain and padlock. Sam and Carlos stop and get out of the van with the bolt cutter, and Sam cuts the locked chain.

While they are doing that, Tony demands, "You guys take your wallets out of your pockets and put them in your bags. If you do get caught, there will be no identification on you. Tell them anything you want to except for why you are doing this and who you are."

After they get the gate unlocked and open, they drive in. Sam closes it behind them and hooks the chain back around it. There's a broken piece of wire sticking out directly behind the bar of the gate, and he hangs the chain ends on the wire,

What an idea! On the outside, it still looks like it's locked. Also, it loosely holds the gate shut. They can just ram the gate with the car if needed to get out of here fast. The wire will break, and the gate will swing open.

They drive up and stop between the trucks and tanks. Carlos backs the van up to the big wooden doors. Tony gets out of the car, walks to one of the tanks, gets in, and starts it. It starts moving. He turns it to the left and heads straight for the power pole, smashing right into it and knocking it over. All the wires break, and there's a shower of sparks and a lot of cracking and popping going on for a while. Tony then drives the tank back to where it was parked before, stops, and gets out.

Pete and Hans get out of the car.

Looking around, Pete says, "That takes care of the light, power, and alarms."

Their eyes take a moment to get used to the dark.

Sam and Carlos get the back doors of the van open. Carlos can open anything. He has a small flashlight. It seems like hours, but it only takes about four minutes to unlock the wooden doors of the armory.

They all walk inside a large room. Tony and Pete have their flashlights. They turn them on. They're in a basketball gym. Tony flashes his light around as they walk through the gym. At the far end, there are two swinging doors. Tony opens one and pokes his head through. He motions with his flashlight for them to come and says, "It's in here." They all walk through the swinging doors.

Right inside is a large walk-in safe with a combination lock on it. Carlos picks the lock, and they all enter the safe.

The M-sixteen rifles are in racks of ten. They are chained and padlocked. The chains are too big for the bolt cutter, and it will take too long to cut through them with the hacksaw, so Carlos starts picking the locks.

While he's doing that, the rest of them start hauling ammunition boxes out to the van. Before they can get back to the safe to get more, Carlos has picked all the locks they need. They get several M-sixteens out and into the van, and now they also have several boxes of ammunition and grenades. The boxes are heavy, and Hans's slowing down. He's getting behind.

From inside the safe, Hans hears the van and car doors slam and the engines start. Before he can drop the box and run out to catch them, they ram the gate and turn right and left at the crossroads. From out of nowhere come two sheriff cars. One goes right past the gate, turns left, and is right on their asses. The other car comes squalling through the gate.

One of the van's back doors opens and closes, and there's a massive boom as the sheriff's car races after them. The grenade explodes just to the right outside of the car. Not under it. The impact blows the car over on the left side and slides to a stop. A big ball of fire that lights up the dark night. The car isn't burning all that badly.

Cowboy starts running the other way toward the fence. He gets there, but before he can start climbing the fence, the other car stops, and Hans hears the deputy get out of the car and the click of a shotgun.

A voice demands, "Hold it right there and don't move, or you're a dead man!"

Hans's facing the fence. He's too scared to move and can hardly breathe. The deputy demands, "Put your hands up against the fence." He searches him and takes his pistol out of his belt. Hans keeps his cool and does exactly what he says.

He handcuffs him with his hands behind his back, then shoves Hans into the patrol car's backseat.

The deputy gets in and drives straight to where the other deputy's car is still burning. He stops the car and gets out, running to the back of his car. Opens the trunk, grabs a fire extinguisher, runs over, and puts the fire out. He puts the fire extinguisher back in the trunk, runs over to the car, and tries to push it back onto its wheels. But he can't.

He returns to the car Hans is in, opens the back door, and demands, "Get out of the car. You're going to help me get that car back onto its wheels."

Hans gets out of the car. The deputy takes the handcuffs off him and pulls his colt 45 out of his holster. He points it at Hans and remarks, "Try anything, and you're dead.

They run to the other car. Hans tries pushing on the right side of the trunk. The deputy is pushing on the right front fender. They can't do it.

Hans asks, "Do you have a long rope or a chain?"

"Yes, I have a rope."

"Get it for me. I have an idea."

He goes to get the rope.

Hans looks around. There's no place to run. There's a slope on both sides of the road and no trees or buildings to run and hide behind. He would kill him if he made a run for it.

He brings the rope. Hans demands: "Get in your car, turn it around and back it up over here on the right side of the road, and call for an ambulance.

He gets the car, backs it over here, and stops.

Hans ties the rope to the wrecked car's front bumper and the other end of the rope to the back bumper of the other car.

Hans explains, "Now pull forward and drag the front of the car crossways on the road."

He drags the front of the car around.

Hans shouts stop. "That's far enough; back up a little way. That's good."

Hans unties the rope and reties it in the middle of the car on the top frame on the right side.

"Now, pull forward kind of fast."

He drives fast and pulls the car back on its wheels.

Hans shouts, "Stop. Now untie the rope."

Hans run around to the left side of the car. Hans tries to open the door, but it's stuck. He pulls harder. The door opens, and he pulls the deputy out and drags him away from the car. The deputy has a big bump on his head. Hans looks below the car. Flames are under it.

As the deputy comes around the car. Hans shouts, "Get over here; the car's still on fire."

The deputy runs up to them. The car explodes, and a big ball of fire lights up the night.

The deputy bends down and checks the other deputy's pulse. "He's still alive and is starting to come too.

He opens his eyes and stammers, "W-where a-am I?"

The other deputy replies, "You have a big bump on your head Tom. Hang in there. Stay with me; the ambulance is on the way."

He stammers, "O-okay, I-I'll try."

The other deputy gets up and looks at Hans and remarks, "Your something else bad guy, the bad guy. I don't know your name. So, I'll call you the bad guy. You just saved our lives. But I can't let you go. The sheriff will kill me if I do. Oh, he will!"

Hans turns his back to him, puts his hands behind him, and politely says, "Do what you got to do." He thinks Pete and others are going to hit the sheriff's office to get the bolts. They'll break him out of jail.

The deputy puts the handcuffs back on Hans, walks him back over to his car, and Hans gets in the back seat.

He gets on the radio and calls for a fire truck.

The ambulance pulls up. The ambulance attendants put the other deputy in the ambulance and heads back to town. The deputy gets in the car and follows them.

The fire truck's coming.

On the way to town, Hans asks the deputy, "What's your name?"

"My name's Frank. What's yours?"

"I'm sorry, Frank. I'm not going to tell you. I'll just be the bad guy to you."

"For saving our lives back there, I'm going to warn you about the sheriff. He's an asshole and has a really bad temper. If you make him very mad, he might kill you. If you do say anything to him, try not to make him mad."

"Thank you. Frank, for the warning. But I think I'm going to make him mad. Because I'm not going to tell him anything."

"You're something else, bad guy".

Chapter 11

Hans Gets Thrown in Jail

Frank's a tall, thin man with blond hair. He's young, probably in his late twenties or early thirties, wearing a khaki uniform with a flat-brim hat of the same color.

They get to the sheriff's office, and he pulls around to the back and parks in a space reserved for sheriff's cars only. He gets out of the car, pulls Hans out, and begins to read him his rights. "Bad guy. You have the right to remain silent. If you give up that right, anything you say may be held against you."

He keeps reading, but Hans's mind does not hear the rest. He's thinking about the first part: you have the right to remain silent. It reminds him of something back in basic training at Fort Ord. It flashes back to him as if he's still there. Just about to get out of basic when his drill sergeant gets them around for a short talk.

He stands on the steps right outside the barracks and explains, "If any of you get captured by the enemy, and they ask you any questions, you don't have to tell them anything. You only tell them your name, rank, and service number. That is all."

Suddenly someone pulls Hans's arm. It's Frank. Hans's mind comes back to the present. He takes him into the sheriff's office and tells the sheriff, "He has no identification on him. But he saved Tom's and my life." Frank explains to the sheriff what happened.

The sheriff's sitting in a chair at a desk. He has a flattop haircut, and his hair's very gray. An older man in his fifties, maybe. He's big around the shoulders and has a fat belly. He has a bulge in his left cheek and chewing tobacco stains on his lips.

He doesn't seem to be too impressed about Hans saving their lives.

He glares at Hans and spits a big wad of tobacco into a big coffee can by his desk.

In a gruff voice, he asks, "What is your name?"

Hans doesn't say anything.

He repeats, "What is your name?"

"My name is Fred," Hans replies in a serious tone. "Private, United States Army. Service number zero, zero, ought, ought, zero, zero, ought."

Oh shit! The looks on both of those guys' faces after that remark. The sheriff doesn't like that at all.

He blurts out angrily, "What in the hell is your real name?"

Hans replies in the same tone of voice he used before, "My name is John. Airman, United States Airforce. Service number ought, ought, zero, ought, zero, zero, ought." Again, that is all he says.

The sheriff gets mad. His face twists into a scowl, and then he gets up from his chair and hawks a gob of that slimy tobacco spit right in Hans's face.

That! Makes Hans mad. His hands are still cuffed behind his back, so he can't wipe his face. Hans just glares back at the sheriff.

The sheriff shouts as he comes around the desk, "You dirty son of a bitch." He swings and hits Hans right in the mouth. He wallops him that he loses his balance and falls back against the wall. His lip's bleeding.

The sheriff backs off a little and demands again, this time yelling at the top of his voice, "Who the hell are you?"

Hans stands up and steps away from the wall. With tobacco spit still on his face and his lip still bleeding, Hans replies, "My name is Gene. Corporal, United States Marine Corps. Service number zero, ought—"

"Dammit, all to hell!" The sheriff punches Hans in the stomach, the face, and all over his body. Dazed, Hans falls to the floor, his hat falls off his head, and the sheriff keeps hitting him.

He is going to kill Hans.

Frank yells, "Help me, Jack." The two of them pull the sheriff off Hans. They saved his life.

Holding the sheriff down, Frank demands, "Cool off, Sheriff. Let the detectives come out and work on him."

"The detectives like hell," the sheriff yells. "We don't need any city-schooled detectives out here. This is my town, my county, and my department. We will do this my way. I don't want the Highway Patrol or anyone else to stick their noses in this. Now, do I make myself clear? I will fire the guy that calls for outside help."

The deputies let him loose.

From the floor, Hans sighs with relief. Hope that dumb shit keeps right on thinking that way; it will be easier for Pete and the other guys to get him out of here and rip this place off.

Looking straight down at Hans, the sheriff laughs and says, "It doesn't do you any good to rip off those rifles because the bolts are right here in that safe. You can't use those rifles without bolts, dumb shit."

He points back behind his desk to a small walk-in safe with a combination lock on it.

Hans doesn't say anything, thinking, Sheriff, you're the dumb shit. Thank you for telling him where the bolts are.

He glares down at Hans again and demands, "Put this bastard in the same cell with those two queers. Let those two have a little treat with him. That might be just what he needs to make him talk. Leave those handcuffs on him so he can't fight them off. That'll be the day somebody pulls that name, rank, and service number bullshit on me and gets away with it."

He laughs as the two deputies, Frank and Jack, pick Hans off the floor. Frank picks up Hans's hat and put's it back on his head. The sheriff picks up a camera off the desk and takes Hans's picture just before they lead him to the cell. One of them unlocks and opens a thick iron door. They go through it and walk between two rows of cells. They take Hans to the last cell on the right. He can hear the sheriff still laughing until the big iron door shuts with a loud clang. Then Hans can't hear a thing.

Frank politely says, "I'm sorry, bad guy, but he's mean."

Hans looks at Frank and just nods. Hans likes Frank. Frank should be the sheriff.

There's a door at the end of the hall. It's locked, and it takes a code to open it.

Hans's stomach, face, and eyes hurt where the sheriff hit him. He feels a little sick.

Then Hans really feels sick and wants to throw up seeing those two men sitting on a bench in the cell.

They're in each other's arms and kissing each other. They stop and look over at Hans.

Oh shit. Hans will kill that sheriff when he gets out of here. Hans was mad earlier but not half as mad as he is right now. That dirty son of a bitch! He hears the big iron door clang down the hall as it shuts.

There's no one else in the other cells.

The two gay guys break away from each other. They both give Hans a girlish smile. The smaller one gets up off the bench and starts walking toward him.

"Hi there, big boy," he says in a high, feminine voice. "My name is Jimmy, and this is Donny. What is your name?"

Hans doesn't answer. He just stands there and glares at them.

Stepping closer, Jimmy coaxes, "Come on, now, don't be bashful. We are your friends. Oh, for mercy's sake, those silly savages out there cut your pretty mouth. I hate policemen!"

He comes closer, and Hans backs up a little to his left and away from him.

Donny gets up from the bench and steps toward Hans, a malicious gleam in his eyes. He suggests, "Let's unzip him and find out how well-hung he is. Maybe we will have an all-day sucker."

Jimmy smacks his lips and giggles, just like a girl.

As Jimmy slowly gets near, Hans judges the distance between Jimmy and him.

Better get him now. Hans very quickly brings his right knee up as far as he can. Then, Hans kicks him right in the nuts by snapping his foot out and coming up hard with the pointed toe of his boot.

Hans steps back. Jimmy falls to his knees.

Hans yells, "I'll kick you in the neck and kill you, or would you like to get out of here?

Enraged, Donny charges at Hans. He quickly ducks and moves to his right. Donny misses Hans and hits the wall with his head and right shoulder. That dazes him, and he falls face down.

Quickly stepping one leg over him, Hans sits on his shoulders. Donny's head is behind Hans. He reaches back, slips his hands under his neck, and pulls the handcuffs up. Crossing his hands, Hans presses down on the back of his head and starts choking him.

Jimmy shouts. "Don't kill him. We'll do what you want." He sits down on a bench holding his nuts.

Hans lets loose of Donny, gets off him, and gets up on his feet.

Donny is coughing and starting to get up. He glares at Hans.

Jimmy yells, "leave him alone, Donny. He says he's going to get us out of here."

Jimmy isn't talking with such a girlish voice anymore.

Donny sits down next to Jimmy, not saying anything and still glaring at Hans.

Hans sighs with relief, walks over to another bench, and sits down. Hans's panting hard, and his wrists are hurting badly from the handcuffs' pressure when he was choking Donny.

Hans explains, looking at the two gays, "Some friends of mine are going to break me out of here. I don't know how or when. When they do, you two get out that door and go just as fast as you can and don't stop or look back. Do you understand?

They both look at Hans and nod.

Donny asks, "How do we get the code for the door?"

Hans replies, "We'll get it from one of the deputies. You two relax and go back to doing what you were doing when I first got here. Pretend I'm not here if you want to. Just leave me alone. Now we wait for something to happen."

Still sitting on the last bench, Hans leans his head against the wall and doses off for a few minutes.

Hans suddenly wakes up to what sounds like something tapping against the glass. He looks up. Directly above his head is a window. It has bars on the inside and glass on the outside. Hans quickly demands in a low voice. "You two lay down and cover up under the blankets like you are asleep."

They did what Hans demanded.

Hans gets up, stands on the bench, and looks out.

There's Sam, grinning at him. He must be standing on something because his face is right there at the window. Hans sighs with relief and grins back. He cannot open the window because it is a solid sheet of glass. Hans turns around, so Sam sees he has handcuffs on. He waves at Hans to get away from the window. He jumps down and backs away.

Sam shatters the window with the butt of his pistol. He keeps hitting it until he's cleared enough glass away to get hold of two bars.

Sam asks, "Are you okay, Cowboy?"

Hans climbs back on the bench and replies, "I'm fine. Just get me the hell out of here."

"Hang in there a while longer, Cowboy. We don't know just how we are going to do this yet. Here, take my pistol. Maybe you can shoot a couple of them from inside. That will help us get in from the outside."

"Dammit, Sam, I can't shoot a pistol with my hands cuffed from behind. They will be coming back after me real soon. They're trying to get me to talk. Get me something else."

"Okay, I will get something better. I will be right back."

Hans hears Sam tell someone, "Let me down and wait here."

Looking out the window and down, Sam has been on Carlos's shoulders, piggyback style.

Sam gets down and runs around the building. Carlos steps back a little and looks up at Hans. He smiles and waves. Hans smiles back.

Sam does not waste any time. Just like that, he's back. He climbs back on Carlos's shoulders, and Carlos steps up to the window.

Sam ties two sticks of dynamite together by a thin short rope, pokes them through the hole in the window, and lowers them down to Hans. He turns so that his hands will be to the window. Hans gets the dynamite in his hands. Sam turns loose from the rope.

Hans asks Sam, "Where in the hell did you get these?"

"Never mind, Cowboy," Sam replies with a grin. "We have ways of getting what we need. Catch this book of matches."

"Okay. When you hear the dynamite go off, get your asses in here and take this place over."

"Okay, Cowboy. We will be ready."

Sam jumps back down off Carlos's shoulders, and they run around the building

Hans jumps down off the bench onto the floor! He sticks the dynamite and matches under a blanket folded on the bench's end. He kicks the broken pieces of glass under the bench and out of sight.

Jimmy and Donny come up from under the blankets.

Hans explains, "Things are starting to happen. Now we wait again. When the big iron door slams shut, you two get back under the blankets and act like you're asleep. As soon as the deputies get in here and get close to you, jump out from under the blankets and attack them. Take control of them, but don't kill them unless you just have to. The door won't open without the code. With my hands cuffed behind me, the only thing I can do is kick them.

While they wait, Hans tries to think of a way to get someone back sooner. There's no way to make enough noise for them to hear through that thick iron door. He gives up on the idea and dozes off again.

Hearing a loud clang, Hans opens his eyes and sits up.

Chapter 12

Hans breaks out of the Jail

Jimmy and Donny quickly get under the blankets. The sound of approaching footsteps comes faintly through the door. Hans quickly checks to make sure that the dynamite's out of site.

Hans looks through the bars in the door. It's Frank and Jack, the other deputy, that helped pull the sheriff off from him. They look first at Hans and then at the two gays with the blankets over them. Jack unlocks the door and opens it, and as they step in, Hans stands up.

Jack says, "I'll be damned! You must have really satisfied them for them to be asleep already. You must be just as queer as they are. What did you do, suck them both or something?"

They seem to be more interested in the guys than Hans. As they approach Jimmy and Donny, Jack keeps right on talking. "Wait till the sheriff hears about this."

Their backs are to Hans. Hans is thinking. He better get them now. He walks softly and quickly, gets behind them and kicks Frank right in the nuts. Pivot to his right on his left foot, and kicks Jack with his right heel square in the nuts. They both groan and fall to their knees.

Hans yells, "Get them now."

Jimmy and Donny quickly jump up off the bench and start hitting them in the head and stomach. The deputies fall to the floor, dazed.

Hans demand, "Get the handcuff key and get these cuffs off me."

Jimmy gets the cuffs off Hans.

Hans tells Jimmy, "Put the handcuffs on the deputies, hands behind them. Hans gets the other cuffs from the other deputy and cuffs him."

Hans pulls the Colt .45 out of Jack's holster and does the same with Frank. Hans points the guns at Jack. He is coming too.

Hans demands, "Give me the code to the back door."

Jack looks up, not saying anything.

Hans pulls the hammer back, points one of the guns to the left of his head, and pulls the trigger. Hans repeats, "Give me the code."

That scares the hell out of Jack. He stammers, "It-its 8642."

Hans runs out of the cell, over to the code box, decodes the door, and opens it.

Hans gets back into the cell; Donny is bent down, choking Jack. Hans quickly Kicks Donny in the head. He falls back against the wall.

Frank comes to.

Hans points both guns at Donny and demands, "Pick the deputies up off the floor, onto their feet. Jimmy, help him. After they get Frank and Jack on their feet, Hans demands, "Jimmy, pick up their hats and put them on their heads."

Jimmy does it.

Hans blurts, "Donny, you son of a bitch. You two get the hell out of here before I change my mine and kill you both."

Jimmy and Donny vanish out the door and into the night.

Jack's coughing a little from being choked, but he's all right.

Hans points both guns at Frank and Jack. Hans explains, "I have some friends outside; they're going to break me out of here. This place's going to be burned down. You will never see me again. You saved my life from the sheriff. With his temper, I bet he's done this before."

Frank replies, "That dirty son of a bitch had killed innocent people before, just like he tried to kill you, and gets away with it because we're too scared of him to do anything about it. Bad guy, you saved my life twice to night. I don't care what you do with the sheriff."

Hans states, "Thank you for the information about the sheriff. I'm not taking your handcuffs off. I'm keeping your guns. Both of you saved my life tonight. We're even. You get the hell out of here and get as far away from here as fast as possible and stay away from the news media. Don't go around front and try and stop this. If you do, you'll be killed."

"Frank, when election time comes. I suggest you run for sheriff. The way you handled things tonight, the good and bad guys worked together as a team to save the other deputy. I think you would make a good sheriff."

There was a surprised look on Jack's face when Hans told Frank that.

Frank smiles and replies, "Thank you bad guy. I might just do that."

Hans puts one of the guns on the bench away from Frank and Jack and puts the handcuff key in Frank's front pants pocket.

Hans demands, "Get the hell out of here and be careful."

They run out the back door. Hans shuts the door behind them, locks it, and arms the code box.

He puts the Colt .45 in his belt, then pulls the blanket off the bench. He drops it on the floor, grabs the dynamite and matches, and holds them all in one hand.

Hans comes out of the cell. He pulls the key out of the lock and runs straight across the hall to the opposite cell door. He unlocks it and opens it wide.

He races out of the cell straight to the big iron door at the end of the hall and leans against it. With the dynamite still tied together, Hans lights the fuses and lays them right against the big iron door. He races back into the open cell, runs to the left corner, and leans against the wall. Just then, the dynamite explodes.

Hans waits a few seconds, coughing from the smoke. He takes the Colt .45 from his belt, goes out into the hallway, and starts walking slowly toward the office.

Smoke continues to pour from the doorway.

Suddenly, Tony shouts, "Hold it right there, Sheriff. Get your hands up and get up out of the chair."

The sheriff yells, "Don't shoot! I will do anything you want, anything. Only don't shoot. Please don't shoot me."

That cowardly son of a bitch.

Hans slowly walks along the hall. The smoke's almost gone by the time he walks into the office.

The sheriff is standing against the wall with his hands up in the air. He's sweating and shaking.

The only thing Hans does is glare at him. He thought he was damned high and mighty when he was pushing Hans around with the handcuffs on him.

Hans looks around. Pete and Tony are standing just inside the door with their guns pointing at the sheriff. Sam and Carlos are to his left, going through the other offices.

They return, and Carlos quickly says, "There's no one else in here."

Sam remarks, "The rest of them must be out on patrol."

Tony asks, "Cowboy, did you hear anything about where they might be keeping the bolts? Are they in that safe?"

Not saying anything, Hans just glares straight at the sheriff and nods.

Shaking and scared, the sheriff stares at Hans and stammers, "Cow-Cow-Cowboy. Th-that's what they call you? Come on, Cowboy. You have the upper hand now. Why don't you say something?"

Tony blurts out, "Shut up, Sheriff, and get the safe open."

The sheriff continues to stare at Hans in disbelief that he doesn't say one word. He turns and starts unlocking the safe.

He gets the safe open.

Tony demands, "Cowboy, watch him."

Still not saying anything, Hans just nods.

The sheriff just can't believe Hans. He stammers again, "W— what the hell is it with you?"

Hans motions with the Colt .45 for him to sit down. He does. Walking to his desk and picking up the coffee can full of tobacco spit, Hans dumps the whole can over the sheriff's head. The tobacco spit goes down his face, back, and ears.

Hans throws the can down on the floor, points the gun at his face, and says in a deep, slow, loud voice, "My name is something. The United States Armed Forces. Service number zero, zero, zero, zero, zero, zero, zero."

The sheriff screams, "No, no, you are mad! You're insane! No! No!"

Hans points the gun at one of the chair's legs the sheriff sitting on and pulls the trigger, shattering the chair leg. Falling to the floor, he sits up on his elbow and yells, "Come on. Don't make me suffer. If you're going to kill me! Get it over with and kill me!"

Hans hears a shot from a pistol, and the sheriff falls to the floor dead. Hans turns around, and Tony stands there with his pistol pointing at the sheriff.

Pete says, "We have all the bolts we need."

"Sam and Carlos," says Tony, "Throw grenades in all the offices and cells. Set the rest of the building on fire and burn this place down."

Pete starts setting papers on the desk on fire.

Hans grabs the camera off the desk, pulls the film out, and exposes it.

He gives the sheriff one last glare and runs out of the building.

They've just gotten clear when the grenades start to explode.

Getting two grenades from the van, Carlos runs to the door of the main office, pulls the pins, and throws the grenades in. He runs back over to them as they explode. The building's really on fire now. There's no way anyone can save it.

Hans walks over to the van, lays the Colt .45 in the van, and gets one of the M-sixteen rifles, a bolt, and some bullets.

Tony says with a grin, "I take it you didn't like that sheriff too well."

Hans just grins back and replies, "Yeah, I think we had a kind of a personality clash. He didn't have to treat me the way he did. He's not going to treat anyone else like that again."

Tony, Pete, and Hans get in the car and get the hell out of there, with Sam and Carlos right behind them. Tony's driving. Pete is in the front seat, and Hans's in the back.

They turn right onto a four-lane highway, and Hans starts putting the bolt in the rifle. Pete looks back at Hans and says, "Think you can still disassemble and assemble that rifle blindfolded, Cowboy?"

Hans grins. "Sure."

Suddenly Pete blurts out, "Oh shit! Look! Here come two deputies."

Hans glances up to see Pete's pointing out the back window. Hans turns and looks, and from out of nowhere, two sheriff cars pull out onto the four-lane highway right behind them. Their red lights flashing, and their sirens blowing.

Tony yells, "Dammit! I was hoping we would be out of here before any of the deputies showed up back here. We can't have any witnesses at all, or we are done." He starts to speed up.

Hans finishes getting the bolt in the rifle and starts loading bullets into the magazine.

Hans says, "I'm ready. Let's not get killed in a car wreck trying to outrun those deputies. Slow down and let Carlos pass us. As soon as those deputies get close enough, I can take care of them with this M-sixteen."

"Tony," says Pete, "Cowboy's damn good with an M-sixteen. He does not miss."

"Okay. Whatever you say," replies Tony.

He slows down.

Hans motions for Carlos to go ahead and pass. He waves his hand to confirm and goes around them. Hans gives Pete another magazine and some bullets. Pete starts loading it.

Hans sits on his knees on the seat. He's sideways, with his left side against the back of the seat.

Holding the rifle low along the back of the seat and waiting for the deputies to come up a little closer.

They inch closer and closer. They're side by side. Deciding they are close enough. Hans straightens up on his knees and brings the rifle to his shoulder. Swinging it to his left, toward the back window, Hans aims at the cars and starts shooting fast and wild. He shoots most of the back window out of the car and sprays bullets all over the sheriff's cars.

The deputies swerve all over the road, trying to avoid the deadly hail of bullets.

Hans hits the grills and radiators, and antifreeze sprays all over. They keep right on coming. He shoots their headlights out. Even in the dark, they don't stop.

His rifle is empty. He pulls the magazine out and throws it up to Pete. Pete throws him a loaded one. He puts it in the rifle and starts shooting again.

This time, Hans shoots low at the car in the left lane and hits the right front tire. The blown tire makes the car swerve to the right and go out of control. It hits the other car, and it swerves right. The deputies are driving so fast that they both lose control and head off the highway into a deep ditch. They hit the ditch and each other so hard that the cars catch on fire. The deputies get out and run away. The cars explode. Hans doesn't tell Pete and Tony that the deputies safely got out of the cars.

Hans sighs, sit back in the seat, and say coolly, "I did it. I did it."

Pete remarks with a grin, "Way to go, Cowboy. Way to go."

"That's good shooting," says Tony. "Now I know why Pete thinks so much of you."

Hans is glad they thought he did okay. Personally, Hans thinks he should have done better. He should have gotten them in the first magazine.

Sighing with relief, Tony says, "We're okay for now. We'll have to get another car and van and get rid of these before we get to Jacksonville."

They catch up with Carlos and Sam and pass them. They drive to the next turnoff, go down a two-lane road for about a quarter of a mile, and then stop.

Carlos pulls up alongside, and Tony says to him, "We have to get rid of these vehicles."

"Okay," Carlos replies. "Just follow us down this road. It's the back way, and it will be safer. There's a small town farther along here. We'll change vehicles there before we go on to Jacksonville."

They all head on down the road.

Hans says with a slight grin, "Well."

Pete turns around and replies, "Well, what?"

"What the hell took you guys so long to get me out of that jail?"

Pete says with a smart-ass look on his face, "We stopped off for a couple of beers."

"Yes, I believe you, assholes. I bet you didn't think to bring me any either."

A big grin comes over Pete's face. His hand comes up with a can of beer in it. "Hell, no. We didn't forget to bring you some. Here, have one." He opens it and gives it to Hans.

He takes a big swig. Boy, that's good! Pete gets Tony and himself a beer.

Hans says with a grin, "You, assholes. This is one hell of a way to get me to forgive you for not getting me out of jail sooner."

They all laugh.

Still laughing, Hans sighs a little and says, "Let's rip off a ship and go for a sail."

While Hans is drinking his beer, as they go down the road, he gets to thinking; Jesus says I must forgive those that trespass against me. Someday Hans will forgive that corrupt dirty sheriff for trying to kill him but not today. Four deputies are still alive, and nobody knows that. Hans will just keep this between Jesus and him.

Hans finishes his beer and throws the can out the broken window. With no back window, the night air feels cool.

Tony says, "We better get rid of this car before we get to town."

Chapter 13

Stealing Another Car and Van

He flashes his headlights. Carlos flashes his lights in recognition. Tony pulls over and stops the car. Then Carlos stops the van, backs up, and stops just in front of them.

As Carlos and Sam walk to the car, Tony turns to Pete and Hans and tells them, "Get the suitcases and put them in the van."

As Pete and Hans do so, Tony tells Carlos and Sam, "We better get rid of the car before we get to town. A cop might spot the back window being broken."

Carlos thinks for a minute, then says, "There's a canal with a ditch bank road about two miles up. We can get rid of it there."

They all get back in the vehicles and take off. Carlos stops the van across the bridge, just past the ditch bank road. Tony turns onto it and stops. Turning to face Hans, he says, "Cowboy, get me two grenades, and then you wait here with Sam and Carlos. Pete and I will take care of this."

"Okay." Hans takes the rifle and gets out of the car. He goes over, gets the grenades, and brings them back to Tony. Then he goes back and gets in the van.

Tony and Pete drive down the ditch bank road about half a mile. The car stops, and Tony turns the lights off. It is so dark out that they can't see them. About three minutes later, there's a massive explosion, and a big ball of fire lights up the dark night. Both grenades must have gone off at about the same time.

Against the ball of fire, Tony and Pete come running back. They get in the van, and they get the hell out of there.

Lighting up a cigarette, Tony asks Carlos, "Do you know your way around these parts?"

Carlos replies, "I lived around here for about five years when I was in high school and a little after. Why?"

"Is there a back road that goes around the town?"

"Yes, there is. We will be coming to it very soon. Turn right. It will take us straight to the road that goes to Jacksonville. There will be a sign that reads 'Jacksonville' with an arrow on it."

"Okay, this's what we will do. We'll go past the turnoff and head into town. We'll not go all the way in. We better not take this van all the way into town. We might get nailed if we do.

"When we do get close to town, stop. Carlos, Sam, and Pete will get out and walk the rest of the way. Cowboy and I will turn around and take the back road around the town.

"You guys get into town and get us another car and van. Then meet Cowboy and me on the other side of town someplace. Got any place in mind, Carlos?"

"Yes," Carlos replies. "When you get to the road that goes to Jacksonville, don't turn. Go straight about five miles. There's a community church on the right. Turn left, go down about half a mile, and pull over. Just wait for us there. It's a gravel road, and only the local people use it."

They drive past the road they'll be turning onto. Carlos points it out as they drive by. He stops the van just on the edge of town, and everybody gets out except Tony and Hans. Tony gets behind the wheel, and Hans gets in the front seat. Tony turns the van around, heading for the back road and driving around town. It takes us about twenty minutes to get to the place where they are to wait for the others.

Tony turns the van around and stops. "Cowboy, how about putting some bullets in a couple of magazines. If a sheriff or some cop drives out here and starts nosing around, you know what you will have to do. There can't be any witnesses."

"Okay, I'll be ready." So far, Hans hasn't killed anybody. He hopes he doesn't have to. If he does have to kill someone, he'll become a murderer.

While loading the magazine, Hans asks, "What will we do if those guys get caught?"

"They won't get caught. We will have to go into town and break them out if they do. Or go steal that ship just the two of us and then come and get them out later with some help."

Oh shit! This's a bigger town. They might have to go get help if they get caught and thrown in jail.

Tony and Hans don't say much after that. Only three cars come down the road, and they all pass. They don't even slow down.

About an hour and forty-five minutes later, Hans beginning thinks maybe they did get caught when he sees two vehicle headlights coming from town. They turn at the corner and head their way. Hans gets his rifle ready just in case they're cops. As they come, they slow down. When they get close enough, It's a car and a van.

The car stops, and a dome light comes on when the door opens. Hans sighs with relief. It's Pete. Carlos drives on past and backs the van up to the back doors. Hans gets out, runs back, and opens both vans' back doors.

They all transfer the rifles, ammunition, and grenades over to the new van. After they get done, Pete closes the back doors of the new van, and Carlos and Sam get in the front. Carlos turns it around and heads down the road the same way they came.

Tony turns the car around and stops. Pete has Hans's rifle and some bullets, and he puts them in the backseat. He stands here with the door open.

Hans has two grenades. He pulls the pins out of them and throws them into the old van. Then Hans runs and jumps into the backseat of the car while Pete gets in the front.

Tony steps on the gas and hauls ass out of there. They turn right at the corner by the church. Hans looks back at the old van just as the grenades explode. Again, a massive ball of fire lights up the night. The ground rumbles and shakes the car like an earthquake.

They turn left onto the road for Jacksonville and are on their way. The car they are in now looks like a new one. It's a white Plymouth. The new van is a yellow Dodge.

They cross the state line into Florida. The sun's just coming up, and the sky is clear by the time they reach the outskirts of Jacksonville.

Luckily, Carlos knows his way around. They follow him as he takes them to a motel with an individual garage for each room. They get a room. Sam and Carlos get a room. Carlos drives the van into the garage, closes the door, and locks it. Tony does the same with the car. They have a short meeting in Tony's room.

At the meeting, Tony explains, "We'll stay here until we can make our next move. We will leave the car and van in the garages and come and go by taxicab. Sam, do you think you can get Cowboy a job on one of Lagno's ships?"

"There's no problem there," replies Sam. "I know somebody who can. He owes me a favor. It might take a day or two, though."

"That's okay. We should all relax for a couple days. We all had a hard night. I'm getting something to eat and then hit the sack for a while. That's what I'm going to do, anyway. You guys do what you want."

There's a little café just across the street, and They all walk over there and get something to eat. After returning to the motel room, Hans shaves, takes a hot shower, and goes to bed. Boy, is he tired!

It's about six o'clock p. m. that evening when Hans wakes up. Tony and Pete are already up and dressed. They're starting to walk out the door when Pete notices that Hans's awake.

Grinning at him, he says, "It's about time you woke up. Tony and I are going over to the café to get something to eat. If you're hungry, you can meet us there."

Hans nods, and they walk out the door. He just lies there for a while, finally gets up and gets dressed. He goes over to join Tony and Pete at the café and meets Sam and Carlos as they leave. They both smile at Hans.

As they walk up to him, Carlos says, "It's about time you got up, sleepyhead. What are you trying to do, sleep your life away?"

They both laugh.

Hans laughs and remarks, "After being cooped up most of the night in jail. I needed more sleep, smart ass.

"Pete told me all of you guys stopped off someplace and had some beers and a good time."

Carlos grins and replies, "Having some beer helped us think how to get you out of jail."

Hans laughs, "Bull shit. And laughs again."

They all laugh, and they walk to their room.

Hans just stands there in the doorway of the café, looking back at them for a moment with a grin. For some reason, Hans thinks, they're picking on him. They're a lot like Pete and Tony. Hans guesses that's why they make such a good team. They wouldn't have gotten away with all this if it wasn't for their excellent teamwork.

After eating, they go to Sam and Carlos's room and have a small meeting.

At the meeting, Tony says, "I am going to make a phone call tonight and get some more men to help take over the ship, some of the same men who were going to help us the day the ship sank.

"They should all be in Daytona Beach, waiting to hear from me. I can get at least six more. They should be here by tomorrow, and we'll pick up the rest of the men in Daytona.

"Now, while I'm making that call, the rest of you go out in the garage and get in the van. Get the bolts assembled in the rifles. Then load all the magazines. Get everything completely ready before we make our next move."

Tony leaves, and they go into the garage, get in the van, and start putting the bolts in the rifles.

Sam starts picking on Carlos, "While I was dancing with the lady at the bar the other night, what did you say to the lady you were dancing with that made her so mad at you that she slapped you on the face and yelled at the one I was dancing with, and they both walk out the door?"

Carlos laughs and replies, "I really don't know. I thought I was being nice. I asked her if she and the lady you're with were sisters?

She softly says, "Yes, we are. How can you tell?"

Carlos replies, "You both look almost alike, except your nose is slightly bigger than hers. That's when she slapped me and walked out the door."

Sam, Pete, and Hans laugh.

Sam politely says, "No, Carlos. that wasn't the right thing to say to a lady."

They all laugh.

In about two and a half hours, they get it all done.

Pete and Hans go over to their room. Tony is watching television and drinking a beer. They walk in and close the door. Pete says, "We're all set, Tony."

"Okay," Tony replies. "There should be six more men here tomorrow afternoon."

While Pete and Hans wash up, Tony adds, "I got some beer on the dresser if you guys want any."

While having a couple of beers and watching television, the news comes on. The anchor lady reports, "Last night, the Georgia National Guard Armory was robbed. Several rifles and a lot of ammunition were stolen.

"Later that same night, the sheriff's office was also robbed. The sheriff was killed. So far, two deputies are uncounted for. Did the robbers take them hostage? If they did, why? The state police don't know if they're dead or alive.

"The robbers got away with the bolts for the rifles they had stolen. They burned the sheriff's office and the jail down.

"They're driving a green Ford van and a dark red Buick with a white top, and the back window is broken out.

"The state police have taken over the investigation. There are no suspects at this time."

There's a surprising look on Tony's face as he shuts off the TV.

He blurts out, "How did anyone know what we were driving? It's a good thing we switched vehicles when we did. And two bodies are missing. That's kind of strange, and we don't have them."

Hans doesn't say anything. It's got to be the two deputies chasing them who told them about the vehicles. The ones Hans let go are in the wind, and that's good. Hope they just keep going and don't look back.

They all go to bed.

The next day, after they all get up, Hans looks out the window. Another sunny and warm day. There's a knock on the door. Hans opens it. It's Carlos.

He comes in and says, "Sam has gone to get you a job on one of Lagno's ships, Cowboy. As soon as he gets back, you will go to the ship. The only thing you can do is sit back and wait."

"Okay, Carlos," Hans replies. "Thank you for telling me."

Carlos leaves.

The first part of the day goes slowly. At about two thirty p.m., the phone rings, and Tony answers it. It's the six men waiting at the airport. He tells them to get in a cab and come on over here. Then he hangs up the phone and goes to the bathroom.

Sam gets back. He comes to our room and says, "Everything is set up." He hands Hans the union papers and false passport and identification.

Sam continues, "The ship is pulling into the harbor right now. You'll be going under the name of Ed Edwards.

Leave your real identification here with Pete. Get your work clothes back on. Pack your bag, get a cab, and get on over there. The name of the ship you are assigned to is the Hawk. So, when you get there, go right onboard. After that, you're on your own."

Tony comes out of the bathroom. He says, "Sam, get yours and everybody else's bags. Go to the bus station and send them to Daytona Beach. I have a man there who will pick them up for us. Cowboy, I will call a cab for you."

He calls one. Then he says, "You will probably get to leave the ship after five o'clock this afternoon. Get in a cab and come back over here. If something comes up and you can't make it, give us a call."

He writes down the motel phone number and gives it to Hans. Tony tells him, "Memorize it and throw it away before you get there."

The cab arrives. As Hans walks out the door, Hans calmly says, "See you later."

On the way, Hans memorizes the motel phone number.

The cab driver turns left toward the pier. On the right is the end of a long, wide building with a dome roof. It has been painted white, but most paint is worn off. Big black letters on the same end read "Lagno Corporation." Just past the building is a paved open space about half the size of a football field.

Four more buildings sit around the open space, two on each side. They all look exactly alike and are set at a ninety-degree angle to the first one. Directly across the open space from the first building is the pier.

The ship is tied up alongside the pier, a small freighter. It looks damn big to Hans. He hasn't seen many ships before. None of the real big ones that is.

It's a dull rust color, with black just above the water. It looks very dirty.

The cab driver comes straight alongside the building to the left. As he gets close to the pier, he turns right and stops about halfway up alongside the ship. Hans pays him and gets out. Then he drives off.

The ship has docked on the starboard side instead of the port side. I wonder why?

Chapter 14

Hans Boards the Ship

They don't have the gangplank up yet, so Hans just stands there and waits.

He looks around. Abreast of the ship, and almost the entire length of it is open space.

About forty feet away from the pier are the wooden boxes. They're stacked on wooden pallets two high, ten long, and two boxes close together.

Directly in line with where the gangplank is, is a space big enough for cars or trucks to drive through. On the other side of the driveway are more rows of the same kind of boxes stacked the same way.

About six feet behind the first row is another row, just like the first one. Behind that is one more row. Behind all of that are the lumber and all kinds of things stored all the way back to the first building.

Dockworkers use one of the ship's derricks to set up the gangplank. This waiting is starting to make Hans a little nervous. They finally get it in place, and a man comes down from the ship and unhooks the shackles from the derrick.

It is late in the day, past 4:30 p.m. It looks like they're letting most of the men go ashore. Come to think of it, it's a good thing they came in late, or they might have loaded those boxes already. Then they would have to think of something else.

Hans waits until the rush of men gets off before going aboard. There must not be too big a crew because it didn't take long for all the men to get off.

Hans starts walking up the gangplank and looks up at the ship. At the end of the plank, just to the right, is a man in work clothes with a hard hat and a military duty belt. He has a small rifle hanging from his shoulder. They must run these ships like the navy, with watch standers.

Just before stepping onto the ship, Hans gets his papers and passport ready to show the guard. Hans steps aboard, face the guard, and coolly says, "Hi." Then he smiles and hands the guard his papers.

He takes them and looks at Hans with a serious look on his face. He doesn't smile as he replies sternly, "Good afternoon."

He looks through Hans's papers. While he is doing that, Hans notices that his rifle is a .30-30 bolt action.

He looks at Hans and asks, "What other ship lines have you worked for?"

Hans replies, "None, sir. This is the first one."

He nods.

A phone is clamped to the railing just to the guard's left. He picks up the receiver and dials two numbers.

He waits awhile. Then he says sternly, "There is a squirrel out here that has papers assigning him aboard this ship."

Squirrel, huh? Since he joined the army back in basic training, Hans hasn't heard that phrase.

He hangs up the phone, and then the smart-ass says, "There will be someone out here for you in a little while, Squirrel."

That word squirrel is starting to piss Hans off so. He just glares at him, not saying one word while he waits. Suddenly Hans gets the feeling that his right back in the army again.

A man dressed in a green suit comes out of a door from the bridge. He's taller and slimmer than Hans, with long, curly, dark hair. He walks up and scowls at Hans.

Turning to the guard, he asks, "Is this the squirrel you called about?"

What the hell kind of outfit is this anyway?

"Yes, Bob," the guard replies. "This is the one."

As Bob guy reaches out for Hans's papers, Hans happens to catch sight of the butt end of a pistol inside his coat.

He turns toward Hans and says, "Come on Squirrel. Follow me."

Hans still doesn't say anything.

Hans follows him back through the same door he came out of. They turn left, climb a ladder to the next deck, turn right, and stop. In front of them is a door with the words "Captain's Office."

Bob knocks on the door. It opens, and a tall, thin man dressed in a brown suit appears in the doorway. He's bald, with short black hair around the sides and back of his head.

Looking at Bob, he asks, "Yes, what can I do for you?"

"Captain," Bob replies, "you are not going to like what I have for you. I have a squirrel here for you, sir. They sent us a man with no experience, sir."

The captain's face turns bright red with rage. He blurts out, "Those dirty sons of bitches. They know better than to sign a squirrel on a Lagno ship."

He glares at Hans. "Get in here right now. Damn it all to hell anyway!"

Following Bob, Hans comes into the office. The captain asks in a gruff voice, "Do you have a name, Squirrel?"

Hans keeps his cool and replies, "Yes, Sir. Ed Edwards, Sir."

God, Hans feels like his right back in the army.

Bob hands him Hans's papers. The captain looks through them and says in the same gruff voice, "Ed Edwards, huh? These papers look too good. They look so good they smell. Boy, my boss is having a lot of trouble with a crook named Bacco. That's why I'm on edge about anybody assigned to this ship. You are going to have to prove to me that you'll be a good worker and that you aren't an inside man for Bacco.

"I am stuck with you, Edwards, so I'm going to have Bob here check you out from one end to the other.

"If you are okay, you'll be a squirrel until I make a sailor out of you.

"Edwards, I don't like you. I don't like anybody. You are guilty until proven innocent. You won't be leaving this ship except to stand watch. I'm giving you the midnight-to-four watch tonight on the pier. Do you know how to shoot a rifle?"

"Yes, sir."

"You'll have a .30-30 rifle with you on watch. Shoot anybody who doesn't belong there. If you don't, you'll be shot. Bob, get him a bunk and a locker, and get him out of here."

Oh shit. How in the hell can Hans get word to Tony without leaving the ship? Just before he starts to walk out, Hans thinks of an idea. He stammers, "C-Captain, sir, may I make a phone call, please?"

The captain glares at him. "What for?"

Hans rakes his brain fast for an answer, saying, "I want to call my wife and tell her I won't be home tonight."

Pulling out a cigarette, the captain thinks for a minute. Then he says, "Okay, but use this phone. That way, I can hear what's going on. Dial nine. That will put you on an outside line."

Dammit. What the hell can Hans say with them listening? It's a good thing he memorized the number. Hans thinks of something. He picks up the phone receiver and dials nine, then the number. It rings. The captain has the speaker on so the whole room can hear the whole conversation.

Hearing a click, and a man's voice says hello. It is Tony.

Hans quickly replies, "Hi. This is Ed. Is Hanna there?" Before Tony can say you have the wrong number, Hans continues. "If she is still at the neighbors, tell her I have the duty tonight on the ship at my new job and won't be home. I've got to stand the midnight-to-four pier guard tonight. Be sure and tell her the midnight-to-four so she will understand. I will see her as soon as I can. I'll talk to you later."

Hans hangs up the phone and says, "Thank you, Sir."

Suspiciously, the captain asks, "Who's that man you talked to?"

"That's her brother, sir."

"Okay. Now, get out of here."

Bob and Hans leave and go to the lower decks. He shows him where the chow hall is. Then they go to a room. Bob opens the door and turns on the light as they step inside. It has four lockers and four bunk beds in it. He shows Hans which locker and bed he can have.

He explains, "You have the room all to yourself. The other men are on the beach tonight, and you will meet them in the morning.

"Relieve the watch at fifteen minutes to the hour. You will take the rifle he has, along with the hard hat and the duty belt with the bullets on it. Now you are on your own. See you later, Squirrel."

He leaves.

Hans closes the door and lays the mattress out straight on the lower bunk bed. He lies down for a while and relaxes. Well, hope Tony gets the idea that from midnight to four is when they'll have to make their move to get into those boxes.

He's thinking about the captain and the men he has aboard. Bet the whole crew will kill anybody for Lagno. Bet if they don't, they'll be killed. There's no way out. That's too bad. Well, if there are some good men on the ship, maybe they'll be able to help them.

For now, though, Hans thinks he'll go find out if their food's as bad as the army. There's nothing else to do.

After eating, Hans goes back to his room. Turning off the light, he decides to lie down for a while and get some sleep before going on watch duty. Hans has a feeling it's going to be one hell of a night.

Well, Hans must have fallen asleep because the next thing he knew, someone was tugging at his shoulder. Hans opens his eyes to a flashlight right in his face.

A voice asks, "Are you, Edwards?"

Hans squints his eyes and replies, "Yes. I'm Edwards."

The man holding the flashlight continues. "You are due to be out on the pier in fifteen minutes. Don't be late."

He turns and leaves.

Hans lies there for a few more minutes to wake himself up, and then he gets out of bed. Since Hans went to bed with his clothes still on, he's almost ready. He washes up and goes out.

The night's a little cool, and the sky is clear, with a slight breeze; Hans can smell the salty air.

Two guards stand watch on the pier. The guard Hans is to relieve is standing at the end of the gangplank. The other one has already been relieved. The guard waiting for Hans asks as he walks up to him, "Are you, my relief?"

Hans says, "I guess I am."

He takes his duty belt off and hands it to Hans. Hans adjusts it and puts it on. The guard gives him his hard hat and the .30-30 rifle.

Pointing, he explains, "You have to walk around, starting right here. It doesn't matter which way you go. Just cover the area heading aft of the ship, along the waterfront, to the end of the pier at those long buildings. Turn left there and go all the way to the other end. Turn left again, go to the building straight across, and then back in line with the gangplank. You need to walk all over, through the rows of boxes, and everywhere.

"The main thing is to keep moving around. Use that rifle if something is going on that shouldn't be. If there's a fire, and it is too big for you to put out, run back to the ship. Tell the guard up there at the end of the plank, and he'll get the fire department out here. Okay, it's all yours, Squirrel. Have fun."

You, assholes, will be the squirrels when Pete, Tony, and the rest of the guys get aboard this thing,

Hans starts walking along the waterfront the way the other guard pointed out to him.

There are pole lights all over the yard. The whole place is lit up.

Hans looks up at the main deck. There's another guard on watch as well. He can watch the whole yard from up there better than Hans can from down here. Hans watches him as he walks to the fantail, turns, and disappears over to the other side. They'll have to make their move when he's on the other side of the ship.

Hans continues to the end of the pier. Along this side of the building are several stacks of lumber. They're stacked two stacks high and extend almost the whole length of the two buildings. Hans walks past the end of the lumber and to the building next to the pier. He looks between them. There's enough room for a person to come through here without being seen from the ship. Hans goes out front and walks alongside the lumber, looking at the first stack of boxes to his left. There are about eighty feet of lighted-up open space from the lumber to the boxes.

Shit! How can those guys get over to the boxes without being seen from the ship? Hans looks down between the first and second rows. Oh, we're in luck. At the far end, there are two more boxes, one stacked on top of the other between these two rows. That will keep the forward guard from seeing anything that's going on between the two rows back here. The same thing repeats between the second and third.

Right at the other end of the lumber, there are eight more stacks of boxes. Hans walks on past and looks to his right. That's the end of that building. There's the driveway that Hans came in on earlier, in the cab, between the two buildings. He stops and looks around.

On his left is a forklift parked next to some other boxes. Hans walks over and gets a look at it. The key is in it.

Remembering what the other guard said about a fire gives Hans an idea. Pete and the rest of the guys will have to come between these two buildings. One or two guys will have to run between the buildings and the lumber to the waterfront and set the stack of lumber on fire. After it gets started, Hans will run over and report it. Then run over here, get on the forklift, and start moving those boxes to make it look like he is saving them from the fire.

Pete and some of the guys can run low behind each box as he moves them across the open space and stacks them on this end between the second and third rows. That's the only way Hans can think to do it.

On Hans's second round, he walks up to the main entranceway, not knowing if his supposed to walk on out toward the road or not. He does it anyway. Just before getting to the end of the building with Lagno's name on it, someone peeks around the corner at him. Hans can't tell who it is. He Holds his rifle ready and slowly walks over.

A voice says, "Cowboy, it's me, Pete."

Chapter 15

Sneaking Pete and the Guys onto the Pier

Hans relaxes and walks on over and around the corner. The building is completely dark. There's no light next to the street. Pete and Tony are standing next to the building.

As Hans walks up to them, Tony asks, "How in the hell are we going to get in those boxes, Cowboy?"

Hans tells them about his plan. "I'll go ahead and make my beat just as if nothing is going to happen. That'll give you guys enough time to get over behind this building and set up. Have two men walk on the sidewalk and cross the driveway far enough away that they can't be seen from the ship. Then they can get between the building and the lumber and run to the pier. Then, when I come back along the outside of the lumber, about halfway, I will take off my hard hat and wipe my forehead. That'll be the signal to start the fire."

Tony nods and quietly says, "Okay, Cowboy, we'll be ready."

Hans goes back around the building and continues his beat. He goes slowly, poking around to give those guys plenty of time to get set up.

Hans comes around along the outside of the lumber and gets about halfway through. Everything is calm and smooth. They better be ready because here goes. Hans takes his hard hat off, wipes his forehead, and puts the hat back on.

Looking back at the lumber toward the waterfront, they're getting the fire started. Waiting for a little to make sure it really gets burning good. Hans can smell and sees the smoke and flames. He hears the fire cracking and popping.

Hans makes his move now. Running over to the gangplank, he just happens to look up at the ship's main deck. The guard has just reached this side. Hans stops and shouts, "Hey, guard on the ship!"

He looks down and sees Hans waving at him. He shouts back, "What the hell do you want?"

Hans points to the fire and yells, "There is a fire in the lumber."

He looks over, waves his hand in recognition, turns, and runs over to the guard at the gangplank.

Hans turns around and runs as fast as he can to the forklift. He climbs on it, swings the rifle's strap over the seat's backrest, and lets it hang. Hans sits down and starts it, then works the gears around until he finds out how they work.

Hans has driven forklifts before, but they're all a little different. He puts it in reverse and backs it over to the boxes. Because the lift is in front, it's easier to see where his going in reverse.

Hans swings it around and lifts the fork to the top box, sticking it in the pallet under the box. He lifts the fork, tilting it back a little and back up enough to clear the lower box. He lowers it just above the pavement and backs it up to the first building so the guys can get behind it. He turns toward the ship.

Hans backs it across the open space just behind the second row and turns around. Four men with rifles and boxes of ammunition run behind the row of boxes. He lines the box up just outside the second row and a little between the second and third rows, sets it down, and backs out.

Hans lifts the fork a little, backs across the open space, and goes for the next box. He brings it across and over the same way he brought the first one. As he sets that one down, four more men with rifles and ammunition run behind the row. Hans goes for the third box, and just as he gets it across and sets it down, Pete and Tony run in behind the row.

Tony turns and gives Hans a thumbs-up. That's all of them. He keeps on bringing the rest of the boxes over. He is just about to get the last one when the fire trucks come hauling ass up to the fire.

Hans waits for them to pass, and then he goes and gets the last box. After moving it, Hans keeps on going and starts moving some of the stacks of lumber. He manages to get four pallets of lumber moved. Hans can feel the heat, smell the smoke, and hear the cracking and popping from the fire getting worse. As he moved the last pallet over, all the rest caught on fire.

The fire spreads to the building behind the lumber. There's nothing more to do. Hans parks the forklift back where he found it and gets off. He gets his rifle and stands there for a while, watching the flames.

More fire trucks come. Then the cops come, sirens going, and red lights flashing. With all that racket and everyone's attention on the fire, those guys shouldn't have any problem getting in the boxes.

Hans decides to walk his regular beat because the guard in the forward section is walking his beat as if nothing is happening.

By the time Hans returns to the boxes he moved, those guys may be about done. There's just enough room between the two boxes in the second row for a person to walk through.

Hans slowly goes back in. They're not in the boxes yet.

Hans whispers, "How come you guys aren't in the boxes yet.?

One of the new guys says, "All the boxes are full of rifles. Look in this box. There's no room for us." He pulls the top right corner of the box open and shines a small flashlight into the box. Hans looks in. Sure enough. It's full of rifles.

Tony sees Hans and waves for him to go out from between the boxes and meet him between the second and third rows.

Hans walks over to Tony and Pete. Hans replies in a low voice, "I just heard about and saw the rifles."

Tony asks, "What are we going to do now, Cowboy?"

Hans replies, "Let me check something." He walks over to the third row of boxes, turns around, looks toward the ship, and sighs. The top stack of boxes on the second row blocks the ship's view, except for the bridge.

He goes back over to Tony and demands, "Bend down low, go between the boxes in the third row and try those boxes." The people from the ship can't see you."

Tony gets the crew and opens one of those boxes, and Tony looks in and sighs. "These are the right ones.''

Hans states. "Tony, I'd better move around. I'll be back."

Tony waves Hans off.

They get them open, and everybody gets in by the time Hans gets back to them.

As Tony is nailing up a box, he explains, "Cowboy, there are small black Xs on each one of these that has someone inside it" He shows Hans one of the Xs. Another box is still open. He hands Hans the hammer and climbs into the box. "Nail this shut for me, Cowboy. I will see you after we get aboard the ship."

Hans nails it back up. He gets the box nailed shut just in time because the fire fighters have turned all the sirens off. The building's still burning, and Hans can hear their voices and the fire's cracking and popping. Other than that, it's quiet.

Now, what the hell can Hans do with this hammer? Holding it close, Hans returns to the forklift, takes his handkerchief out of his back pocket, wipes the hammer to get the fingerprints off, and drops it in the toolbox.

With a sigh of relief, Hans starts his rounds again. The plan went well. It went very well except for those boxes full of rifles. That's the proof of Lagno's gun smuggling.

Just before Hans gets relieved, they put the fire out. As he returns aboard the ship, nobody says a word to him, and he doesn't try to talk to anyone. Hans goes straight to his room and lies down, not bothering to take his clothes off again.

Suddenly Hans feels someone tugging at his shoulder. Hans opens his eyes and looks up. The lights are on in the room. It's Bob. This time, he's wearing work clothes and a hard hat. He also has a pistol in a holster on his belt.

Still tugging Hans's shoulder, he says in a demanding voice, "Edwards, the captain wants to see you right now. You have a lot of explaining to do about that fire this morning."

Hans sighs with relief. He thought for a minute that he had checked him out and found out that there was no such person as Ed Edwards.

Hans gets up and follows Bob. They get up on to the main deck and step outside. It's daylight, warm and sunny, and the crew's already loading the wooden boxes onto the ship. They go on up to the captain's office. Bob knocks on the door, and they go in.

The captain's sitting behind his desk. He's also in work clothes, and he has some papers in his hand. He sets the papers down on his desk and says, "Edwards, it sure seems like, since you came aboard this ship, things are starting to happen around here that generally don't happen. There's no way of telling yet how the fire got started. But in time, the detectives will find out. They always do.

"I'm not accusing you of anything yet, but I can hardly believe that a man who has never worked around these kinds of things before would know exactly what to do when that fire started except to just report it.

"No, Edwards, it just seems a little strange that a fire starts when you're on guard. And right after you reported it, you didn't hesitate one last little bit of running over, get on that forklift, and move those boxes and lumber.

"If one of my regular men had done what you did, I would immediately give him a raise in pay and pat him on the back because that was a brilliant move. But with someone with no experience, that move is too smart to suit me.

"Another thing. Who gave you the authorization to drive that forklift anyway? I only have five men I allow to drive that stuff down there. You need to have a special driver's license for that. That's the law.

"Edwards, just so you understand me, I don't like you, and I don't trust you. I believe that you are responsible for that fire and that there's a reason for it.

"Now, I don't want to hear any bullshit from you. I just want you to get out of my sight. Go down and watch them load the cargo. You can do anything you want for now, but don't leave the ship.

"Bob, go and get him a hard hat.

Bob gets Hans a hard hat and goes out onto the main deck. Hans walks over to the starboard side and looks down at the pier. He starts thinking about all the things the captain implied. It's scaring the hell out of him.

What the hell did Hans do to make him so damn suspicious of him? Is it just him? Or does he get that way with every new man?

Hans just happens to glance over at the gangplank. Five men are coming up it. Four of them look big and mean. As a matter of fact, they look more like gorillas than people. There are two in front and two in the back. They're wearing dark suits. In the middle is a taller, older man. He's almost bald, with short gray hair around the sides and back of his head. He's wearing a light tan suit.

Hans glances over at the guard standing at the end of the gangplank. He picks up the phone receiver and dials two numbers. He waits a bit and hears him say, "Captain, Sir, Mr. Lagno's here, Sir." He hangs up the phone.

Hans looks back at the taller man. So, that's Lagno. He wonders why he's here. Oh shit! Hope he doesn't stay aboard when this ship goes to sea.

Just before Lagno steps onboard, the captain comes out of the door at a run, races over to the gangplank, and waits for Lagno to step aboard.

He stammers, "M-Mr. L-Lagno, w-what a surprise that you're here. Welcome aboard, Sir."

Lagno steps aboard, shake the captain's hand, and replies sternly, "Thank you, Jenson. Looks likes you had a problem during the night."

The captain stammers, "C-come into my office, and I will explain w-what happened."

As they all start walking to the door, Lagno says, "Yes, Jenson. I would definitely like to hear more about that fire."

They disappear into the ship.

Oh shit. Hans hopes they don't call Him in there for anything. Well, if they do, he'll just stick to his story no matter what they have those four gorillas do to him. If they kill Hans, Tony and the others will be on their own. They'll have to figure out some other way to get out of those boxes.

Well, there's nothing that can be done now anyway. Looking back down at the pier again, they're just starting to move the boxes that Tony and the guys are in. There's a man on the forklift that Hans used. He's setting them down close to the ship.

The derricks lift them up over and lower them down into large holes called holds. The ship has five holds, three in the forward half and two in the aft. They're putting the boxes with the guys in them in the last hold back aft.

Hans goes over to that hold and looks down in. They're stacking the boxes four wide, five long, and four high. There's still enough room in that hold for a man or men to get in there and move around. At the deck of the hold are four doors, two on each side of the ship. They lead to a passageway just outside the hold. After the holds are full, they close them with a big heavy hatch. Hans will have to get into the hold from one of the doors below the deck.

The boxes the guys are in are all aboard now, and they're all in the same hold, in the top stack and the stack just below. Hans will have to find a way to climb up to them. Once he gets a few of the guys out, they can all help each other get the rest out.

After they close the hatches, Hans hears a voice say, "Hey, Edwards."

Hans turns around Bob's coming toward him. He says, "The captain wants you in his office right now."

Hans follows Bob to the captain's office, not looking forward to what's going to happen. Hans is getting scared all over again.

They walk into the captain's office. Yes, Lagno and his four gorillas are still here. The captain does not say anything. He's shaking like he is nervous or something, and he looks like a boy who has just gotten his ass chewed out by his father.

Looking straight at Hans, Lagno says in a stern voice, "You are Edwards, the man who knows it all. Tell me all about that fire this morning."

Hans stammers a little and tells him his story.

In the same stern voice, Lagno says, "That was a smart move you made, but I agree with the captain that you made too smart of a move. In time, I guess we'll really know.

"Edwards, maybe we will meet again someday. I hope not, for your sake. The only business you should have with me is through my name and the ship. If we need to do business again, that might be a problem because it might not be too healthy for you."

Hans just stands here, not saying anything.

Turning to the captain, Lagno says, "Jenson, I have to go. You better put more guards out on the pier from now on. I lost a lot of supplies in that building. Don't let that happen again."

The captain stammers, "N-no, sir, I won't."

Lagno and his four gorillas leave, and the captain tells Hans to get the hell out of his office. Hans goes down to his room for a while.

Hans gets to thinking. No wonder the captain is like he is. He's scared to death of Lagno. If the captain makes a big mistake, bet Lagno would put a hit on him and have him killed.

Well, Hans is going to have to be careful. They'll be watching him like a hawk, so he'll have to kill anybody who gets in his way when he goes into the hold to get those guys out. After sitting in his room for a while, Hans returns to the main deck. On the way up, he notices that nobody's in the passageways. Out on the main deck, he sees why there's nobody below the decks.

Hans bets there aren't more than two hundred men on this ship because it looks like the whole crew is up here. They're all standing along the starboard side. Most of them are waving their arms and hands at something on the pier. They're also yelling down to the pier. It all looks kind of strange.

Hans goes over and looks down. There are some women and children down there. It looks like the crew's families have come to see them off.

Hans looks over at the gangplank. They're hooking the derrick cable up to it. Then a voice over a loudspeaker says, "The ship will be underway in thirty minutes."

Now would be an excellent time to get those guys out of the boxes while most of the crew's up here instead of waiting until after they get out to sea. Hans will have to try to find a place to hide them. He turns and starts down to the lower decks. He goes down four decks to get to the one that leads to the hold doors.

Chapter 16

Getting Pete and the Guys out of the Boxes

Hans heads back aft on the starboard side. The passageways run in all different directions. Every so often, he steps through an oval-shaped doorway. It doesn't open all the way to the deck. He needs to step over that part.

Hans gets back to what looks like a hold, but it's the wrong one. Printed on the door are the words: "Fourth Hold." So, Hans keeps going. Between the holds is a passageway that stretches over to the other side. Just past that is the hold he wants to get into. Hans's lucky. The door's unlocked. He goes on back, and the other door is also unlocked. Just past that is another passageway to the other side of the ship. He stops and looks down through it. Just about halfway down, on the left, is a door. "Supply Room" is printed on it, padlocked shut.

That will be a good place to hide the guys. Carlos can get that lock open. Hans turns around, returns to the hold door, and goes in.

There's just enough room to squeeze in. Hans closes the door and can't see a thing, so he feels along the starboard wall. A few feet in, he feels some iron bars shaped like a ladder going straight up the wall.

Now Hans needs to find some tools and a flashlight. He looks around as he leaves the hold, but nobody's around.

Going further aft, Hans comes to the end of the passageway. He goes up a deck at a time, trying to find something along the way. He goes up two decks to a passageway that goes further aft. At the end of that one, there's one going across to the other side.

Just inside that, and to the left is an open door. Just above the door, a sign reads "Damage Control."

Hans slowly looks in. It's a big room. There's only one person in here, to his left and at the far end of the room. The man is sitting on a tall stool at a high workbench, working on something. Over to Han's right, on the wall, hangs everything he needs, a wood saw, an axe, along heavy rope and a crowbar.

Just to the left is a big deep sink with three Faucets. The one on the left has a sign just above it that reads "Salt water only." And it has along garden hose attached to it. The hose is rolled up and hanging on the wall just to the left of the sink.

Just inside the door to Hans's right is another workbench with a rubber hammer and flashlight.

Hans slowly and softly walks into the room. The man's back is to Hans. He doesn't see or hear him. Hans reaches over and quietly picks up the hammer. Hans brings his arm up over his head, and when he gets close enough, he swings down and hits him on the back of his head. He doesn't even groan as he falls to the deck. He's knocked out cold. Hans rolls him under the work bench.

Hans lays the hammer back on the workbench and gets a pair of leather gloves. He picks them up and puts them on. They're a little big, but they will do. He takes the rope, puts it over his shoulder, grabs the rest of the things, and leaves the room.

Just outside, a chain hangs through a wrought-iron handle welded to the wall, with an unlocked padlock at the end of it. This door is a little different from the others. To dog the door down airtight, there are wheels at the center that control all the dog latches at once, one on the inside and one on the outside. One of the cross-members of both wheels extends past the wheels, about a foot, for leverage. Hans closes the door, wraps the chain around the extended part of the wheel, and locks it with the padlock, thinking that might help stall someone for a little while.

Hans goes straight back to the hold as fast as he can. Once back inside, he closes the door and turns on the flashlight. He gets to the ladder and puts everything on the deck except the crowbar and flashlight.

Hans climbs the ladder to the third stack of boxes and flashes the light around. Three of them right in front of Him have Xs stamped on them. He pries open one and looks in. This is the first time his gotten a very good look inside one of them. It holds a short, odd-shape pipe about sixteen inches around. They crated them up in wooden boxes to look the same as the boxes the guns came in.

One of the new guys is in the box Hans just opened. He says, "Leave the rifle and things in the box for now and go down and bring the axe and saw back up here."

Hans opens the following box. In it is another new guy. Pointing his finger to the inner box, he explains, "If you knock on some of these boxes and you get a knock back, it means someone is in there. That's if you can't find the X. They will be in the inner boxes. There's someone in the one right next to mine."

Nodding, Hans replies, "Okay."

The first guy comes back up the ladder with the axe and saw. Hans takes the axe from him, gives it to the other man, and tells him, "Chop through to the next box."

As he does, the first guy says, "There's someone inside of mine also."

The two men switched off the axe and saw to get to the other boxes. Hans moves to the forward box and pries it open with the crowbar. Sam looks at Hans and grumbles, "Dammit, Cowboy, it's about time. I got to piss so damn bad. I can't hold it any longer."

"Why didn't you piss right there in the box?"

"Because I was afraid someone might see a wet spot, asshole!"

Sam pisses clear down to the deck. While prying open another box, Hans says, "Sam, when you get done, you can go down the ladder. Bring up the rope you pissed on all back up here."

"Oh shit." He goes down the ladder to get the rope.

After getting the following box open, Hans tells the man inside, "Go down the ladder and tell Sam that when he gets back up here with the rope, he can start lowering the rifles and ammunition down to you."

Hans climbs up to the top. There's just enough room between the top of the boxes and the hatch to crawl through. He finds two more with Xs on them. He gets one open, and while opening the other one, Hans can faintly hear a voice over a loudspeaker say, "The ship's now underway."

He can feel the ship starting to move. He gets that box open, and Tony pops his head out.

Tony must have also heard the speaker because he asked, "Why didn't you wait until we were clear out to sea?"

Hans tells him, "Because everyone is still up on the main deck and not down here. There's a supply room just outside the hold to hide everyone."

"Okay. That's fine with me."

He grabs his rifle and other equipment and climbs out of the box. Then he goes over and starts helping Sam and the other men.

Hans crawls on over to the other side. On top are two more boxes. He gets one open, and it's Carlos. He tells him, "There's a supply room just outside to hide everyone in, but it's locked."

Climbing out of the box, he replies, "No problem, Cowboy. Just let me have one man to go with me."

Hans opens another box and tells that guy, "Go with Carlos."

Hans takes some of the rifles and ammunition across to the other side, where the ladder and the guys are. He gets one of them to come back over and help him get the rest of the things.

Pete and the other new guy are in the following two boxes. One of the other guys lets them out, just as the other guy and Hans get the last things over from the previous two boxes. They get everybody out and everything down to the deck.

Carlos sticks his head in the door of the hold and says, "All set. Come on, let's go."

They carefully pick everything up and go out of the hold and around the corner into the supply room. Hans can't believe it when they get out into the passageway. There's still nobody around. They all get inside the supply room.

Carlos found the light switch and turned on the lights.

Closing the door, Tony sighs and says, "Okay. So far, so good. Cowboy, you're doing one hell of a job. It's hard to believe we got this far. Now, when we make our next move, we will store what we don't need here. Carlos has the lock and found a spare key hanging just inside the door.

"Cowboy, I want you to meet John. He knows all about ships and will be our caption. John and the rest of you guys, this is Cowboy." They all shake his hand."

John's an older man, in his late fifties, maybe. He's about as tall as Hans but a little thinner and has long red hair covering his ears and neck.

Tony continues, "Cowboy, you better get back up on the main deck with the ship's crew. Just as soon as we get a lot farther away from land, you get down here and let us know. We will make our move then. If you can't get back here without getting into trouble, we'll make our move in an hour and a half. The ship should be far enough out by then."

Hans heads for the main deck, acting just like nothing has happened. He decides to stay one below the main deck and go as far forward as possible. That way, if some of the ship's crew sees him, it might look a little better. Hans needs to be as far away from that damage control room as he can get before someone finds that guy he hit in there.

Coming to the end of the passageway, Hans goes up to the main deck and comes out at the ship's bow. No one notices him. Most of the crewmen are still up here. Nobody even pays any attention to Hans. They're too busy watching the landscape as the ship leaves the bay and heads out to the open sea.

Hans walks over to the starboard side, leans his hands on the railing, and looks around along with the others.

No one speaks to him, so he doesn't make any effort to speak to them. One reason is he will probably need to shoot some of them before they get complete control of this ship, so there's no sense in getting acquainted.

The ship's out on the open sea now. It turns a little south and picks up speed. The salty-smelling air has grown cooler. Hans looks around and notices that as land gets farther and farther away, the crew is slowly disappearing down to the lower decks. He knows it will be just a matter of time before someone finds that guy in the damage control room.

Someone might also try to get in that supply room, but that doesn't bother Hans because Tony and the others will take care of that.

Hans hears one man say to another, "There's a line starting up from the mess hall. It must be noon. Let's get in line before it gets any bigger and get something to eat."

Hans's looking over at the bridge and where the crews lining up. They're just outside the door on the starboard side. That leads down below the deck to the mess hall. Hans sighed with relief. That's why the crew is slowly disappearing. They're going to eat. Maybe the rest of the damage control crew is in that line. Maybe no one has gone back to the control room yet.

Come to think of it, Hans hasn't eaten at all yet today. He will just get in that line along with everybody else. By the time He gets through it and gets something to eat, they should be away from the land, far enough for Tony and the guys to make their move.

Hans steps in line, and it continues to grow behind him.

Hans finally gets through the chow line. The mess hall is full of men eating. He gets his tray full of food, walks through the mess hall, and finds a little table against the wall at the far end. It's just big enough for two people. Hans sits down here next to the wall and starts eating.

Someone sits down at his table. Not paying any attention to him, Hans keeps on eating, but he just happens to glance over at his tray and sees that he ate about half of his meal before he sat down. He must have gotten up from where he was eating and come over here.

Wondering why he moved, Hans looks up at him. He's a thin man, older, in his seventies, maybe. His face is dark from the sun and very unshaven. His whiskers and hair are white, and his hair is all messed up. He stares Hans right into his eyes. He's spookier than hell. Getting a little annoyed at him, Hans blurts out, "What the hell's your problem, old man?"

He puts his forefinger in front of his mouth. And goes. "Shh." He says in a low voice, "Boy, you're up to something, aren't you?"

Hans doesn't say anything.

The old man continues. "I have been watching you ever since you came aboard. That is, I have been watching you most of the time. The way you handled yourself at that fire during the night, the way you got right in there and helped. You knew just what to do. You're cool. You are too cool to be just another seaman aboard this ship."

Chapter 17

The Hijack

"So, what?" Hans remarks, "The captain feels the same way you do, so why in the hell did you come over here and tell me this?"

The old man replies, "Let me tell you something. You better be up to something. Because they'll kill you before you ever see land again. They have already passed judgment on you. Don't go to sleep tonight. While we're out at sea, Bob and some others will hit you over the head, take you up on deck, and throw you overboard. When the caption gets mad at someone, he has him killed and thrown overboard. They just disappear. There are no dead bodies on the ship. If there are any witnesses, they also face the same fate. We all know what's going on. We just can't prove it."

The old man's voice changes into a kind of pleading sound. "Son, I have been in this floating prison for over thirty years. Once a man is assigned to any Lagno outfit, they become a slave for life. There's no way out but death."

"I ran away once, about twenty-five years ago. I went clear out west. In less than a year, they found me. They kidnapped my daughter and two sons and threatened to kill them. They threatened my wife, also. I had to come back to save them.

"Everyone here has about the same problem. They're all too scared. They're so scared that they will kill you if ordered to.

"Lagno's power hungry. He wants to own and will own the whole island and everyone who lives here if somebody doesn't stop him. I have little pride and little faith left in me until now. I have prayed every day that someone like you would come aboard this ship since

I have been here. I have just been a scared old fool. If it's not too late, I will do anything I can to help you."

Then suddenly, he gasps. His eyes get big! His head falls right on his tray of food.

Hans looks about halfway down his back, a switchblade knife sticking out of it. The old man's dead. He quickly looks over to his right. Bob's standing there with a shit-eating grin on his face.

He steps up, reaches over, and pulls the knife out of the old man's back. He wipes the blood off the blade on the old man's shirt, closes the blade, and sticks the knife down in his boot.

Bob remarks, "We should have retired that old man years ago. The older he got, the looser his mouth got."

The only thing Hans can do is glare at Bob. That puts a puzzled look on his face because he thinks he scared the hell out of him. Well, he did for a minute. But most of all, he's just pissed him off.

The old man wanted to help. Well, he did. He opened Hans's eyes to a lot of what's going on around here, and he believes his every word.

Suddenly a voice comes over a loudspeaker. "Medical men to the damage control room. Man's unconscious. All personnel concerned, please report to the damage control room."

Oh shit. Somebody found him, and he's still unconscious. Glaring at Hans more suspiciously than ever, Bob says, "Edwards, since you came aboard this ship, there have been some unusual things going on around here. I think I will get someone to watch you all the time. Even when you sleep or shit.

"Now, come on. You and I are going to have a look at that man together. Let's go. I will follow you."

Hans leaves his unfinished meal and heads out of the mess hall. Just before Bob follows, he demands to two of the men in the mess hall, "Get rid of the old man's body. Throw him over the side."

Hans walks toward the bow. Bob stops him and says, "The damage control room is back aft. Don't act innocent with me."

They walk back to the damage control room, and neither of them says another word. Hans's trying to think of a way to get away from him but can't come up with anything.

They get back to the damage control room, and just before walking in, Hans sees that the padlock is unlocked and the door is wide open.

They step inside the room. There are about three men in there. Two medics are bending over the man. Bob walks over to them and crouches down to look at them.

Hans starts looking around, wondering what the hell he can do to get himself out of here. Hanging on the wall, just to the right of the door, are several CO_2 fire extinguishers. He learned how to use them in the army. Looking at them closer, they all have a thin wire seal on them to show they're full.

They're designed to cut off the air to put a fire out. If Hans can get some of those bottles to shoot out the gas and then get the door closed, dogged down, and locked, the men here will suffocate.

Looking back over to Hans's left. At the far end of the room, under the workbench, are two large trash cans made from fifty-five-gallon drums, and they're full of dirty throwaway grease rages, papers, and all kinds of garbage. The grease rages will make a lot of smoke. An astray and a book of matches sit on top of the workbench.

Hans understands there's no other way. He's got to kill them. Slowly backing away from the other men, he goes over to the trash cans. Reaching over, he gets the book of matches.

Suddenly Hans changes his mind about killing them. He notices the sink and the hose hanging there and some gas masks. They can use the hose and gas masks to put the fire out and not use the CO-2 bottles.

The other men are still watching what's being done to that guy. Hans takes a match, lights it, and then touches it to some of the dirty rages and papers in one trash can. It starts burning. He lights another match and does the same thing to the other can. The fire's burning good. He pushes the drums over, and the burning trash falls out onto the deck all over the place. Hans can smell the smoke, and it's thick.

The smoke's so thick that Hans can't see the other men

Hans runs out of the room, closes the door, and shuts it down tight. He puts his left shoulder under the extended cross-member of the wheel to hold it shut because they're trying to get it open from the inside. Grabbing the chain from the wrought-iron handle on the wall, he lets it hang and then grabs the first end with his left hand, crossing the chain under the extended part of the wheel cross-member, holding both ends of the chains in his left hand. Hans takes the padlock with his right hand and locks the chain as close as he can to the extended part of the cross-member, just like he did before. Then he pulls his shoulder out of there.

The wheel gives a little turn but stops when the chain comes tight. There's no way those men can get out of there now. They should be able to put the fire out before all the air's, gone.

With Hans's shoulder still hurting from that wheel handle, he turns and runs down to where Tony and the guys are hiding. He bangs on the door. It opens a little at first, and then it opens wide.

Standing in the doorway, Hans shouts out, "Let's go now."

As Tony and Pete both come out with M-sixteens rifles in their hands, Tony orders, "Take Pete and me and show us where the captain's office is, Cowboy. Then come back here with the others. As soon as you get back here, get your rifle and some ammunition, and make your move with the rest of the guys here."

They drape two blankets from the supply room over the rifles. Hans takes Tony and Pete straight up to the captain's office.

Just outside the door, Tony says in a low voice, "Okay, Cowboy, get back down with the rest of the guys."

Pete grins and slaps Hans on his shoulder. Hans grins, waves, and heads back down. Just as he gets back inside the supply room, a voice comes over the loudspeaker. "This is the captain speaking."

Hans looks at Sam and Carlos, puzzled, and says: "What the—"

Sam goes, "Shh."

The captain continues. "All deckhands and derrick operators assemble on the main deck immediately. All hands and derrick operators."

That is all he announces.

Sam hands Hans a rifle and some ammunition and says, "Cowboy, we'll all wait a few minutes. We want to give those men a little time to get up there on the deck. I want you to lead John and four others to the engine room. Then show me and two others to the mess hall. We can hold some of them there.

"You and Carlos stay down on this deck and go all the way to the bow. From there, go on up to the main deck and watch. Just as soon as they get hold number one empty, wave up to the bridge to Tony. He'll have the captain send men from the mess hall to hold number one, and I will lock them up."

They wait about five minutes, and then Sam asks, "Are you ready, Cowboy?"

Hans replies, "Yes. I'm as ready as I will ever be."

"Okay, let's go and shoot or capture anyone who happens to be in the way."

They get to the door heading down to the engine room. John and three men go on in and down. On the way to the mess hall, five men come around the corner just in front of them. They all point their rifles at them. Sam tells them, "Turn around and go back into the mess hall."

They turn and start back

Hans tells one of the guys, "Go around to the front entrance of the mess hall. That way, you can stop anyone from coming back out there.

"Okay," he replies, "I am on my way."

There are seven men coming out of the mess hall when they get there. One of the five men heading back yells, "Go back! They have guns!"

The seven men look at them coming. Four of them turn back, but three come toward them and dart around the corner.

The five men who turned around were between them and the three men who ran around the corner. One of the guys pushes through them, runs around the corner, and starts shooting. He stops at the corner. As they come by, he says, "I got all three of them."

There are only about twenty people left in the mess hall, counting the cooks. They're cleaning up and closing it down. Sam makes the cooks and their helpers come in and sit down. The guy Hans sent around to the front entrance comes in with six more captives, and he quickly says I shot four others, but about eight men got away from me." He shut and dogs down the door.

Keeping his eyes on the men they've taken hostage, Sam says, "Cowboy, you and Carlos can go head forward now. We have things under control here."

"Okay," Hans replies. "Come on, Carlos, let's go."

Carlos and Hans exit the mess hall. They close the door. Then they go around the corner and down the passageway, stepping over the three dead men. They turn left on the starboard side of the ship and head forward.

They're just passing hold number three when they hear a voice yell, "There's two of them with rifles. One of them is that new squirrel. Let's get them!"

They look through the passageway. They see two men coming at them. They both have a pistol. They're pointing them at Carlos and Hans. Carlos commands, "Hurry, Cowboy. follow me forward and around a corner." They make it right before the men start shooting. They stop just past the corner. The passageway they're in heads across to the other side of the ship.

Carlos says, "We don't dare try to stick our rifles around and shoot back. Let's run to the end of the passageway and go through the door and around the corner." They run to the door, which is closed and locked from the other side. There's no way they can go in.

Carlos blurted, "I can't pick this lock."

About halfway back the other way is another CO_2 bottle hanging on the wall.

Suddenly Hans remarks, "Come on, Carlos, I have an idea." They run over, and Hans takes the bottle off the wall and runs back to the corner.

In the other passageway are two doorways. Hans carefully lays the bottle on top of the bottom seals, with the nozzle head pointing aft on the edge of the corner. Hans takes the butt end of his rifle and points it straight at the nozzle head, holding the rifle by the barrel.

Watching what Hans's doing, Carlos asks, "What the hell are you trying to do with that?"

Hans replies, "Just watch."

Hans hit the nozzle head twice. Bullets from those men's guns slam into the butt of his rifle. The third time, Hans hit the nozzle head hard, and it breaks.

F-w-w-w-w-w... Just like that, it's gone. One great big crash. Bang and nothing. Slowly looking around the corner, the CO_2 bottle got both of those men and put a hole right through the ship's starboard bow. The hole is big enough for a basketball to fit through.

Running around the corner toward the hole, Hans shouts, "Oh shit, come on!"

Carlos's right behind him. He shouts, "Damn you, Cowboy, you put a hole in the ship."

Hans replies, "No shit. Come on, let's get it plugged."

The hole is just above the waterline, but every time the ship bobs down, it drops below, and water gushes in.

They run as fast as they can, jumping over the two dead bodies on the way to the bow.

With water splashing all over them, they make it to the hole and grab onto door seals to keep from getting washed back down the passageway.

There's a wall just to the left of the hole and an open doorway to a passageway leading across to the other side. Hans gets to it and unlatches the hook that holds it open; he closes it and starts to dog it down. The water comes in and pushes him back, but he catches himself on another door seal.

The ship comes up, and Hans steps up to the door again and finishes dogging it down. Hans has to dog each latch one at a time to hold it shut. The ship goes back down, and Hans runs behind the door to close off their passageway.

Carlos has it ready to close when Hans comes through. He slams it shut, and starts dogging it down, and Hans helps him. They did it. There's no way any more water can get in the ship unless some dumb shit opens the doors.

They both lean against the door and sigh with relief.

Carlos says with a grin, "Cowboy, the more I get to know you, the more you amaze me. When I first met you. I was thinking, why in the hell does Pete like this Cowboy guy so much. You didn't impress me at all. But now that I got to know you, I wouldn't have come up with the idea to hijack this ship, and I wouldn't have thought about using the fire bottle the way you did. I'll follow you anywhere, Cowboy."

Grinning back, Hans replies, "I never could make an excellent first impression. I could wear a three-hundred-dollar suit or be dressed like I am now and still not make a good first impression. I hated to go looking for a job for that reason. I gave up trying. What you see is what you get, and what you get is what you see, right, wrong, or otherwise.

"The fire bottle thing, I've seen that happen before. A man walking down some steps, holding a fire bottle on his shoulder, is the wrong way to hold it. He tripped and fell. He dropped the bottle on the nozzle head and broke it. The bottle went clear through the base Headquarters. Luckily it was on a Sunday, and nobody was in the building."

Carlos grins and nods.

They take a quick look at the dead men. That CO_2 bottle smashed clear through them both. What a mess!

They run aft until they find a ladder heading to the next deck. They go up and run forward and up to the main deck.

The day is still sunny and warm.

That's where most of the ship's crew is. What a sight. They're dumping all the wooden boxes and other cargo over the side. They finished hold number one. Hans and Carlos go over and look down.

Hans waves to the bridge and gives a thumbs-up to show they're done. The captain's voice comes over the loudspeaker, letting Sam know the hold's empty. A few minutes later, Hans looks down in the hold. The captives from the mess hall are coming in the hold. Sam's standing inside the door talking to five of the captives. He's not holding his rifle on them. There not arguing, just talking.

Carlos and Hans step back from the hold when they close the hatch. Numbers two and three are empty now, also. An hour later, they have the aft half of the ship empty. They close the hatches on all the holds.

The captain's voice again comes over the loudspeaker: "Now that the ship's empty, all hands and derrick operators report to holds number one, two, and three."

They are almost done locking the ship's crew up in the holds. Then they all get together right outside of hold number three on the port side. Hans closes the last door. He looks around and notices they are short one man. Hans locks the door and asks Sam, "There's one more man, isn't there?"

Sam lights up a cigarette and explains, "We lost one man when we were in the mess hall. One of the cooks put a butcher knife in his back."

"We lost just one man through all of this. That's not too bad because we're all damn lucky any of us made it at all."

"Don't hold your breath, Cowboy. This thing isn't over yet.

We will walk through this whole ship and look in every room and corner to ensure we got the whole crew.

Hans implies, "Be careful. Some men might still be alive when you get to the damage control room. The one with a green shirt has a gun and a knife."

Sam says, "Thanks, Cowboy."

Chapter 18

Tying up Loose Ends

Hans asks, "When I was up on deck looking down in the hold you were putting the captives in, I saw you talking to some of the captives. What was that all about?"

Sam laughs a little and replies, "The captives talking to me are glad we took this ship over. They say that most of them are glad. When someone does something wrong, he doesn't get fired; he gets killed. There's no way out. Lagno and the captain are complete mad men."

Hans replied, "One of them told me the same thing just before they killed him right in front of me. They told you the truth."

Sam looks surprised and replies, "Oh really, I didn't believe them.

Sam suggests, "You can go up and tell Tony and Pete that we have everything under control."

"Okay. I will see you later. Be careful, you guys."

Hans goes to the other side of the ship and heads up to the captain's office. He gets about halfway up the ladder and looks in at the next deck and the captain's door when he stops. Standing in front of the captain's door is a man. His back is to Hans. Suddenly, in his right hand, a knife appears. He pulls open the door and hurls it into the room.

Hans runs up a couple of steps, aims his rifle at him, and shoots him in the back. He falls to the deck.

The captain gets up from behind his desk and comes around it. Someone else starts shooting. The captain falls to the deck, and the shooting stops.

Running the rest of the way up the ladder and to the door, Hans steps over the dead man's body and looks into the office.

Pete's lying face down on the deck, with the knife sticking out his back. Hans didn't shoot that man in time to save Pete. He calls out, "Tony, are you okay?"

Tony replies, "Yes, come in."

Hans steps in and closes the door. To his right is a ladder going directly up the bridge from the captain's office. He looks up. Tony's standing about halfway up it.

Looking down at Hans, he explains, "I was keeping a watch on the men up there on the bridge. I wasn't down here."

Before Hans can say anything, two men appear at the top of the ladder with pistols in their hands. He swings his rifle up at them as fast as he can and starts shooting, getting them before they can shoot back. One falls back, and the other falls down the ladder. Tony drops down the ladder and gets out of the dead man's way.

Hans quickly asks Tony, "Are there any more up there?"

"No. Just those two."

He bends down over Pete and pulls the knife out of his back. He rolls him over on his back and whimpers, "Oh God, why? Just when we have everything under control. I should have stayed down here. I could have saved his life."

Hans clears off the top of the captain's desk, and then Tony and Hans pick up Pete and lay him on the desk.

Hans looks down at Pete, and it's starting to sink in that he's dead. His best friend. Hans starts crying and bends down and hugs him.

Hans starts thinking, what's he going to do now without Pete. He's feeling all alone. Guess he depended on him a lot more than he thought he did. Hans can't pull himself away from him and can't stop crying.

Hans whimpered, "Oh Tony, I didn't shoot that man fast enough to save Pete's life. I could have shot him sooner if I had gotten up the ladder a little earlier." Hans pulls himself away from him, gets one of the blankets used to cover the rifles, unfolds it, and spreads it over Pete's body.

Watching Hans, Tony says sadly, "Oh, Cowboy. Please stop lamenting about your actions. Don't go blaming yourself for this. It happened, and there's nothing we can do about it."

Hans replies, "I know, Tony. I'll suck it up and move on. But not right now."

Tony politely says, "We'll have to get John up here. He has been a sailor all his life. He's supposed to take command of the ship anyway.

"Why don't I page John over this microphone?" Hans suggests. Tony doesn't say anything. He just nods.

Hans takes the microphone and calls for John. Shortly after, he enters the office. He sees what happened, and Tony says, "Go up to the bridge and take over the ship, John. It's all yours."

As John starts up the ladder, he politely says, "Just as soon as you can, I'll need a couple of the guys up there to help me.

"Okay, John," replies Tony. "Just as soon as Sam and the others get up here."

Hans gets back on the microphone and calls for Sam and two of the guys to come up.

While they are waiting for Sam, with tears still falling from his eyes, Hans explains to Tony, "One of their men told me everyone who goes to work for Lagno becomes his slave and prisoner."

Tony lights up a cigarette and replies, "I hope you didn't believe him."

Hans implies, "Yes, every word. Especially when they killed him right after he told me."

About this time, Carlos, Sam, and two guys enter the office. Tony tells them, "Pete's dead," and he shows them his body.

Tony orders, "You other two guys go up to the bridge and help John." They go.

Hans starts thinking about the captives and states, "We can't just kill all the captives. Let's tell them that this ship is a Bacco ship now and tell them they are free from Lagno and can go home to their families."

Tony thinks about it for a while and says, "Oh shit, I didn't even think about Lagno's crew. We'll have to kill them all. There can't be any witnesses, or we're done.

 Sam blurts out, "No, most of them are glad we took this ship. Let's go all the way and kill Lagno. He's crazy, they say. The way they pleaded, I believed them. I won't kill them."

Carlos states, "Those men got hired not knowing what they were getting themselves in to. They're innocent people just trying to make a living for their families."

Hans explains, "Tony, if we kill all of them, we are no better than Lagno. Maybe even worse. We're supposed to be the 'good' bad guys. No more; I'm not going to kill them. I will kill only those that are trying to kill me."

Tony was surprised at the words of his fellow mates.

Looking straight into Tony's eyes, Hans replies, "That corrupt dirty sheriff had that look in his eyes that he was going to kill me. Two deputies pulled him off me; they saved my life.

Tony states, "There weren't any deputies in the sheriff's office when we stormed in there, just the sheriff himself."

Hans replies, telling a lie, "The other deputies must have gone out on patrol before you guys got there. They might have been the deputies that were chasing us right after we burned the sheriff's office down."

Carlos indicates, "Lagno has a lot of bad people working for him and has a lot more good people working for him. Let's focus on the bad people and leave the good ones alone."

Tony Just stands there for a mount. Then he states, "Your right. I was getting carried away. We'll kill only the ones we just have to."

Suddenly one of the new men comes into the office. He states, "There's a room with the word "Storage" on the door. It's padlocked, shut from the outside. I can hear voices coming from inside, and they sound like women.

Hans looks over at Tony and states, "Your dad did say Lagno is human trafficking young teenage girls. They must have smuggled them aboard right after I got aboard and was in the captain's office, being interrogated by the captain. Because I don't have any ship experience, I was suspected of being Bacco's inside man right from the get-go."

Tony looks at Hans and shakes his head. "Wow, Cowboy, you're something else. You went ahead and pulled this off anyway."

Trying not to think about Pete, Hans's starting to feel a little better, for now anyway. He takes the microphone and announces, "Attention, everyone, we are holding captive. Your captain's dead. This ship now belongs to Antonio Bacco. So, when we pull into port, you are all free to go home to your families. You will never have to fear the name Lagno again. You are free to make a new start just as soon as we dock."

Tony walks over to the ladder and says, "I'm going up to the bridge and helping John. After we tie up the ship at Daytona Beach, we will let Lagno's crew get off. We can hold them in a building on the pier until we are loaded and ready to pull out to sea, just in case some of them try to cause trouble.

"Carlos, Sam, and Cowboy, go down and check out that storage room. Then Sam and Carlos go down to the engine room and give the others a hand. Cowboy, you come back up to the bridge. I'll think about what I'm going to do with those girls."

Carlos picks the lock and opens the door to the storage room. They go in. The room's big and full of young teenage girls and bunk beds. The girls don't say anything. They look scared to death.

Carlos comments. "Relax, we're not going to harm you. Just hang in there a little longer. When we pull into the port, you all can go home."

One of the girls states, "Two girls died, and four girls are sick."

Sam indicates, "Two of Lagno crew you saw me talking to Cowboy in the hold are medics. I'll go get them."

He leaves.

Carlos and Hans stay with the girls, and they show them the sick girls.

Sam gets back with the medics. They're tending to the sick girls.

Sam and Carlos go down to the engine room.

Hans goes back up to the bridge.

At about four-thirty that afternoon, they tie up at Daytona.

John looks out over the pier and says, "My crew's down there waiting. I better go out on the deck and let them know it's me."

He leaves.

Tony tells Cowboy, "Go down and check on how Sam and Carlos are doing with the enginemen."

Hans goes down to the engine room. It looks like Sam, Carlos, and the others have everything under control.

"Yes. We're all done down here."

"Let's go back up to the main deck."

Once they get up there, they go over to where Tony and John are standing at the end of the gangplank as they watch John's crew come aboard.

Tony tells John, "Pick out some of your crew that is good with rifles."

"Sam," he says, "Take them to the supply room and give them the rest of the rifles and ammunition."

"I found the ship's armory when we were looking through the ship," replies Sam. "There's several .30-30 rifles, ammunition, and some pistols."

"Okay," says Tony. "We will arm as many men as we can with rifles and ammunition and get all of Lagno's crew off the ship."

Sam takes the men and leaves.

Tony turns to John and asks, "How many men do you have?"

"Two hundred and eighty-five."

That is about fifty more than Lagno has on here.

"Just as soon as we get rid of Lagno's crew," says Tony, "start loading up the ship with lumber, cement blocks, and everything that's on the pier that's supposed to be loaded."

"Okay."

After standing there and listening to them talk, Hans finally gets a word in. He asks John, "Do you have any welders on your crew? I had to make a torpedo out of a fire bottle and put a hole in the bow big enough that a basketball could fit through. It's at the starboard bow.

"How long will it be before you're ready to pull out of here?"

John sighs and replies, "We'll get the hole fixed, and thank you for telling me about it. Around 9:30 or 10 p.m. tonight, we will be ready to pull out."

Hans turns to Tony with a grin. "It looks like we did it. John and his crew have everything under control. I feel that I have done enough around here for a while. I'll see you guys at ten o'clock tonight. I'm going to find a bar and have a whole bunch of ice-cold beers. If anybody wants to come along, that's fine with me. If not, that's fine with me, too."

Hans hands his rifle, ammunition, and hard hat over to Tony.

He grins and takes them. "Get lost, Cowboy. I hate to admit it, but you deserve it. Be sure to get back here by ten o'clock and stay out of trouble. Most of all, stay out of jail."

Hans runs down the gangplank to the pier, then around a building, and to the street, looking for a bar. If there's no bar, he'll get a taxicab.

The day is sunny with a warm breeze, and the air smells clean and fresh.

At the street, Hans stops and looks around. A sign reads "BAR" right across the street and a little to his right. Hans walks over and goes in. It's a small neighborhood port bar. It's clean but not real fancy. There's a nice-looking little café in the back. The bar is to his right, and some booths are to his left. A couple of them are empty.

Hans steps over to the bar and orders a pitcher of beer and one mug. Then he takes them over to one of the booths and sits down.

Hans fills the mug up and gulps it down. That sure is good! He fills it up again, this time drinking it slower.

Hans feels relaxed and relieved. It's a big load off of his mind. It's hard to believe that they hijacked a ship like pirates back in the olden days. Hans wonders what will happen next.

Hans starts to feel sad again, thinking about what happened to Pete.

But that thought doesn't last long. Hans hears a voice say, "Think you can just sneak off the ship without inviting your friends, Cowboy? Hans looks to his left. Sam's standing there with a grin on hie face.

Hans laughs and says, "Hi, sit down." Sam sits down just across from him. Hans looks over toward the bar. Carlos's coming with a pitcher of beer and two beer mugs. He sits the beer and mugs on the table and sits down next to Sam.

Carlos remarks, "Hi, Cowboy; want some company?"

Hans replies, "Sure, it's about time we get together and have a few beers."

Sam indicates, "John has his crew taking care of everything. We felt kind of in the way. Tony told us to join you for a beer."

Hans laughs and remarks, "Unofficially, you're my babysitters to keep me out of trouble, laughing again." they all laugh.

Carlos pours the beer into the mugs and tops off Hans's mug. Hans's pitcher is empty. He gets up and walks back to the bar to get a refill. He gets back and sits down.

Hans asks, "Did they get the girls off the ship?"

Carlos replies, "John's going to have his crew take them to a Catholic church close by and drop them off.

Hans sighs, "That's good.

He laughs and remarks, "When Lagno finds out what happened to his ship and all the guns and girls he lost, that will piss him off."

They all laugh.

Carlos remarks, "There were drugs in some of the other boxes we opened. We're damn lucky we found the right boxes to get into, or we would have had to drop everything and run out of there as fast as we could."

Hans states, "I would have had to run out of there with you, or they would have killed me.

Sam and Carlos light up cigarettes and drink their beer. Hans asks, "Where and when did you guys meet up?"

Carlos explains, "We both were on the Fort Lauderdale police force for about four years. Sam and I were partners. I got shot five times. I had a bullet proof vest on each time."

Sam stated, "I got shot three times. Then one night, we got Tony out of a jam. He offered us a job to be his bodyguard. We quit the police force and now work for Tony."

Hans remarks, "You're still getting shot at with this job."

Carlos replies, "Yes but not nearly as bad as it was on the force. Plus, we get paid a lot more money."

Hans asks, "How come none of the guys got married and have a family?"

Sam replies, "I almost got married while working one night. She was walking the streets and dealing drugs. I caught her. She's now in prison.

Carlos remarks, "I just haven't found the right one yet. I'm not really looking that hard ether."

Hans states, "Carlos, we were talking about first impressions earlier. The first time I met you and Sam. You two were so serious; I got the impression you guys don't like anybody, and if someone looked at you wrong, you would shoot him.

"The more I got to know you, you're not that way at all. You say you'll follow me anywhere. The same goes for me. I'll follow the both of you anywhere."

They both grin, and Carlos replies, "That sounds good to me."

Sam quickly says, "Me too, Cowboy."

They all shake hands. The three of them become friends, not just working partners.

More people come in, and a group of ladies comes in. They start playing the Jukebox.

People are dancing. Hans tells the guys, "I'm going to give it a try." he gets up and goes and asks one of the ladies to dance. She accepts. Sam and Carlos found some ladies to dance with.

This's a real friendly place. By nine p.m., Hans's feeling no pain and having a good time.

Starting to feel a little hungry, they go in the back to the café and get something to eat. Then they make our way back to the ship.

They get aboard. Sam Says, "See you later, Cowboy."

Hans replies, "Okay."

They go down below decks.

Hans finds Tony and John at the bridge and tells them they're back.

They just laugh and tease Hans for being drunk. Not caring, Hans just laughs and teases back at them because they had a good time. Hans goes down to his room and goes to bed. It's about nine-thirty the next day when Hans wakes up. He knows they're at sea. He can feel the ship rocking and swaying.

Hans still can't stop thinking about Pete. He's trying not to think so much about him and keep from crying. Hans is supposed to be a tough guy. "Come on, get on with it. Quit thinking about Pete."

Hans starts thinking. Lagno's going to really be pissed off when he finds out about his ship and that all his cargo is gone. He's going to come after them with both barrels loaded.

Chapter 19

Mr. Bacco Learns That Pete's Dead

Hans gets up and looks in the mirror. There's about a three-day beard growth, and he feels filthy, so he shaves and takes a hot shower. Feeling good after that, and having slept almost twelve hours, he doesn't feel any hangover from last night.

Hans has two sets of work clothes with him. He puts on a clean set and heads to the mess hall, wondering if John brought some cooks aboard. The mess hall's open, so Hans goes in and has breakfast and coffee.

After breakfast, Hans goes up to the main deck. The sun is warm, the sky's clear, and the wind's calm. For the first time since being aboard this ship, Hans can look out across the ocean water, relax, and enjoy the beauty of the deep blue sea.

He wanders around the main deck and talks with some of the crew for a little while. Then he goes on up to the bridge. He goes up the starboard side of the ship so he doesn't have to walk through the captain's office, where Pete's body is. Afraid He might start crying when he sees him.

When Hans arrives, Tony, Sam, Carlos, and John are up on the bridge. A man wearing a phone headset is standing by to call down to the engine room to give orders to the enginemen.

John smiles at Hans and says, "Well, good morning, Cowboy. It's about time you got up."

Tony and John laugh.

Sam and Carlos just sit there, not laughing or saying anything, with innocent looks on their faces.

Hans grins, "Thanks a whole lot, you guys. You all act like I am the only one around here that ever takes a drink now and then. Just because you guys can't hack it, that's not my fault."

They all laugh. It's good they're all-in good spirits, even though Pete's dead. Hans knows they're concerned and feeling bad about it but going around moping about it won't bring him back.

Tony has been staring out the front window at sea with a cup of coffee and a cigarette in his hand. He turns to them and says, "Well, now that everybody's here, I'll tell you what we are going to do now. I don't know where Dad is.

"As soon as we get to the island, Sam, Carlos, and I, with some of the ship's crew, will take the bodies of Pete and our three other men who were killed off the ship and to a funeral home. We will have to get a hold of the three men's families and let them know. As for Dad, we will just have to wait for him to contact us. Until then, we're going to continue right on just as we have planned.

"John, this ship is all yours. You just keep bringing the supplies over. Don't let Lagno get this ship back. The rest of us are going to go ahead and start building the casino.

"John has his crew cleaning up the dead bodies of Lagno's crew. They're feeding them to the sharks. Cowboy, you stay up here until John's navigator and some of his other men get back from having breakfast. The rest of us can go below or do whatever you want until we pull in."

Tony and the rest of the guys leave.

Watching out over the sea, John takes a sip of coffee and a puff from his cigarette and says, "There's really nothing much for you to do, Cowboy. Just look out to sea on all sides. Let me know if there's another ship, land, or almost anything that isn't water."

Hans nods.

Before looking out to sea, Hans glances around the room. The bridge is the highest room on the ship, and it has a row of windows that go all the way around. Hans can look out for miles, clear to the horizon. Right below some of the windows are desks for the navigators to do their work. On one of the desks is a coffeepot with a spout at the bottom. There are some clean cups right beside it.

Hans remarks, "Think I'll have some coffee."

John replies, "Go ahead and help yourself, Cowboy. "

"Tony brought your hard hat up here. It's on the other desk."

Hans pour's some coffee, goes over, picks up his hard hat, and puts it on.

"Thank you, John."

John has not moved. He keeps looking out to sea. He sighs and states, "Boy, it sure is good to have a ship again. Thanks to you guys and Mr. Bacco, I get a ship, and my crew can get back to work again. Cowboy, I had a ship once a lot like this one, but that damn Lagno put me out of business. That son of a bitch! I hate him just as bad as Bacco does.

"When I found out someone like Bacco had the balls to fight against him, I decided to join in and help, even if it meant getting killed. Without a ship, I might just as well be dead anyway. The sea is my life.

"Cowboy, if you need any favor, just let me know. I will do the best I can for you."

Hans replies, "There might be one. After this ends, you can give me a free ride back to the States. Then I can go back home to Idaho."

"That, I can do."

The navigator and the other men come back up to the bridge, so Hans tells John, "I'll see you later."

Hans goes down and out on the main deck. He wanders around, enjoying the warm air and sunshine, visiting some of the crew, making small talk, nothing important.

After a long time, he hears someone say, "There's land."

He goes over to the port side and looks south and a little east. against the horizon. There's land.

About an hour later, they're heading into the harbor. Tony and the guys are over on the starboard side, and Hans goes over and joins them. Tony's busy talking to Sam.

Hans steps up to the railing and looks over at the pier they're going to tie up.

On the pier are tractor-trailer rigs with flatbed trailers and men standing around them. Five men dressed in suits are standing next to one of the trucks in the middle of the pier, close to the waterfront.

As they get closer, Hans recognizes that one of the men wearing a suit is Mr. Bacco.

Pointing to him, Hans shouts, "Tony, your dad, is on the pier, waiting for us. He has trucks down there, also."

Tony comes over, looks to where Hans's pointing, and says in a serious voice, "Well, I'm glad he's here."

Tony waves at his dad. He waves back in recognition.

The four men with him are his gorillas. They look just as mean as Lagno's gorillas.

They get the ship tied up and the gangplank set up. Mr. Bacco and the four other men start up the plank. Tony stands at the edge of it.

Mr. Bacco steps onto the ship. With a big grin on his face, he joyfully says, "I can't believe it. You guys hijacked this ship, one of Lagno's ships. You guys did a damn good job."

Nobody says a word or even smiles. Mr. Bacco notices that, and he looks at all of them. The grin comes off his face.

Tony looks at his dad with a sad look on his face and bluntly says, "Pete's dead."

Mr. Bacco does not say anything for a minute. He just stands here with a sad look on his face.

He asks, "Where is he?"

They all go up to the captain's office, where Pete's body is. Mr. Bacco looks at him. He covers him back up.

Looking at Pete's face again, Hans starts fighting back the tears.

Mr. Bacco looks at Hans and his tears. He asks, "Pete was your best friend, wasn't he, Cowboy?"

Hans nods.

Mr. Bacco replies. "Cowboy, I'm so sorry for you. He was one of my best men."

He shakes his head no and states, "I was going to have a big dinner for everybody tonight. But I think we will cancel that until tomorrow night. I will tell you of further plans then. I don't think Cowboy feels up to dinner tonight, do you?"

Hans stammers a little, "S-Something Pete told me back in Vietnam when some other good friends of ours got killed." Pete stated, "You have to suck it up, tough it out, Cowboy, and move on. Feeling sorry for yourself won't bring them back.

"I agree with Pete. Let's move on. The dinner will help take my mind off him. It wouldn't be right for everyone else if we didn't have the dinner because of me, if that's okay with you, sir? Please don't feel sorry for me. I don't want anybody to feel sorry for me. It's not anybody's fault that Pete's dead. It's more my fault because I couldn't stop it in time."

Mr. Bacco smiles at Hans and politely says, "Cowboy, you're a good man. We'll have the dinner tonight, around seven p.m., at the same place we always have it."

Tony phones for a couple of ambulances to get Pete's body and the bodies of the other three guys off the ship. Mr. Bacco leaves with his four men. Tony tells John to start unloading the supplies.

Tony turns to Hans and commands, "Cowboy, go down and get your bags. Let's get a cab and go to the airport to get my car. "Sam, you and Carlos can also go with us and get your cars. We'll come back here and get some of the rifles and ammunition. They still might come in handy before this is over."

Hans asks Tony, "What are you going to do with Pete's car? Or can I have it?"

Tony thinks a little and replies, "You might as well take it. Go to the office and get the keys out of Pete's pocket before the ambulances get here."

Hans goes and gets the keys.

They get the cars and get the rifles and ammunition off the ship. Hans drives straight to his apartment. Just before he goes up. Hans opens his bag up and pulls out his dirty pants and shirt. Put the M-sixteen's barrel in one pant leg and wrap the shirt around the rest. Hans throws a whole bunch of loaded magazines in his bag. With the rifle covered, no one will notice him carrying it up to the apartment.

After going in and setting his things down, Hans goes back out and checks the mailbox. The only thing there is the phone bill. He goes back up to his apartment.

He opens the phone bill, looks at it, and puts it on the table. He takes the rifle from the pants and shirt, puts it in the bedroom closet next to his bags, and then puts the dirty clothes in the box in the closet.

Hans goes out to the kitchen. He gets a beer from the refrigerator, goes into the living room, sits down, and just relaxes.

Hans gets ready for dinner.

Around 6:30 p.m., he drives over to the hotel.

Hans's the last one here, so he walks right into the banquet room. Sam, Carlos, John, Mr. Bacco, and his four bodyguards are here. Everyone's dressed in suits and is seated at the same long table. There's a place close to the middle of the table. Hans sits down.

Mrs. Bacco's here, looking beautiful again. She is wearing a long black dress and is the only woman here. She smiles politely at Hans but says nothing.

There's nothing much to talk about during dinner, just small talk. Hans doesn't say much and lets the others do the talking. He keeps glancing over at Mrs. Bacco, and it seems like she is glancing away from him every time he looks over. Dammit, this is dumb. Hans quits glancing at her and quietly eats his dinner.

After everyone gets through eating, Mrs. Bacco excuses herself and leaves the room.

That woman shakes Hans up so much. He feels more relaxed after she's gone. God almighty! At first, he was a bit bashful in high school, but this is ridiculous.

Now Hans's thoughts go back to business, and he waits for Mr. Bacco to tell them what will happen next.

Chapter 20

Hans Meets Joannie

Mr. Bacco takes a cigar from his coat pocket and lights it. He explains, "Now there's going to be an addition to our plans. We're going to build a sixteen-story hotel on top of the casino. John, the ship is yours. Just keep right on bringing the supplies over.

"Tony, you will be going with me to the court hearing.

"Lagno and I will be in court, trying to hang each other. One of us or both of us will get a prison sentence out of this. If I go to prison, I want you to go right on as planned. I won't be there forever.

"Sam, Carlos, and Cowboy, you stay here on the island and help out here. You guys won't be doing any manual work. You will be more like security guards. You will have your M-16 sixteen rifles with you and other rifles someplace close by so that you can pass them out to the men just in case Lagno's men should try something. They're tough men, but they're builders, not fighters. Your job is to protect them in any way you can. At night, there will be several pit bulls locked inside the fence.

"Okay, that is all I have to say except that you guys have done a damn good job so far, and I have something here for you."

He pulls some brown envelopes out of a briefcase he had by his side. As he gives them each one with their name on it, he says, "Don't open these until you get home tonight."

After that's all over with, Hans drives back to his apartment.

He goes on up and fixes himself a drink of bourbon and water. Then opens the envelope that Mr. Bacco gave him. Boy, what a happy surprise: it's full of crisp hundred-dollar bills. FIVE

THOUSAND DOLLARS!

Hans takes the money and puts it in the dresser drawer, still having plenty of money left from the last time he got paid. He really hasn't had the time or the place to spend much of it.

Well, that's all right. He will be able to save some of that for when he goes home to Idaho.

After a couple of drinks, Hans goes to bed but can't go to sleep right away. He starts thinking about Mrs. Bacco again. Boy, what a feeling it would be just to hold her in his arms, kiss her, and make love to her. Suddenly, he feels himself getting turned on. Oh, he wants her! She's so beautiful. She's too beautiful and too good to ever be for him. Dammit, there are lots of women in this world. There's a lot of them right here on this island. Boy, he needs a woman and needs one bad. He'll have time to find one or two, or maybe three, starting tomorrow. Especially since he has Pete's car.

Guess Mrs. Bacco is the only woman he has really been close to in a long time. That's probably why his getting a crush on her. Hope that's the reason, anyway. Finally, he relaxes enough to fall asleep.

The next morning, Hans puts on his work clothes and wears his hard hat. It's about seven a.m. The day is sunny and warm, with no wind.,

Hans gets some breakfast.

He pulls out onto the road and turns left. Suddenly about five cars are coming straight at him. He doesn't know what to do. Then it dawns on him: He's in the right-hand lane. Quickly turns into the left-hand lane just in time.

Hans sighs. Oh shit, that was close! That's one sure way to learn how to drive on the left-hand side of the road. Dammit, He knows better than that, too, just from riding around on this island. He's so used to driving in the States that he completely forgot.

Then Hans goes to the site where the casino is to be built.

Mr. Bacco has already got a crew started. There's a big hole dug for the basement and foundation. There's a big chain link fence around it, and several men are there.

Sam, Carlos, and Tony are all dressed in work cloths, with hard hats on. Mr. and Mrs. Bacco are standing close by as Hans comes through a big open gate. Just as he walks over to them, Mr. Bacco takes his cigar out of his mouth and quickly says, "Good morning, Cowboy."

Hans replies, "Good morning, sir."

Looking over at Mrs. Bacco. Of course, she's just as beautiful as when she was before. She's dressed in a black pants suit for mourning for Pete, maybe.

She coolly flutters her eyes at Hans and smiles. She doesn't say a word. His heart skips about ten beats, and a big lump comes in his throat. He doesn't say anything. He just smiles back at her and looks back at Mr. Bacco, trying to keep from embarrassing himself.

Never in Hans's whole life has he had a woman turn him on so fast and as much as she does. With her being married to the big boss, keeping cool and looking innocent about the whole thing when she's around is hard.

Standing right beside Mrs. Bacco is a muscleman. He's about six feet tall with a dark crew haircut, clean-shaven. He is probably around twenty-five years old. He's wearing tight pants and a T-shirt. He looks like a weightlifter. He's probably never done a hard day's work in his life. Bet he couldn't keep up with Hans in a hay field. He just stands there staring at Hans. He must be her bodyguard. The one Pete was talking about.

Mr. Bacco and Tony are talking all this time, but Hans doesn't hear what it's about.

Then a big man walks up. He's wearing work clothes and a hard hat. He's over six feet tall and has broad shoulders. He has slightly short black hair just below his hat and a curly black mustache.

Mr. Bacco introduces him to Hans as Jeff Bates and says, "Jeff, this is Cowboy."

Jeff remarks, "It's good to meet you, Cowboy." They shake hands.

Hans replies, "It's good to meet you, Jeff."

He looks at Hans, kind of strange. Can't figure out why. Looking back at him, though, he seems familiar. Think Hans has seen him someplace before. Maybe that's why he looked at Hans like that. He might have seen him before, also.

Hans politely asks, "Were you in the army?"

He gives Hans a dirty look and bluntly says, "No, I haven't been in the army, and no, I've never seen you before."

Hans replies. "I'm sorry I asked."

Mr. Bacco explains. "Jeff's my new contractor. He tells me he's not afraid of Lagno and will take the job."

Mr. and Mrs. Bacco and her bodyguard leave.

Jeff shows Tony, Sam, Carlos, and Hans around and introduces them to some of the men working here.

Jeff states, "You guys get your rifles and some ammo and get started with your patrol." He and Tony walk away.

They walk over to Carlos's beige color van. There are a lot more rifles and ammunition in it. Hans gets an M-sixteen and five magazines.

Just before walking away from them. Carlos remarks, "This part of the job is going to get boring until something happens."

Hans replies, "I agree, but I'd rather be bored than get shot at or killed."

Sam remarks, "I'm with you, Cowboy."

They just patrol the place, watching for anything that might indicate trouble from Lagno's men. They walk in different directions by themselves, meet in places, and stop and talk for a while.

When Hans patrolled by himself, he would stop and visit with some of the builders.

Jeff walks by and smiles, and keeps going. Damn, he still looks familiar. He's thinking back to the guys and the teachers Hans knew in high school but can't seem to place him. Oh well, maybe he reminds Hans of someone who kind of looks like him. It doesn't matter anyway.

Tony walks over. He states, "I have to leave now. I'm going to the States today with Dad. We'll be on the airplane around five p.m. I don't know how long I'll be gone. A week or more. I'll see you when I get back."

Hans replies, "Thank you for letting me know, and good luck."

Tony leaves.

At about 4:30 p.m., the men began shutting down for the day. By five o' clock p.m., most everyone has gone home. The dogs are brought in, and the gates are closed and locked. Sam, Carlos, and Hans leave also. Sam has his own car, a blue ford.

At the apartment that evening, Hans sits down, has a couple of beers, and relaxes for a while. Tonight, he'll clean up and go out and raise a little hell. Maybe he'll find a woman someplace. Hell, with all the money he has, what's a hundred dollars? If he wants to, he'll get one of those high-class prostitutes. That will do for a starter until he can meet someone steadier. That way, he can get this silly notion out of his head about Mrs. Bacco.

Mrs. Bacco—that's the only name Hans really knows her by. Old man Bacco doesn't call her Jennifer, Jenny, or anything else when Mrs. Bacco is out in public. Oh well, the whole damn thing's kind of crazy anyway.

After shaving and showering, Hans puts on his suit with a string tie, Western hat, and boots. Goes to a real nice-looking hotel. The night air is quite cool. It's a good thing Hans has his suit jacket on. He walks into a cocktail bar and lounge. The lights are soft, not too bright, and it smells a little smokey. He sits at the bar and orders a beer.

There are about four couples and a couple of men by themselves. No single women at all. Well, it is early. Slowly, he drinks his beer.

After finishing two beers, the place still hasn't gotten any busier. Hans's getting bored, so he leaves.

Comes to another real nice hotel and walks into the lounge. This one has soft lights and no smokey smell. It's a little busier than the other one, but the patrons are all couples again. Hans sits down at the bar. Maybe better get a mixed drink. It might look better in these high-class places. Hans gets a bourbon and water.

Just to his left is a piano. A man walks over to it, sits down, and starts playing soft classical music. He's good. Hans sits there and listens to four or five songs, and then he just happens to look over his left shoulder. Sitting at a small table is a woman.

She's looking straight at Hans, and she smiles. He smiles back at her. She's not bad looking, but she's not overly good-looking, either. But what the hell? He can do worse.

She has long blonde hair and blue eyes, and she looks to be about twenty-five years old. She is wearing a long, backless purple dress. The front is like a halter top, barely covering her large breasts.

Thinking, he picks up his drink, gets up, and walks over to her table. "Hello," Hans says softly. "May I buy you a drink?"

She smiles at Hans again and replies, "Yes. Please sit down, Tex."

He pulls up a chair and sits down. A cocktail hostess comes over, and she orders a Tom Collins. Hans orders another bourbon and water. She's holding a cigarette. He picks up a book of matches by the ashtray and lights her cigarette.

She takes a puff and politely says, "My name's Joannie."

After Hans introduced himself, she asked, "Are you a big Texas oilman or cattle rancher?"

Naturally, she thinks he is from Texas. Well, Hans's not going to tell her any differently. He knows more about cattle than he does about oil, so he'll be a cattle rancher.

Hans grins slyly and replies, "I have a small ranch."

She grins back at Hans and says, "Small ranch, huh? I don't believe you. How many thousands of acres do you have?"

Hans replies with the same sly grin, "Oh, about five is all."

The cocktail hostess brings the drinks over. Hans pays her for the drinks, and she leaves.

Before Joannie can ask another question, Hans asks, "Where are you from?"

She takes a sip of her drink and replies, "I'm from a little town just outside Milwaukee. My daddy's a doctor. We don't have much, just a house, double-car garage, swimming pool, boat, and camping trailer. Daddies into a little real estate business also. He buys and sells lots all over the place."

She has it made for an overnight hooker. She acts like a permanent hooker looking for a rich husband. Wonder who is fuller of shit, her or Hans?

Well, Hans thinks he will try to find out just how far he can bullshit her along before breaking her poor big-pocketbook heart.

Hans invites her to have dinner with him. After that, they have a few more drinks and do some dancing. While they're dancing, a group of people comes into the lounge, about six women and three men, sitting down at a round table. To Hans's surprise, one of the women is Mrs. Bacco. Hans looks for Mr. Bacco, but he's not there. He remembers he and Tony are gone. She's not sitting by any of the men. Looking back at Mrs. Bacco and she's looking straight at Hans. Twirling Joannie around, Hans winks and smiles at Mrs. Bacco. She winks and smiles back, and gives Joannie a dirty look. Joannie and Hans dance a slow dance. She puts her arms around him and kisses him. Then she invites Hans up to her room for a nightcap. They walk into the elevator, and Hans looks back at Mrs. Bacco. She takes a sip from her drink and looks at Hans. The elevator door closes.

Up in her room, things work out just right. After making love to her, he ended up spending the whole night with her. Hans didn't have to spend near the money he thought it would take.

The next morning, while they're getting dressed, Joannie asks, "Will I see you again?"

"Yes, you will tonight," Hans replies.

Hans goes home and changes into his work clothes, goes out and has breakfast, and goes to work. The morning is a little cooler and a little cloudy but no rain.

Hans gets to the job site. The foundation, basement, and rough plumbing, are done. They're starting on the floor.

Sam and Carlos are always there before Hans gets here.

Feeling good about the time Hans had last night, Hans walks over to Carlos's van and happily says, "Good morning, you guys."

Carlos looks over at Hans and asks. "Why are you in such a good mood this morning?"

Sam remarks, "Oh, I bet Cowboy got laid last night. I can tell by the gleam in his eyes." They both laugh.

Hans laughs and asks, "When are you two going to find some women? You're always together. People are going to start thinking that you're queer,"

Carlos blurts, "That will never happen."

Sam laughs and replies, "We don't kiss and tell. We keep our women a secret."

They all laugh, and Hans gets a rifle and some ammo and starts walking his beat.

The sun is getting warmer, and the day is going slow with nothing happening. Finely 4:30 pm gets here. They all go home. It's Friday night with two days off.

Hans has a couple of beers at the apartment and gets cleaned up. Around 7:00 o' clock p.m. He goes over to the Hotel where Joannie's staying. First, Hans looks in the lounge. She's not there. Hans goes up to her room. A "do not disturb" sign hangs on the door knob; he's going to knock on the door anyway, but he finds the door is open a little.

Chapter 21

Hans and Mrs. Bacco get together

Hans hears Joannie laugh and remark, "If you want me to do that to you, you have to give me another two hundred dollars."

A man's voice grumbles, "Oh, all right. Here are your two hundred dollars."

Hans laughs a little to himself and thinks. That's good she has forgotten all about him. I'll get out of here and go to some other place.

Hans gets down to the lounge and starts walking to the front door. He just happens to look over to the right at the far end of the bar. A woman is sitting there by herself. She looks a little like Mrs. Bacco, but her back is to Hans. Maybe in the back of his mind, he wants it to be Mrs. Bacco. Looking straight ahead of him, there's a table and a big leafy indoor plant in between the table and her. Hans walks over to the table and sits down behind the plant. He wants to make sure it's her before he goes and does something stupid. She's dressed in a blue pants suit. She gets up and goes to the left of the bar and into the restroom. Leaving her drink, handbag, and a book at the bar.

A cocktail hostess comes over, and Hans orders a beer.

Her being here last night with some friends could just be a coincidence. But being here again, in the same place, the next night by herself. Hans doesn't think that's a coincidence.

The woman comes out of the restroom. It's Mrs. Bacco, all right. She sits back down at the bar, takes a drink, picks up her book, and starts reading it.

The cocktail hosts bring Hans a beer and leave.

Hans takes a drink." Well, here goes." Getting up from the table, he takes the beer with him and walks around the big leafy plant toward the bar. He stops at the bar just to her right and leans on it, looking straight ahead.

Hans remarks, "On the farm, they have a saying. When the cat's away, the mice will play."

Hans turns his head toward her and looks straight into her eyes. She looks at Hans.

He smiles and calmly says, "Hi."

Her eyes get big, and she smiles and replies, "Hi, Cowboy, what a surprise. And what do you mean about the cat and the mice?"

Hans laughs, "You never heard that? Don't take this seriously; I'm only kidding. It's just a saying. It means while Mr. Bacco is away, Mrs. Bacco will play."

She laughs and implies, "That's cute. And you are right. No, I never heard that before."

"My name's Jennifer, but don't call me that in front of my old man. "Oh no. You're not here to get with that thing you were dancing with last night, are you?"

Hans laughs and replies, "Yes, I am, but she's up in her room fooling around on me right now."

There's a surprising look on Jennifer's face at what she just heard.

She asks, "What's she doing?"

Hans laughs again and explains, "I know she's a hooker. I just met her last night. I haven't been with a woman in a longtime. I ended up going to bed with her and got what I wanted. "She's looking for a permanent free meal ticket. She thinks I'm a big Texas cattle baron.

"I went up to her room to find out that she had another man in her room. She's bleeding every dime she can get out of him. I hope she doesn't go too far with him and get herself killed. Don't worry, I don't love her."

Jennifer's eyes twinkle, and she states, "Cowboy get away from her. She's no good. She'll take everything you have and leave you with nothing. You can do a lot better than her."

Hans thinks this will probably blow it with him and her, but here goes. He looks straight into her beautiful brown eyes and replies, "You're right. I can do a lot better than Joannie. But there's one little problem. You're married."

Jennifer's eyes twinkle even more. She doesn't say anything.

Hans continues, "I'm completely consensual. The rest is up to you. If I offended you, I'm sorry. It won't happen again, I promise."

Jennifer's eyes are still twinkling and staring into him like she's in a trance. Hans thinks okay, I'm going to try one more thing. He puts his left arm around her shoulder, reaches over, and kisses her lips.

She throws her arms around Hans tight, and her tongue goes into his mouth. She squirms with delight. They stop kissing, and they hug each other.

She softly says, "I love you, Cowboy."

Hans replies, "I love you, Jennifer! Let's get out of here.

She softly says, "Okay."

She picks up her handbag and book.

As they walk toward the door, arm in arm. Hans looks to his left. The elevator door opens, and Joannie and a big and tall muscleman step out, turn left, and walk into the restaurant.

Hans laughs to himself. The muscleman's Jennifer's bodyguard. Now he knows this isn't a coincidence. She set him up with Joannie so he couldn't get together with her tonight.

They get in Hans's car and drive straight to his apartment. After they're in, Hans turns on a light, closes, and locks the door. He takes her by the hand and leads her into the bedroom. He turns on a small lamp by the bed, takes her in his arms, and kisses her.

Hans asks her, "May I make love to you right here, right now?"

She smiles and replies, "I bet I can get my clothes off faster than you can."

Watching her undress gets Hans so turned on that he damn near forgets to get undressed himself. Unable to take his eyes off her beautiful naked body as she lies on the bed, Hans lies down beside her. He kisses her, and they both start feeling each other's bodies. Her body is smaller than any other woman he's ever been with. Her breasts are small but firm. Making love to her is so fantastic that Hans needs to control himself. He doesn't want to reach a climax too soon. He's hanging in there, and from the sounds, she's making and the way she's moving all around, Hans knows his satisfying her. They both reach a climax at the same time.

Hans kisses her and softly says, "I love you." Then he lies back on the bed for a while. Not saying anything.

Jennifer interrupts the silence, "I'm hungry. Are you hungry?"

Hans replies, "Yes, but I don't have any food here. There's a café across the street. We can go over there."

Jennifer implies, "Let's not go back out tonight. I'll call for service."

Hans laughs, "This isn't a hotel. I don't have room service here."

She laughs, "They do have pizza delivery here, just like in the States."

She gets up out of bed and asks, "Where's the phone?"

Hans replies, "In the living room on the countertop."

She walks out of the bedroom into the living room, calls, and orders some pizza.

Hans put on a pair of pants, no shirt.

She puts her panties on and asks, "May I have one of your T-shirts?"

Hans replies, "sure." He gets her a black one. It's big enough to cover her just above her knees.

The pizza gets here. They sit at the kitchen table, eat a lot of it, and put the rest in the refrigerator.

It's late. They return to bed, kiss each other goodnight, and fall asleep.

The next morning after Hans shaves, showers, and gets dressed, he goes out and into the kitchen. Jennifer's in there. She's dressed.

Hans joyfully says, "Good morning, beautiful."

She looks over at him, smiles and replies, "Good morning, handsome." She pours him a cup of coffee and sets it on the table.

Hans walks over to her, puts his arms around her, and kisses her.

She pulls the pizza out of the refrigerator and sets it on the table. They sit down and have the cold leftover pizza for breakfast.

During breakfast, Jennifer says, "We better go back to the hotel we were at last night and get my car. I need to go over to my hotel and freshen up and pack a few thinks, and I'll come back over here around twelve noon."

They finish the pizza.

It's a bright sunny warm day with a little breeze. Hans drives her over to her car. It's a bright red corvette convertible. They kiss. She gets out of the car and gets in hers, starts it up, and puts the top down. She smiles and waves at Hans. He smiles and waves back to her. After she drives away, Hans goes back to his apartment.

Hans pours some coffee, takes the empty pizza carton out to the garbage, and cleans off the kitchen table and her cup.

Hans starts thinking about Jennifer. Wow, he has gone to bed with Mrs. Bacco, and they made love. He's not dreaming. It really happened. Wonder if he's excited about having sex with Jennifer or about having sex with a woman his not supposed to be with, who is married to someone else, not him. He thinks it's some of both. Wonder how long this will last. Is this just a one-night stand, or is this permanent? It seems too good to be true. Right now, Hans is happy.

Just before twelve noon, there's a knock at the door. Hans opens it. It's Jennifer. She smiles and remarks as she walks in. "I'm back."

Wow, she's dressed in cut-off blue Jeans, a pink blouse, and sneakers and is holding some full grocery Bags. She puts them on the table. She empties the bags and puts everything in the refrigerator.

She says, "I'm going to cook dinner for us tonight."

Hans just stands there, not saying anything, completely surprised at what's going on here.

She continues with a smile, "I haven't always been a mob boss's wife. It's been a long time, but I can cook. You need cookware. Let's go over to the shopping-center and get what we need."

Jennifer walks over to Hans, smiles, and puts her arms around him, and he puts his around her and kisses her.

Jennifer asks, "Is that okay with you, Cowboy?"

Hans grins and replies, "Sure, that sounds great. Let's go get what we need."

When they return from the store, it's time to start cooking. Jennifer starts getting the beef roast ready to put in the oven. Hans peals some potatoes and cuts some green beans. She gets the roast in the oven, puts the potatoes in a pan of water, does the same with the green beans, and starts the cooking.

Jennifer wipes her hands on a paper towel. She looks at Hans, smiles, and joyfully says, we have got some time to kill before dinner. Let's go to the bedroom. Making love is an excellent way to build up an appetite."

After they make love, she puts Hans's black Tee shirt on, Hans puts a pair of jockey shorts on, and they go into the kitchen for dinner.

She pours some red wine.

Hans fills his plate with some of everything she cooks. He tastes it and happily says. "Wow, this is delicious. You're a good cook, Jennifer."

She smiles. Her eyes twinkle she replies, "Thank you. I'm glad you like it."

Hans takes a drink of wine, smiles, and politely says, "You're welcome."

During dinner, Jennifer explains, "We're going to have to be more discreet. Antonio tried to call me last night, and I wasn't there. You're going to have to be alone every night from now on. We can get together most every night after you get off work until seven p.m. Because he calls around eight p.m. When he's here on the island, we won't see or hear from each other. I will call you when he's gone."

Hans replies, "I can be discreet. I better not call you. He might answer the phone. I'll give you my phone number." He writes his number down and gives it to her.

After dinner, she washes the dishes, and Hans dries them.

They both get dressed.

Just before she leaves, she says, "I'll call you around eight-thirty tomorrow morning."

Hans walks her down to her car. They hug and kiss and say, "Good night, I love you."

She leaves.

Hans goes back into the apartment.

He walks into the kitchen, gets a glass, and pours some more of the wine Jennifer brought.

He goes into the living room and sits down on the couch, picks up the T. V. remote control from the end table, and turns the TV on.

The ball game just ended, and the six o'clock evening news is coming on late.

The anchor lady reports, "The F.B.I. is beginning to think that last month's Georgia National Guard Armory robbery, the Sheriff's office rips off, and the hijacking of Deano Lagno's ship might be related. The Hawk is the name of the hijacked ship. It has completely disappeared. The name probably has been changed.

"We got in touch with the Deano Lagno's corporation but haven't been able to reach Mr. Lagno for comment."

"A survivor from Lagno's ship doesn't want to be on camera." He explains, "The hijackers let all the crew members go free. They saved our lives from Lagno. Lagno's a mad man. Anybody that gets hired on his ship becomes a slave for life. If anybody quits, he ends up disappearing. I think Lagno kills him. No one gets fired; they just disappear. Out at sea, in the darkness of the night, it's easy for anybody to just disappear, especially with a little help. He's killed and thrown over the side of the ship. I will probably get killed for reporting this. But someone needs to tell this. Lagno's also human trafficking young teen age girls from the U. S. to all over Europe. Plus, he is dealing drugs and smuggling guns. I just can't prove it. We weren't allowed to have cameras. I would be killed before I could testify in court. The rest of the survivors are too scared of Lagno to come forward and say anything. I have reported more than I should have."

The anchor lady comes back on. She reports, "That was one who survived the hijacked ship."

"Turning to other news."

Hans changes the channel and finds a western movie. When the movie ends, he goes to bed.

The next morning, Hans has just gotten out of the shower when the phone rings. He comes out of the bathroom into the living room to the countertop between the living room and the kitchen and answers the phone.

He quickly says, "Hello."

Jennifer's soft voice says, "Hi, handsome. Are you up and ready?"

Hans replies, "I'm up, but I'm not dressed yet."

She remarks, "Stay undressed. I'll be there in about twenty minutes. I love you." She hangs up the phone.

Just before nine a.m., there's a knock on the door. Hans looks through the peep hole. Jennifer is standing out there. He opens the door wide enough for her to walk in. She's dressed in the same cutoff blue jeans and a green blouse.

She comes in. Hans closes the door and locks it.

She looks at Hans and remarks, "Wow, you really didn't get dressed. Let's go into the bedroom right now."

She takes his hand and leads him into the bedroom.

Later, while they get dressed, she asks, "Do you have any swimming trunks?"

"I sure do."

"How would you like to take a tour of the island and go swimming at Paradise Cove and maybe do some kayaking?"

"That sounds good. Let's go."

Hans gets his blue swimming trunks. They head out the door. He locks it, and they go to her car.

Another sunny, warm day with a slight breeze. The weather has been great since Hans has been here and still is.

Hans looks at the Kentucky, U. S. A. license plates on Jennifer's car.

He asks, "Are you from Kentucky?"

She smiles and replies, "Born and raised on the farm, just like you."

They get in her car. She starts it up. The radio comes on, and Patsy Cline is singing "Sweet Dreams."

Hans remarks, "Wow, you are country."

Jennifer's eyes twinkle, and she replies, "You can take the girl out of the country. But you can't take the country out of the girl.

"Where's that café you were telling me about? Let's get some breakfast."

"Just straight across the street, into the shopping center, and turn right into the parking lot."

They walk into the café and sit in a booth. Hans states, "This isn't a fancy place like you are used to, but it's a comfortable neighborhood café."

Jennifer replies, "This is fine, Cowboy. I'm more down to earth than you think I am just because I'm married to a rich mob boss want-to-be. I'm just Jennifer."

Hans laughs and says, "Wow, the things that come out of your mouth sure surprise me, and he laughs again."

She laughs.

After breakfast, they get into her car, and she drives down the road.

There are some palm trees and pine trees. Hans can smell the pine as they drive through the countryside. There are some small hills, but most of the island is flat, with a lot of green grass.

Now, they're coming to some farm country. There are citrus fruit trees and banana trees. They also grow honeydew, cantaloupe, watermelon, and squash. They drive by cattle, goats, horses, chickens, and a lot more. He's surprised that there are so many farms.

Hans gets so interested in the countryside and the farms that he and Jennifer don't do much talking,

Jennifer breaks the silence by asking, "Do the farms remind you of your home, Hans?"

"Yes, it does. My Dad's farm is too far north, and it's too cold for citrus fruit and banana trees. But Dad grows just about everything else. I never really thought about anything like this here on the island. But people here have got to eat too."

Jennifer states, "You and I have a lot in common. We're both raised on the farm. I was in the 4-H club. I raised four calves. At the county fair, I won second place the first year and first place the next three years. I kind of miss those days.

"I grew up and came to the Bahamas on vacation. That's when I met Antonio.

"Antonio has a house in Kentucky, not far from where my parents lived."

I ask, "Why didn't you stay in Kentucky?"

She replies, "I like it here. I wouldn't want to live here, but it's a good place to visit. That's why we're staying at a hotel.

"Besides, if I had stayed in the States, I wouldn't have met you."

Hans laughs a little, "That's right."

They're coming alongside the ocean on the left.

Jennifer asks, "See those rocks sticking out of the water, about fifty yards out from the beach, almost like a fence or a wall?

Hans replies, "Yes, and further over to the right of these are some more."

As she drives up the road and continues, "That separates the ocean from the cove. Those buildings close to the beach are up on vertical beams to keep them safe from the high tide. There are apartments called villas. Villas on the higher ground don't have vertical beams under them. People rent and stay in them."

Some people are on the beach, some are swimming, some are kayaking, and so on.

She turns off the main road onto an unpaved parking lot and parks her car. She puts the top up. They get out of the car. Hans picks up his swimming trunks off of the seat. She opens the trunk, gets a small bag out of it, and closes it.

She softy says, "There are some changing rooms in the beach bar."

They put their arms around each other, and he kisses her. They walk, holding hands, along a board walk to a red building called the red bar. Inside they found the changing rooms.

Hans gets his swimming trunks on and goes out of the room, holding his clothes and waiting for her. She comes out wearing a red two-piece bikini.

Hans remarks, "Wow, you are beautiful."

She smiles and replies, "Thank you."

They take their clothes out her car and put them into her trunk, and get some sunscreen and they rub it on each other.

They go over to a water sports shop and rent two kayaks, two paddles, and two life vests. Jennifer pays for everything. Hans offers to pay.

She softly says, "You can pay for dinner. Hans replies, "Okay."

They put their life vests on, take the kayaks and walk out in the water.

Jennifer laughs and suggests, "Let's race out to those rocks. I bet I can beat you.

Hans agrees, "Okay, let's go."

She's good. Hans thinks she's done this before, and she wins and laughs. Of course, Hans really didn't try to pass her.

Hans laughs and remarks, "I'll beat you back to the beach.

This is fun. They laugh a lot. She wins again. They go out one more time, and Hans wins that one. Going back to the beach. Suddenly the wind kicks up, and a wave tips Hans over. In the water, he goes.

Jennifer laughs, "You're all wet."

Hans laughs. "No shit." He gets back in the kayak, and they head back to the beach. She wins again. A few clouds are moving over them, the wind is getting intense, and the waves are big.

Hans suggests, "Let's stop; the water is getting too rough; you might tip over and get wet like me. This was fun, and I'm tired."

Jennifer teases, "You tired, huh, can't hack it. Oh, poor baby." She laughs. They both laugh.

She agrees, "I'm tired too. I'm ready to quit. This was fun."

They turn everything they rented back into the water sports shop. They get their clothes out of the car, go into the bar's changing rooms, and change back into them.

Hans thought about getting a beer. But this beach bar's not a regular bar. To get a drink or something to eat, he would have to go to an" Order Here" window and move over five feet to the left to a" Pick up Here" window, and there's a big line of people at both windows.

They decided to leave. Hans drives. Jennifer leans her head on his shoulder and falls to sleep.

They stop at the café where they had breakfast that morning to have dinner.

At the apartment, they make passionate love.

Just before she leaves, they kiss each goodbye over at her car.

She softly says, "I'll call you tomorrow after you get off work."

Hans replies, "I should be here around five p.m. Thank you for a great day."

 She leaves.

In the apartment, Hans settles down on the living room couch with a beer. He turns the T. V. on and scans through the channels, finds the Gary Cooper black and white movie, "High Noon," in progress, and starts watching it.

Around 8:30 p. m. the phone rings. Hans answers it, "Hello."

 Jennifer's voice says, "Cowboy. Antonio just called me. He won't be calling anymore tonight. I don't want to be alone tonight. May I come over to your place?"

Hans replies, "Sure, come on over."

She softly says, "Thank you. I'll be right over."

She hangs up the phone.

Hans gets another beer and goes back to watching the movie.

Just before nine p.m., there's a knock on the door.

Hans opens the door. Jennifer walks in smiling with a paper bag in one hand and a small suitcase in the other and sits them on the kitchen table. Takes a bottle of vodka and some drink mix out of the bag. She fixes herself a drink. She takes the drink, picks up the suitcase, and walks toward the bedroom with a smile. She demands, "Close the drapes, turn the T. V. off, take your clothes off, right here in the living room; I'll be back."

Hans does what she demands.

About fifteen minutes later, she comes into the living room wearing a short blue shear top just below her hips, a blue shear hose, a blue garter belt, and blue high-heeled shoes. That's all she has on.

She remarks, "Now, don't I look better than anything on T. V.?"

Hans doesn't say anything. He just nods.

She walks closer to him.

He leans forward.

She grabs the back of his head, bends down, and kisses him.

They make love on the couch, on the floor, on the kitchen table, and in bed. The only thing that comes off is her high-heeled shoes.

Hans's like country singer Buck Owens sings: "I've got a tiger by the tail." Wow, he sure does.

The next morning Hans is dressed for work, and Jennifer is dressed in her cutoff jeans and green blouse.

At the café having breakfast, Jennifer asks, May I have your apartment key? I'll go to a lock shop and make me a copy."

Hans replies, "Sure, that's a good idea." He gives her the key.

In front of the apartment, they hug and kiss. She gets out of the car and goes up and into the apartment. Hans heads down the road for work.

Hans gets to the building site. Today he's the first one here. He starts flipping through the radio channels, trying to find Jennifer's country station in her car. He finds it. It surprises him that country music is popular in the east and here on the island.

Hans gets out of the car and looks around. The ground looks like it has been raining earlier. He looks up at the sky. Now it's just partly cloudy, sunny, and warm with a little breeze.

The work men are starting to show up. Jeff unlocks the gate, and everybody walks in. Hans waits by his car for Carlos to get here, so he can get a rifle.

Sam walks over to him and says, "Good morning, Cowboy."

"Good morning. Why's everybody getting here late?"

Sam quickly says, "It was raining hard about an hour ago. They thought they might have to cancel work today. But it stopped raining, and that's why they are late."

Hans remarks. "I didn't get any rain at my place."

Carlos finely gets here. They get their rifles and ammo, go through the gate, and start walking their beats.

As Hans's walking, he comes upon one of the builders, a black man named Elmo. He's about as tall as Hans and a little heavier.

Hans politely says, "Good morning, Elmo."

He looks over and replies, "Good morning, Cowboy."

Hans asks, "What year is that pickup truck of yours."

Elmo replies, "It's a nineteen forty-five Ford."

A black man standing beside Elmo remarks, "Wait until you see what's under the hood."

Elmo suggests, "Meet me over at the truck at lunchtime, and I'll show you."

Hans replies, "I'll be there." He walks away.

At noon Elmo waves Hans over, and he follows him to his truck. He puts the hood up when Hans gets there and eats his lunch while looking at the engine.

Elmo explains, "This's a brand-new engine. The car was in an accident. The engine is the only thing that wasn't wrecked. Just as soon as I can, I'm going to get all the dents taken out and repaint it the same color, red. No more beat-up red pickup anymore."

Hans remarks, "Wow, this's great. Elmo, I'm Jealous. I would like to do something like this."

They went back to work. That was his excitement for the day.

The rest of the day is slow and boring.

At four 4:30 p.m., Hans goes to his place. Jennifer's car is there.

Hans goes up to the room. The door is locked. He knocks on it. The door opens. He walks in and closes and locks the door.

Jennifer is standing with a big smile, wearing nothing but that blue shear outfit she had last night.

They put their arms around each other and kiss each other.

She softly says, "Dinner will be ready in about an hour. Want to take a shower and freshen up. I'll be lying in bed waiting for you."

Hans can smell dinner cooking and replies, "Okay."

He takes his shower.

They make love.

They get dressed and have dinner. Its fried chicken, potatoes, gravy, and corn on the cob. Another good dinner.

Jennifer hands Hans the apartment key.

Right after dinner, there's a knock on the door. Hans goes to the door and looks through the door peep hole. Sam and Carlos are standing in front of the door with two women.

He turns around and quickly says, "It's Sam and Carlos with two women. Should I let them in?

Jennifer thinks for a bit and asks, "Can you trust Sam and Carlos enough not to tell Antonio about us?

Hans replies, "Yes, I think we can."

"Okay, go ahead. They'll find out about us sooner or later anyway. Come in the bedroom and get me when they're in the living room."

They knock again.

Hans opens the door.

Sam holds two twelve-packs of beer and states, "Hi, Cowboy. This is Mary and JoAnn."

The ladies softly say, "Hi, Cowboy." They shake hands.

Mary has shoulder-length red hair, blue eyes, a nice shape, and is about as tall as Hans. She's dressed in brown shorts, a brown sleeveless blouse, and brown sneakers. She's with Sam.

JoAnn has longer dark brown hair, brown eyes, a nice shape, and is a little taller than Mary. She's dressed in red shorts and a red blouse with red sneakers. She's with Carlos.

Carlos's standing there with a box of poker chips and a deck of cards in his hands. He remarks, "Now you've met our girlfriends. Let's meet yours."

Hans implies, "You two gentlemen are going to be in for a big surprise. Come in."

They all get in and look around.

Hans states, "I'll be right back." He goes into the bedroom and gets Jennifer.

Just as they walk into the living room, Jennifer says, "Hi to Sam and Carlos."

Sam and Carlos's eyes get big, and Carlos smiles and calmly says, "I'm surprised, all right. But not all that surprised. The way you kept staring at Cowboy and would look away when Cowboy looked at you at the dinners we had before. I had a feeling you two would get together sometime."

Hans introduces Mary and JoAnn to Jennifer.

Carlos suggests, "How would you all like to play some poker? Just for fun, not for real money. I brought some poker chips and a deck of cards.

Sam indicates, "I brought some beer."

Hans replies, "That sounds good. Let's play."

Jennifer politely says, "You go ahead and play. I need to go over to my hotel. My father is going to call me tonight. But I will be back. And I'll beat all of you, and she laughs."

Mary remarks, "JoAnn and I had to wait for our fathers to call us earlier." She winks at Jennifer.

Jennifer just smiles back at her, not saying anything.

Hans thinks these two ladies are here without their husbands. When the cats are away, the mice will play.

Jennifer gives Hans a kiss and leaves.

The rest of them start playing and drinking beer. Hans loses the first four hands, then wins two.

Jennifer gets back, fixes herself a drink, gives Hans a kiss, and sits down. Jennifer ends up winning. Hans lost all his chips; the rest did better than him. They all had fun. Around 11:30 p. m, they put the chips and the cards back in the boxes.

Sam suggests, "Cowboy, you keep the rest of the beer."

Hans replies, "Thank you."

They all leave.

Jennifer and Hans go to bed.

A mostly rainy week later, Jennifer and Hans are like an old married couple, except when she goes to her hotel to wait for her phone call from her husband every night. Then she comes back to Hans's place. It sure is good having dinner almost cooked when he gets home.

Hans comes home from work one night and goes in. Jennifer isn't here. There's a note on the countertop. It reads, Dear Hans.

Chapter 22

Blind Date

"I went over to my hotel room to get some stuff. When I walked in, the phone was ringing. "It was Antonio. He tells me he'll be there in about two hours. I came straight back over here to write this note. You know the drill. I'll call you when I can. I love you. Jennifer.

Well, Hans is on his own until further notice. He gets a beer and looks in the refrigerator, and finds some leftovers to heat up in the oven for dinner.

After dinner, he cleans up the table, washes, and dries the dishes.

He takes his beer, goes into the living room and turns the T.V. on.

The anchor man reports, "There are still no suspects in the Georgia National Guard Armory and Sheriff's office robbery, along with the hijacking of Lagno's ship.

"Deano Lagno can't be reached for comment about the ship's hijacking."

Hans turns the news off and starts thinking. Lagno doesn't want the law or the news nosing around. The media must not know about the court battle between Lagno and Bacco.

Hans finds a John Wayne western move and goes to bed around ten pm.

The next morning, he sleeps in. It's Saturday. He made some coffee and finished the leftovers for breakfast.

He is feeling lonely without Jennifer here. He really got used to having her around. Well, maybe she'll be back over here by Monday.

Hans drives to the shopping center to get some groceries and a couple of cases of beer.

Around three pm, there's a knock at the door. Hans walks over and looks through the peephole. Tony and two ladies are standing at the door. He opens it.

Tony quickly says, "Hi, Cowboy. I'd like you to meet June and Amy. This is Hans. He's also known as Cowboy."

The lades shake Hans's hand, saying, "Hi, Cowboy." At the same time.

Hans replies, "Hi, ladies. Come on in."

As they all walk in, June's a little shorter than Tony. She has blond hair down to her shoulders, with blue eyes. She's a little bigger and heavier than Jennifer and good-looking. She's dressed in a colorful blouse, yellow shorts, and white flat shoes.

Amy is a little shorter than Hans. She has long light red hair down past her shoulders, with blue eyes. She's a little thinner than June and good-looking. She's dressed in a colorful blouse, but different from June's, with black shorts and flat black shoes.

Hans politely says, "Please sit down. Would you like some coffee?"

The ladies sit down on the couch. Tony hands Hans a brown envelope and sits down between them. They politely refuse the offer of coffee.

He takes the envelope into the bedroom, puts it on the dresser, and comes back into the living room.

Tony lights up a cigarette and remarks, "It's after 11:30 am. How about something a little stronger, like a beer?"

June and Amy both light up a cigarette. Amy replies, "Yes, a beer sounds good."

Hans just grins, not saying anything, and goes and gets the beer.

He gives them all a beer and sits down in an opposite chair.

Tony takes a puff from his cigarette and a drink from his beer and explains, "Dad's giving a dinner party tonight. I don't know how you feel about blind dates, Cowboy. But Amy's your date for tonight. If that's okay with you, Cowboy?"

Wow. What a surprise this is. Hans looks over at Amy. She looks straight at him. Smiles and winks at him. Not saying anything. Hans, thinking Jennifer isn't going to like this. But I can't say: No, thanks, because I'm sleeping with your dad's wife, Jennifer. I better play along with this.

Hans replies straight at Amy, "It's okay with me. If it's okay with you, Amy? I'm completely consensual. It's your call.

Amy replies, "It's okay with me, Cowboy. It'll be fun."

Tony quickly says, "Good, that takes care of that. June will be with me."

I look over at June. She smiles and takes Tony by the arm.

Tony continues, "I wanted you to meet them now before I dropped it on you tonight, Cowboy. The dinner will be at seven p.m. tonight at the same hotel where we always have dinner. Meet us in the lounge at 6:45 pm, and we'll all walk into the banquet room together.

"Thanks for the beer, Cowboy, and we'll see you tonight."

Amy and June softly say, "It's nice meeting you, Cowboy. Thanks for the beer."

Hans replies, "Nice meeting the both of you."

They all leave.

Hans closes, locks the door, goes back into the bedroom, opens the envelope, and counts another five thousand dollars. He puts the money in the dresser drawer, returns to the living room, sits back down, and drinks the beer.

He sure wasn't expecting Tony to come over here with two women. That doesn't seem like something Tony would do. Now Pete would do something like that but not Tony. They're not that close of friends. Wonder where Tony found them. Something seems a little phony. Things went too easy. Got a feeling they're hookers. Oh well, who cares. Old man, Bacco pays for it all.

Hans starts getting ready for dinner.

He puts on his blue suit, a white shirt with a blueprint, a drawstring tie, his black western boots, and a blue western hat.

Hans gets to the hotel around 6:30 pm. Walks into the lobby and stops and looks around, hoping Jennifer might be there so he can tell her about his date, so she won't get mad at him. But she's not here.

He walks into the lounge. There are a few people in there. The lights are dim, and he can smell the cigarette smoke here. Tony and the lades aren't here yet. Hans's a little early. He sits down at a round table. A cocktail hostess comes over. Hans orders a glass of beer on draft. She leaves.

He looks over toward the door. June walks in, talking to Amy with Tony right behind them.

Amy's wearing a bright blue tight straight minidress just below her thighs. The top has a bare back and is strapless, with matching blue high-heeled shoes. She's holding a small handbag. She looks much better than she did this afternoon.

June is dressed in a tight, long, red dress. The dress is sleeveless with a bare back, with red high heal shoes. She, too, is holding a small handbag. She looks quite attractive.

Tony is dressed in a dark grey suit.

Hans stands up and waves at them.

Tony quickly says, "There's Cowboy over there. Come on."

As they walk up, Hans smiles and politely says, "Wow. Hi, beautiful."

Amy softly says, "Hi, Handsome. Wow, I want your hat."

Hans takes his hat off and gently places it on her head.

She remarks, "It's going to cost you to get this back."

Hans laughs and replies. "That's what you think."

They all sit down at the table.

The cocktail waitress brings Hans's beer and takes their order.

Hans looks over at June and politely says, "And, Hi to you too, beautiful."

She softly says, "Thank you."

Hans laughs and remarks, "Here sits a lucky thorn between two roses."

June and Amy smile, and Amy softly says, "Oh, you're sweet."

Tony sighs and bluntly says, "Cowboy, are you sure you don't have a girlfriend stashed around here some place that you're not telling anyone about? I hate to admit it, but you are much better with the lades than I am."

Hans's thinking. Oh, Tony, if you only knew. You would kill me.

Tony looks at his watch and suggests, "It's seven o' clock lets go."

They all get up from the table. They all take their drinks with them. June takes Tony by the arm, and Amy does the same with Hans. Amy and Hans walk behind Tony and June into the banquet room. The lighting is softly dimmed, and there are lit candles on the tables and indoor plants in planter boxes in the center, almost the whole length of the table. There are twice the people here. They put two long tables together side by side. That way, more people can sit at the ends of the tables. Everyone that's here is seated at the table. The Baccos isn't here yet.

Sam and Carlos are here with Mary and JoAnn. Mary sits next to Sam, and JoAnn sits next to Carlos. Sam looks over at them, smiles, and quickly calls, "Hey, Tony and Cowboy, it's good to see you." Carlos doesn't say anything. He just smiles and waves. Mary and JoAnn smile and wave. Hans smiles and waves back at them. John's here and is with a lady. He introduces her, "This my wife, Cindy." Jeff's here with a lady. He introduces her, "This is my friend, Wendy." Tony and Hans introduce June and Amy to everyone.

The men are dressed in suits, and the ladies are dressed in cocktail dresses.

Four seats are left on this side of the table. Amy and Hans walk over to the far side, just to the left corner of the table. Hans pulls a chair out just to his left for Amy. She sits down. Hans sits down to her right. June sits just to Amy's left, and Tony's to the left of June. This end of the table has two seats open. Hans hopes Jennifer sits down just to his right. That way, he can explain to her about Amy before she gets mad at him.

The cocktail hostess comes in, and everybody orders a drink. Hans gets another glass of beer.

Most everybody is already smoking cigarettes, and the room is getting thick with smoke and smells like it.

John looks to his right and quickly states, "Here they are now." Most everyone looks over at the Baccos. Hans's back is to them. He doesn't look around.

Instead, he looks over at Amy. When she sees Mr. Bacco! She gets a scared look on her face that turns mean.

Mr. Bacco's deep, slow voice politely says, "Good evening, everybody. It's good to see you all here."

Hans hears them walk past him and around to this end of the table and stop.

Hans looks up and over at Jennifer and smiles. She looks down at him and smiles back with a puzzled look. She looks at Amy, still wearing Hans's hat.

She's dressed in a yellow sleeveless, straight dress, which hits just above her knees, with white high-heeled shoes.

She's just as beautiful as ever.

Mr. Bacco has the same grey suit and vest, and he continues, "For those who don't know me. I'm Mr. Bacco, and this is my wife, Mrs. Bacco."

Sam quickly says, "This is Mary, and that's JoAnn with Carlos."

Tony says, "this is June, and that's Amy with Cowboy."

John and Jeff introduce their ladies.

Jennifer replies, "It's nice to meet all of you tonight. Please have a good dinner and a good time."

Mr. Bacco pulls a chair out for Jennifer. She sits down.

Mr. Bacco Suggests, "You all may go ahead and look over the menus and find something to eat. In the meantime, I need to discuss something with my son, Tony. We'll be back shortly." Tony gets up from the table, and they leave the room.

Looking normal again, Amy politely asks, "Does anybody know where the restrooms are?"

Jennifer replies, "Go out the door, turn left, and it's just to the left of the elevator.

Amy politely says, "Thank you."

She and June get up from the table and leave the room.

Everyone else is looking through the menus and talking to each other. They are paying no attention to Jennifer or Hans.

Jennifer leans over toward Hans a little bit and softly asks in a low voice, where did you find that thing you brought in here, and why is she wearing my favorite hat of yours?"

Hans leans toward her a little and replies in a low voice, "She's a blind date. Tony brought her and June over to my place around three p.m. this afternoon and introduced me to them. And asked if I would bring her to the dinner party tonight. I didn't want to do this, but I'm playing along with this. I couldn't tell him:" No, because I'm sleeping with your dad's wife."

She gets a surprise look on her face, grins a little, sighs, and nods.

Hans continues, "I think she has a room here. I'll find out for sure. When this is over. I'll tell her I had a good time and go home. Just try to pretend she's not here and don't worry about it. I'll get my hat back. I love you."

She softly says, "I love you too."

Amy and June come back into the banquet room and sit down.

Amy finishes her drink and asks, "Where's the cocktail lady? I would like a refill."

Hans replies, "She'll be around shortly. In the meantime, please take a look at the menu and find something to eat."

She remarks, "I'm just so thirsty, and I'm not that hungry."

She grabs Hans's beer and gulps it down before he can stop her.

She takes his arm, leans on his shoulder softly, and says, "Thank you, Cowboy. I'll be fine now."

Wow, Hans wasn't expecting that. He just looks at her, sighs, and replies: "You're welcome, I guess,"

Hans looks over at Jennifer. She's trying to keep from laughing and shakes her head.

June softly says, "Amy, I'm having the Chef Salad, and I can't eat all of it. I'll ask for an empty plate, and you can have some of that if you want."

Amy replies, "Okay."

Mr. Bacco and Tony come back into the room and sit down.

Hans politely says, "It Looks like everybody's ready. All we need now is a waitress,"

Two cocktail hostesses come with their drinks, and two waitresses are behind them. They take everybody's order.

Jennifer Softly says, "It's my turn to go to the restroom. Please excuse me." She gets up from the table and leaves the room.

Mr. Bacco looks over at Hans and states in his slow deep voice, "Cowboy. Tony has told me a lot about you, that you're the master mind of the hole ship campaign and that you got a job and went aboard as an inside man. You were very brave to do something like that. If it wasn't for you, we wouldn't be building the casino today. Thank you."

Hans was surprised to hear him talk shop in front of all these other people.

Hans replies, "Your welcome, sir, and thank you. I got the idea started, but Carlos and Sam came up with the idea for everything else. It was a team project."

Hans just happened to glance over at Jeff. He had a stern look, staring at Hans. Jeff sees Hans looking back at him. He smiles at him and nods, then looks away. Damn, he looks familiar.

Amy is staring straight at Mr. Bacco with a serious look on her face again.

Jennifer comes back in and sits down, and right behind her come the two waitresses with the food.

When everyone gets their dinners, John has a suggestion. "Before we get started. Let's hold each other's hands. I have a prayer I would like a share with you."

We all take each other's hands.

John begins,

"Dear Lord Jesus. Thank you for getting us through all these challenging weeks and months passed. Please help us get through all the next challenging times ahead of us.

"Please have a place in your Kingdom for Pete and the three other men we lost. Please help Mr. Bacco get through his fight for freedom and justice.

"Thank you for letting us all get together tonight and have this big meal.

"Please forgive us for all our sins, and thank you for listening to this prayer. Amen."

They all say, "Amen."

The room gets quiet; Everyone's eating and not talking mush.

Hans sets his beer on the right side of his plate, so Amy can't grab it.

Hans looks over at her plate. June gives Amy half of her salad. That's a big salad. More salad than they can eat. Even Hans wouldn't be able to eat all of that.

The Prime Rib is good. Everything must be good. No one's complaining.

About twenty minutes later, most everyone is done with their dinner. Hans finishes his beer and politely says, "it's my turn to go to the restroom."

Hans gets up from the table and walks out of the room. Just outside the room are Bacco's gorillas standing there. Two on one side of the doorway and two on the other. Hans smiles and nods to them. They smile and nod back.

While in the restroom taking a piss. Hans starts thinking Amy is acting strange. Wonder why she drinking so fast? Is it because Bacco scared the hell out of her? But why?

On his way back to the banquet room, some hotel staff pushes a piano into the room, and some band members are right behind the piano.

JoAnn comes out of the banquet, comes over to Hans, and softly says, "Hi, Cowboy, it's good to see you." She gives him a hug.

"Hi, JoAnn. It's good to see you."

She continues, "Your date just took another one of your beers. She's drinking boiler makers."

Hans shakes his head and replies, "Thank you, JoAnn." She walks into the restroom.

Hans walks into the room. Most everyone is up from the table, moving around and talking with one another. Jennifer's over on the other side of the table talking to Mary.

Hans sits back down at the table next to Amy. She looks at him, grins, and slurs a little, "H-hi C-Cowboy. A-are y-you mad a-at me? H-here you c-can have y-your h-hat back."

Hans takes the hat, sits it on the table upside down, and replies, "No, I'm not mad."

The band is starting to play. It's classical music. The music is good enough to dance to.

Hans asks Amy, "Would you like to dance?"

She looks at him, smiles, and replies, "Okay."

Hans gets up from the table, takes her hand, and helps her. They walk out on the dance floor and start dancing. The music isn't fast but not real slow ether. Amy isn't too drunk. She's still on her feet. Hans looks over, and Sam and Mary are coming out on the dance floor, and right behind them come Carlos and JoAnn. Everybody else is out on the floor except the Baccos. They're watching them all dance. He looks happy, and Jennifer looks bored and is watching Hans. Hans wishes it was Jennifer that he was dancing with.

Amy is smiling. Hans asks, "Are you having fun?"

Still smiling, she nods.

The music stops. Sam and Mary come over to them.

Sam suggests, "Let's change partners, Cowboy."

Hans looks at Amy. She smiles and nods. Mary does the same.

The music starts up again. Hans Looks around, and everybody else has changed partners.

Mary and Hans dance over by the Baccos. Over the loud music, Hans yells, "Come on, you two, there's room for two more out here."

Pointing at Jennifer, "She needs some cheering up."

They dance away.

The music stops. Mary softly says, "Thank you for the dance, Cowboy."

Hans replies, "You're welcome, and thank you."

Mary walks back over to Sam.

Amy is sitting back down at the table, drinking her drink and my beer.

June is sitting next to her but not talking to her. Hans looks around for Tony, but he's not here.

The music starts up again.

Hans thinks he'll let Amy sit there and drink.

Hans walks over to June and politely asks, "Would you like to dance?' She looks at him, smiles, and replies, "Yes, I would." She gets up from the table. They walk out on the dance floor. The dance is a slow dance. They start dancing.

June quietly says, "I'm sorry about Amy."

"Don't be sorry. It's not your fault. "Does she have a room here at the hotel?"

"Yes, we both have our own rooms."

"That's good. The way she's drinking, she's not going to last much longer. Is she a good friend of yours?"

"No. I just met her yesterday. We work for an escort service. We were told to meet with Tony in the hotel lobby this afternoon and drive to your place to meet you for the dinner party tonight."

"Did Tony set this dating thing up?"

"No. It was his dad. I don't think Tony knows we're from an escort service."

"Well, June, I'm not surprised. I kind of had a feeling about this whole thing that it's something like an escort service all along. I won't tell Tony. I'll let you do that if you want. Thank you for the dance."

Hans walks her back to her seat.

The band's taking a break.

He looks around. Jennifer is talking to John and his wife.

Hans goes over to the table, picks up his hat, and puts it on.

Hans thinks he'd better go sit with Amy. He looks at her. Her head is bowed down. She's sitting there, passed out. He looks around, but no one notices her. June is talking and laughing with Tony. Thinking he'll just let her sleep, Hans walks away from the table.

Mr. Bacco walks up to Hans and asks, "Where's your girlfriend, Cowboy?"

He replies, "She's sitting there at the table. I'm sorry to say, she's drunk. She likes boiler makers more than she likes me. Blind dates and I don't work out for some reason. Maybe better luck next time. But thanks.

Mr. Bacco asks, "Are you mad at her?"

"No. Just disappointed. I'm fine."

"Good. I got something I want to talk to you about in private. Please come with me."

Hans follows him out of the room, through the lobby, and outside.

The night air is a little cooler now than it was today, with no wind. Looking up at the night sky, the stars are bright and fill up the sky.

They walk on a paved walkway, with a green lawn on both sides to a park bench, just under a tree. There's a pole light about ten feet further on up the walkway. They have lots of light. They sit down on the park bench. Out and around, Bacco's four gorillas have spread around them about fifty feet away for their privacy.

Mr. Bacco chuckles a little and starts to speak in his same slow deep voice, "I met my wife through the same escort service I got for you and Tony. It was her first night with the service. Even though she didn't show it, she was so nervous that she got drunk, just like your date did tonight.

"She didn't look like the type that would be working for an escort service or be a hooker. I decided not to force myself on her and get to know her better. I started taking her to dinner, the beach, and the movies. I stopped thinking of her as a hooker but as a woman. By the sixth date, she was ready, and we made love. I talked her into quitting the escort service and moving in with me. About three months later, we got married."

"She didn't have any money and didn't have the skills to get a good job. "She has a high school diploma.

"I had the money and thought about sending her to a business school if she wanted too. But I got selfish and thought that if she got an education, she might get a good job and leave me. I never offered her the school, and she never asked. The first four years were good. We had a lot of fun together.

"But with the ongoing feud between Lagno and me and the building of the casino, things started to change between her and me. This casino thing has been a nightmare for her.

"The thing of it is, the more we are getting into this court battle, I think I'm not going to win. If I go to prison, I won't get out alive. Even if he goes to prison, he'll still have me killed and get away with it. If I kill him, I won't get away with it.

"Lagno's trying to get me for embezzling. But he can't prove I did it. I didn't steal from him, but I can't prove I didn't. The only thing he has on me is circumstantial evidence.

"I'm trying to sue him for failure to fulfill the contract. I can prove that.

"Lagno has some smart and shrewd attorneys."

"After I'm dead and gone, please stay and help Tony build the casino. After it's all done, you can do what you want.

Hans's thinking. Why is he telling him about his personal life?

Mr. Bacco continues, "Now I'm having this meeting here tonight with you and only you because of my wife.

I'm not blind, Cowboy. The way my wife looks at you and how you look at her. If you two haven't gotten together yet. Maybe you should. My wife is in love with you, Cowboy. My marriage with Jennifer is over. We haven't slept together for a long time."

"Hans, I thought about having you killed because of my wife. But it's not your fault that my wife feels the way she does about you. I don't blame you for how you feel about her. She's beautiful, and I can't blame anybody for wanting her. I like you, and you're a good man. I can't forget you saved my life once. I'm not going to have you killed. I'm saving your life. That makes us even. No matter where God sends me. I will rest easy knowing that Jennifer's with you, that you will be good to her, and that both of you will be good to each other."

Hans is surprised to hear about all the things Mr. Bacco's telling him. He suspects that he and Jennifer are together. He says he's not going to have him killed. He's very nice to him. This all sounds way too good to be true.

Mr. Bacco says, "Cowboy, that's all I have to say to you. Thank you for listening to this old man's problems. And I think we solved one of them. You go back to the party. I'm going to stay out here for a little while."

He puts out his hand, and Hans shakes it.

Tears are falling from his eyes and down his face.

Hans is thinking. Is he going to kill himself, or shoot Hans in the back while he is walking back to the hotel or both?

Hans replies, "Thank you for telling me everything. I sure wasn't expecting this.

"But maybe I better stay with you. If not, please be careful. Please don't do what I think you're going to do.

"Sir, we've all sinned against God. I ask him to forgive me of my sins at least twice a day, sometimes more. You can start now if you haven't asked God to forgive you of your sins. It's not too late. I know you're feeling down. It sounds and looks like you're ready to give up. Suicide is premeditated murder of yourself. God won't accept that. That's not an option.

"Pete's up there watching over us right now. He's saying, "It's okay to feel sorry for yourself for a little while. But come on, boss. Suck it up and move on. It's not your time yet."

"Come, let's walk back in together. You don't have to go back to the party. Just have your four friends here go with you up to your room. I'll send Mrs. Bacco up to you."

Mr. Bacco smiles and replies, "Okay, Cowboy. You see right through me. You knew what I was thinking. You're a good man, Cowboy.

But don't send Mrs. Bacco up to the room. I might forget to stop feeling sorry for myself, look into her beautiful eyes, and know I have lost her. I might get mad at her and kill her, then kill myself."

"Take her home with you. You and she now belong together."

He puts his left hand on Hans's right shoulder, and they walk into the hotel. They get inside and shake hands, and he and his four gorillas walk to the elevator. The door closes.

Hans walks toward the banquet room. Just before He gets there, two security guards are coming out of the banquet room, holding Amy with her arms around their shoulders. She's still passed out. They stop right in front of Hans.

One of the guards asks, "Are you the man that brought this woman here with you?"

Hans nods.

"She has diabetes. She shouldn't be drinking at all. Do you know who she is?"

Hans shakes his head.

"She's Deano Lagno's daughter. I suggest you leave the island now."

Hans blurts out, "Wait. She's from an escort service. How do you know she has diabetes? And how do you know she's Lagno's daughter?"

The guard replies, I found insulin, and her ID shows her name as Lisa Lagno in her handbag. Lagno does have a daughter named Lisa. She's only twenty years old. We should have you arrested for giving alcohol to a miner."

Hans's thinking. Tony needs him for his gun. He'll keep him out of jail.

Hans demands, "You better call an ambulance. Don't just take her up to her room. She might not wake up. You and the escort service will be under investigation, not me."

They lay her down on a couch and called for an ambulance.

No wonder she looked at Mr. Bacco so scared and mean.

Did Lagno set up his own daughter in this escort service to get her into this dinner? Lagno's an asshole, But I don't think he would do this to his own daughter. I bet the bored little rich girl did this on her own, trying to impress Daddy, gets scared when Mr. Bacco comes in, and gets drunk.

Shit, she knows where Hans lives.

Hans goes into the room. The band's still playing, and everyone's dancing except for Jennifer. Hans walks over to her.

She looks up at Hans, smiles, and asks, "Where have you been?"

"I've been with you, husband. We had a long talk. I didn't admit to any thing, but he knows about us. He's up in his room, and he doesn't feel good. Don't go up there. Come home with me. I'll explain on the way. Let's go. I've had enough of this place for tonight.

Jennifer softly says, "Okay, let's go."

She gets up, and they leave.

As Jennifer and Hans are walking out, holding hands, through the parking lot to his car. Hans starts getting paranoid. The shape that old man Bacco's in, the talk that he and Hans had might just be to keep him occupied while he has someone booby trap his car and have us both killed. Old man Bacco was way too nice to him. They stop.

Chapter 23

Car Bomb

Hans looks at Jennifer and demands, "Let's take a taxicab home. I have a feeling that both cars might be booby-trapped."

They turn around and quickly walk back to the hotel. Just as they get there, a cab pulls up and stops. People get out of the cab and they get in.

On the way to the apartment, Jennifer leans against Hans, puts her arms around him, and kisses him. She softly says in his ear, "Oh Hans, I'm scared."

Hans replies, "Me too."

They don't say anything the rest of the way home.

The cab driver stops at the apartment building. Hans pays him. They get out of the cab and quickly enter the apartment, turn on a light, close the door, and lock it.

Hans reaches into the kitchen cabinet, gets a bottle of whiskey, opens the refrigerator, and gets a beer.

Hans remarks, "It's time for me to have a boiler maker."

"I learned from one of the security guards that Amy is really Lagno's daughter. Her real name is Lisa."

Jennifer gets a surprise look on her face, sighs, and shakes her head.

She fixes herself a drink.

They drink their drinks and go into the bedroom. Hans gets the rifle from the closet and leans it against the wall beside the bed. They go to sleep in each other's arms.

The next morning, they don't think it's safe to walk over to the café. Jennifer fixes ham and eggs for breakfast.

While eating, Hans tells her about Antonio and his talk last night.

After breakfast, while doing the dishes, the phone rings. Hans answers with a polite Hello.

Tony's voice says, "Hi, Cowboy. Did you have a good time last night? Sorry about Amy."

Hans laughs a little, "Guess what. Amy's real name's Lisa Lagno, his daughter, and yes, I had a good and interesting time. Thank you."

Tony replies, "Maybe that's why she got drunk.

"I'm calling you, Cowboy, to let you know that Dad and I are going back to the States in about an hour. We need to meet with his attorneys this afternoon. I'll talk to you when we get back. But who knows when that will be? Goodbye!"

He hangs up the phone.

Hans pushes the hang-up button down and releases it, and calls Carlos. There's a click and a hello.

Hans says, "Carlos, this is Cowboy. Can you and Sam come over here? I might need your help. I'll explain when you get here.

"Cowboy, our ladies are here."

"Bring them with you. Jennifer's here."

"Okay, we'll be there in about twenty minutes. Bye."

He hangs up the phone.

Hans looks over at Jennifer and says, "Tony and your old man are leaving for the States in about an hour. Sam and Carlos are on their way over here. They are bringing Mary and JoAnn with them. Will you keep the ladies company?"

Jennifer nods.

"Sam, Carlos, and I are going to your hotel to find out if the cars are booby-trapped. I'll need your car keys."

She hands Hans her car keys.

He asks, "Do you know how to shoot that rifle in the bedroom?"

She nods, "When Antonio and I first got together, we went target shooting with the same kind of rifle."

"Good. If something goes wrong while we're gone, use the rifle and shoot to kill."

There's a knock at the door. Hans goes to the door and looks through the peep hole. It's Sam and Carlos with the ladies. He opens the door.

"Hi, everybody. Come on in."

Mary comes in first. She hugs Hans and softly says, "Hi, Cowboy." JoAnn does the same. Sam and Carlos come right behind them.

Hans looks over at Mary and JoAnn and politely asks. "Would you ladies mind staying with Jennifer and keeping her company while Sam, Carlos, and I take care of some business?"

JoAnn replies, "No, we don't mind. We'd be happy to."

Hans says, "Good."

Hans goes over and gives Jennifer a kiss, and says, "I'll see you later."

She demands, "Be careful, Hans. All three of you be careful."

Sam, Carlos, and Hans go out the door and close it behind them.

They get down the stairs. Sam asks, "Where's your car?"

Hans replies, "It's at the hotel, along with Jennifer's car. I think they might be booby-trapped with a bomb. I hope not. I'll explain on the way."

They all get in Carlos's van and head down the road toward the hotel.

Hans tells them about the talk with Bacco and who Amy really is.

Sam remarks, "Amy wasn't drunk last night. She faked it. I started watching her. She pulled one of those potted plants on the table close to her, like some of the other women did, to get a better look at the plant. When she thought no one was watching her, she would pour her drink into the dirt in the planter box, keeping her hand around the glass. I couldn't see if it was empty or not. She would lift the glass up to her mouth, act like she was drinking out of it, and take your beer, Cowboy, and drink it like a chaser. Amy repeated that about four times.

"An ambulance driver came into the lobby. Mary and I went out of the banquet room and watched Amy sitting on a sofa, talking to the ambulance driver. She got up and walked to the elevator, and the ambulance driver left."

Hans replies, "She found out what she needed to know, and faked being drunk, to get out of there.

"Now, the reason why I have you guys with me today is that last night, when Jennifer and I were walking out to our cars, I got paranoid, thinking that while Bacco was keeping me company, he had someone plant bombs in our cars.

"Bacco suspects Jennifer and me. I didn't admit anything to him. But I didn't deny anything either.

"I know a lot about explosives. But I've never built a bomb, nor have I disarmed a bomb. I'm hoping that one of you, or both, can disarm a bomb. Let's hope we don't have to, and I'm just being paranoid."

Carlos remarks, "It's hard for me to believe Mr. Bacco would do something like that to your car."

They pull into the hotel parking lot. There are not many cars there.

Carlos points up ahead to the left, says, "There's your car, Cowboy, " and points a little farther up ahead to the right. There's Jennifer's car."

No other cars are parked close to them. That's good.

Carlos parks the van on the left side of Hans's car. They all get out.

As Carlos comes around the front of the van. He asks, "Do you keep the doors locked?"

"Yes, even when I'm in the car and driving."

Carlos suggests, "First thing, let's check all the doors to make sure they're all locked." They checked. They're all locked.

Carlos continues, "Let's look inside without opening the doors." Nothing there's out of the ordinary inside.

"I'm going to look under the car." Says Carlos. He gets down on his knees, bends his head, and carefully looks all over under the car.

Carlos gets up on his feet and says, "There's nothing under the car. Now let's unlock the trunk and open it very slowly, Cowboy. I'll look for any wires."

Hans unlocks the trunk and slowly opens it. Carlos bends down, sticks his hand under the lid, and slowly feels all of it. He gets a small flashlight out of his hip pocket and flashes it inside the trunk.

"Okay, Cowboy, open it up all the way. We're all clear back here. The only place left to look is under the hood.

They all go to the front of the car.

"Now we're going to do this the same way we did with the trunk." Says Carlos.

Hans finds the hood latch and opens it just like he did with the trunk. There are no wires to the hood. Hans opens it up all the way.

Sam quickly says, "There it is." He's pointing at the fire wall just behind the engine. There's a two-inch thick by four inches wide bar of C-4 about eight inches long, fully armed, and taped vertically to the wall on the driver's side, with a digital timer taped to it. It has three cords.

Carlos says, "I have a manual some place in the van. I'll try to find something close to this one to help me disarm it." He walks over to the back of the van and opens the back doors.

Sam looks over at Hans and sighs, "Wow, Bacco really is trying to kill you."

"Yes, it sure looks that way, and when he finds out he didn't get the job done, he'll try it again."

Carlos comes back with a manual. Looking at the bomb and the manual, he states, "I found something that might work."

Carlos reads the manual to them.

"If there are two red detonator cords, cut the second cord.

"Otherwise, if the last cord is white, cut the last cord.

"Otherwise, if there is more than one blue cord, cut the last blue cord.

"Otherwise, cut the last cord. The top cord is the first cord.

"Cowboy, there's a cord cutter in my toolbox. Get it for me, please."

Hans goes and comes back with the cutter.

Hans suggests, "I'll cut the last cord. Because none of the cords are the same as the manual."

Carlos agrees, "Okay, Cowboy, give it a try."

Hans cuts the last cord. The timer starts to count down. That didn't work. Hans starts praying, "Dear Jesus, please forgive us for all our sins." He cuts another cord. The timer goes faster. He cuts the last cord. The timer goes even faster.

Sam demands, "Here, Cowboy, take my knife and cut the tape from the timer."

Hans cuts the tape and pulls the timer away from the C-4. There's another cord hidden behind the timer. The cord is too short. He pulls the timer, and the blasting cap comes out with it. The timer still won't stop. He throws it down on the ground and pulls all the blasting caps out of the C-4. He takes the knife, cuts the tape from the firewall, pulls the C-4 away from the car, runs to the front, and throws the C-4 as far as he can out into some weeds and tall grass.

They all get behind Carlos's van and wait for the timer to stop. Carlos picks up the timer and cuts the cord to the blasting cap. The timer stops.

Carlos laughs and sighs, "You disarmed it, Cowboy. Way to go."

Hans sighs and prays, "Thank you, Jesus. Amen."

Sam and Carlos both say, "Amen."

Hans asks, "How is a bomb supposed to explode when he gets in and drives?"

Carlos replies, "From the ignition switch."

Hans looks down at the starter. There's a cord connected to the ignition cable at the starter. He reaches down and cuts it off.

He looks around. Nobody is paying any attention to them, not even security.

Hans suggests, "Let's take a look at Jennifer's car."

Sam and Carlos get in the van. Hans gets in his car. They drive over to Jennifer's car.

They do the same thing they did at his car. Hans opens the hood slowly, and Carlos feels all around. Hans opens it up all the way and looks in.

Carlos blurts out, "It's all clear. There's no bomb anywhere."

Hans shuts the hood and says, "Thank you, Jesus, again."

They all sigh and blurt out, "Amen, again, yea."

Hans looks over at Sam and smiles as he hands him Jennifer's car keys.

Sam's eyes open wide, "You mean I get to drive the Corvette? Wow, I'm putting the top down."

He's like a little kid with a new toy.

Hans laughs and bluntly says, "Now remember, a red sportscar is psychologically a lot faster than a white sportscar or any other color. Because of that, the insurance on a red sportscar is a lot higher than on other colors of sportscars. Don't drive too fast and end up upside down in a ditch someplace."

Sam laughs and replies, "Okay, I'll be careful, Cowboy."

Hans laughs and suggests, "Let's all get the hell out of here and go over to my place and have a couple of beers."

Carlos replies, "Oh, that sounds good. Let's go."

They all get in the vehicles and leave.

They get to the apartment. Sam puts the top back up and locks the car. They all go in. The ladies are sitting at the kitchen table, laughing, smoking, drinking, and playing cards. Jennifer's not smoking.

Hans remarks, "Our business is taken care of. Everything's okay, and it's time for a beer."

Jennifer smiles, sighs, and softly says, "That's good, and here are your beers." She reaches into the refrigerator and gets them some beers.

Sam, Carlos, and Hans sit in the living room with their beers.

Sam asks, "What are you going to do now, Cowboy?"

Hans replies, "I'm going to put a piece of clear tape over the end of the hood and grill and check it every day. If the tape is broken. I'll know that someone opened the hood.

"If I come to work in a taxicab, you'll know that's what happened.

"Tony and Mr. Bacco have left and returned to the States. I should be all right until they get back here. If there's another dinner party, Jennifer and I aren't going to be there."

Carlos states, "I have some clear tape in the van. When we leave, we'll put some on the hood of your car. Just show me where you want it,"

In the kitchen, Mary yells, "Yea, I win. Game over." They all laugh.

JoAnn asks, "Are you guys ready to go?"

Sam replies, "Yes, we're ready."

They all get up and wait for them to come out of the kitchen.

Jennifer quickly says, "Thank you two for your company. It was fun."

Mary replies, "You're welcome."

Hans politely says to Jennifer, "Come with us. I want to show you something."

They all go outside and down by the cars. Mary and JoAnn get in the van. Carlos brings a roll of wide clear packaging tape in a tape gun over to the car.

Jennifer and Sam are watching him.

Hans explains, "Put about two inches of the tape near the end of the hood on the driver's side. Roll the tape over the front of the hood about two more inches on the top just above the grill. Press the tape down hard enough that no one can see the tape.

"Tomorrow morning, before getting into the car, I'll look here where the tape is, and if the tape is broken, I'll know the hood has been opened.

"Now, let's do the same thing to Jennifer's car."

Sam remarks, "That's a good idea. We better do that to our cars."

Carlos nods.

Hans demands, "Jennifer, you get in the habit of checking that tape before you get into your car at all times. If the tape is broken, don't get into the car. If you need to go someplace, call a taxicab."

She nods with a scared and worried look on her face.

Carlos gets Jennifer's car taped.

Hans says, "You guys, thank you. I couldn't have done it without you."

Carlos laughs, "Hell, Cowboy, the manual I have wasn't worth a damn. You and your guts, grit, and wits. You disarmed that bomb. You were great. I couldn't have done it any better than you did."

Hans sticks out his hand to shake theirs.

Sam remarks, "Handshake hell. This deserves a hug, my friend." He gives Hans a hug.

Carlos agrees, "We've been through a lot together these passed months. You're a good friend, Cowboy." He gives Hans a hug.

They get in the van and head down the road.

Hans looks at Jennifer and suggests, "Let's get back inside before someone takes a shot at us."

They run up, go in and in close and lock the door.

They go into each other's arms and kiss.

Hans explains, "My car had a bomb in it. Your car didn't have a bomb in it."

Jennifer starts to cry, "Oh Hans, what are we going to do?"

"I don't know, but now, I'm going to take a shower. Let's call for a pizza later, have some drinks, watch TV, then go to bed and make love."

"That sounds good. But let's both take a shower together, then make love, and do the rest later."

The next morning while eating breakfast. Jennifer says, "I'm going to my hotel, packing everything I want to keep, and check out of the room."

Hans agrees, "That's a good idea. You have a lot of stuff there, don't you?"

She replies, "I'm not going to bring everything, just the fancy dresses I like. The rest of them I'm going to just leave hanging there."

After breakfast, Hans hugs her, gives her a kiss, and heads out the door for work. He gets out the door, closes, and locks it.

It's cloudy and cool. It looks like it could rain.

Hans gets to the cars and looks at the tape on the hoods. They're not broken. He gets in the car and leaves for work. At work, everything is normal except for some occasional rain.

Hans gets to the apartment. Jennifer's not there. He goes in, closes, and locks the door.

He gets a beer and decides to call Mom before Jennifer gets home.

He calls home but gets a pre-recorded message saying, "This number is no longer in service." He dials directory assistance, but they can't help either.

Chapter 24

Car Chase, Explosions at the Building site.

Now Hans knows why Mom never called. She doesn't have a phone, or maybe they had the number changed. He doesn't have a clue why?. He'll have to wait until she calls.

He's not going to say anything to Jennifer until he knows what he's going to do.

He gets another beer and sits down on the living room couch.

Jennifer comes in carrying two suitcases. She sets them down on the floor and softly says, "Hi. I have more stuff in the car."

Hans gets up, walks over to her, gives her a kiss, and follows her back to her car. There's one large box and another smaller one. Hans takes the large box, brings it in, and sets it on the bedroom floor. She gets the other box, closes and locks the trunk, brings it in, and closes and locks the door.

Hans brings the boxes and the suits cases into the bedroom and sets them on the floor.

Jennifer suggests, "Let's go over to the café for dinner tonight. I'll unpack them tomorrow.

Hans agrees, "Let's go."

When they return to the apartment, Jennifer fixes herself a drink. Hans gets another beer. They watch TV for about an hour before going to bed.

In the morning, Hans drives to work and walks up to Sam and Carlos.

Carlos looks at Hans, smiles, and says, "Good morning, Cowboy."

Hans replies, "Good morning."

Sam asks, "Is something wrong, Cowboy? You look like you're worried about something."

"Last might I tried to call home. But the phone's been disconnected. I hope nothing wrong. I'll just have to wait and hope mom calls me."

Hans goes over to the van to get a rifle and some ammunition. At the van, he gets some extra magazines and locks them in the car. He might need them for the rifle at the apartment.

After putting the magazines in the car, Hans happens to look around at the dirt parking lot that everyone kind of made just by driving their cars in and out. That's when he noticed that there were a lot more cars parked there in the past month, and a lot of them were missing today. Looking around, he notices one vehicle that is not there: Elmo's old, beaten-up, red Ford pickup. As a matter of fact, Hans hasn't seen him now for about a week. Maybe he's sick. But there are too many cars missing. All of them can't be sick, especially considering the good weather here, except for some rain.

Hans walks back over to the building and starts walking the beat. He gets around to the other side of the building and walks over to Carlos.

Hans suggests, "Come with me, please. I want you to have a look at the parking lot. It's not as full as it normally is."

They go back around the building, and Carlos says, "It sure doesn't look right. Thanks, Cowboy. I will tell Sam."

Hans continues his beat. Farther on up, Jeff, the contractor, is walking across Hans's pathway up in front of him. Hans yells, "Hey, Jeff, where's all your help? Are they sick or something?"

Jeff stops suddenly and looks back at Hans. He just glares at him.

Jeff doesn't say a word. He just turns his head and walks away.

Wonder why he's acting so damn strange. He probably has enough problems on his mind without Hans being nosey.

The next morning, after getting to work, Sam, Carlos, and Hans look over at the parking lot. It looks like there are fewer cars today.

Carlos says, "I will count the cars that are out here today and then count them again tomorrow,"

Every day, fewer men show up for work. Over the next three days, three cars are missing per day. Why the same number every day? Hans doesn't know. Everything else is normal. On the fourth day, three more cars are missing.

As they look out over the parking lot, Sam reaches up, scratches his head, and says, "Something's going on. That's for sure. I wish I knew what,"

It's Friday night, and Jennifer's not here.

Hans gets a beer.

The phone rings. Hans answers it, "Hello." A man's voice asks, "Is this Hans Metzger?"

Being a little suspicious and carful, thinking it might be Lagno or one of his men. He asks, "Who wants to know?"

The man explains, "I'm Ace Smead, a friend, and neighbor to Hans's parents."

Hans thinks something is wrong at home. He replies, "Hi, Ace. This is Hans. How are you?"

Ace continues, "I'm fine, thank you. Your dad gave me your phone number in case something went wrong. Well, something has gone wrong. I hate to have to be the one to tell you this, Hans. Your folks were killed in a car accident.

"The day before they left, your dad told me that your mom has health problems and blood in her stool. The little hospital here in town isn't set up for anything like that yet. They drove to Caldwell and got the treatment done there.

"I didn't know anything about the accident until I saw it on the six o'clock news on the day it happened. They were coming up the steep white bird mountain on the way home.

A logging truck going down the mountain burned up his breaks and couldn't slow down or stop. He lost control and hit your parents head-on. They were killed instantly. The truck driver's body is missing."

"Before all of this happened, your dad asked me if I would take care of any funeral arrangements if something happened to them before you get home. The funeral is prepaid. You don't have to worry about that, and there's a will. I have a copy of it.

 When you get home, the farm's all yours. The sooner, the better. Because a heavyset woman named Mrs. Blake has been trying to get your dad's farm for a long time."

The conversation leaves Hans numb, unable to comprehend how to react.

Composing himself, Hans replies, "Yes, Ace. Dad told me about her. That looks a little suspicious about the missing truck driver's body. He might still be alive, and maybe the accident just looks like an accident! It might have been set up by Mrs. Blake. Mom and Dad may have been murdered! I'll get home just as soon as I can."

Ace quickly says, "Wow, Hans, you could be right. I never would have thought of that. I know the sheriff. I'll ask him if he looks into that."

Hans says, "Don't be surprised if the sheriff doesn't look into it. Rich people like Mrs. Blake have been known to bribe the law into looking the other way."

Ace replies, "I don't think our sheriff can be bribed. He's straight as an arrow.

"I have your five cows at my place, so I can feed them. They'll be here when you get home. I go over to feed your chickens and gather their eggs. That's all I can do, Hans, and I'm sorry."

Hans replies, "Thank you for calling me and letting me know and for everything else." They both say goodbye. Hans hangs up the phone.

Oh my God, no. It's starting to really sink in. Mom and Dad are both dead. They're innocent. Why did they have to die? Things were starting to go good for them. They weren't in the war, but they're Hans's heroes. Why did Pete and some of the other friends in Vietnam have to die? They're heroes, a lot more than Hans was.

Hans starts to cry. He blurts out, "Jesus, you sure have a strange way of punishing me. Everything I try to do goes wrong. I can't win. Why didn't I get killed in Vietnam? I'm still alive. I'm just a loser. Come on, Jesus. **Where Losers Live, Heroes Die**? The loser lives. That doesn't make sense.

Hans wipes the tears off his face with a paper towel from the kitchen and softly says, "Jesus, I don't mean to take this out on you. I'm sorry. Please forgive me. I guess there's a reason you want me to live. Maybe someday I'll know why."

Hans stopped crying. It's time to suck to up and move on.

Jennifer walks in with a pizza and sets it on the table.

She looks at Hans and sees tears still falling down his face.

She asks, "What's wrong?"

Hans walks over to her, takes her in his arms, and holds her.

Hans sadly replies, "Mom and Dad were killed in a car accident."

"Oh, no, Hans. After what's been happening around here, and now on top of everything else, your parents get killed!"

They have no appetite for the pizza but attempt to eat some of it.

The weekend's cloudy, raining, and windy. Monday's cloudy, but no rain. At work, the same thing happens. Fewer people are coming to work.

Driving home that night after work, Hans comes upon a bar that he passes by every day but never stops at. Suddenly, he sees that old, beat-up red pickup of Elmo's parked in front of the bar.

He decides to go in and check this guy out. Pulling up right beside his truck, Hans stops, gets out, and walks into the bar.

Aside from the bartender, there are only four people inside. The man Hans is looking for is one of them. He's dressed in work clothes and looks as though he has been working all day because his clothes are very dirty, and he seems very tired. He doesn't notice as Hans comes in, walks to the bar, and stops beside him.

Acting like He always does when seeing him at work, Hans makes a smart-ass remark, saying, "What's the matter? Won't that red truck, with your new engine, make it to work anymore?"

Hans leans on the bar and grins at him. Elmo's eyes get bigger than hell when he looks at Hans.

He stammers, "C-Cowboy,"

He grabs his drink and gulps it down, choking on it. He looks at his watch and stammers, "I-I g-got to get h-home. I-I am l-late now. I'll talk to y-you l-later."

He gets off the stool and darts straight out the door.

Oh shit. Hans has scared him to death. Something's wrong. Wonder where he's working now.

Looking around at the other people but not recognizing anyone else, Hans leaves without getting a drink and goes home.

Hans tells Jennifer about Elmo.

She states, "Oh, I'm getting worried. Something's going to happen soon.

The next morning, after getting to work, Hans walks over toward Carlos, who's opening the back doors to the van. Soon Sam drives up with someone with him. Recognizing Tony, Hans stops and waits for them. They get out of the car and come over to him. Neither one of them has a happy look on their face. About then, Carlos walks up, too.

Tony hands Carlos and Hans another brown envelope.

Hans politely says, "Thanks, Tony. I'll put this in my car.

Tony lights up a cigarette and then breaks the bad news, "Lagno gets a one hundred thousand dollar fine for breach of contract and is free and clear. My Dad has been sentenced to prison. They gave him ten years, just on circumstantial evidence. They got him for embezzling with no actual proof. We are going to have to continue building the casino without him.

"What's this about the fact that fewer workers are coming to work daily? Sam told me on the way over here."

"Things are looking a little fishy around here already," says Carlos. "Just as soon as Jeff gets here, I will ask him what's happening."

They watch as workmen slowly arrive. Hans starts to tell Tony and the others about the black man, Elmo, whom he stopped to talk to in that bar last night, but Jeff walks up before he can finish.

Tony turns to Jeff and asks, "What seems to be happening to your help? They can't all be sick."

Jeff gives Hans a mean look.

He looks back at Tony and replies, "We have been getting low on supplies. Without them, there's nothing for the men to do. I'm letting some of them have some time off with their families. Most of them do a lot of fishing this time of the year, right off the coast. John will pull in sometime today with more supplies. I will have them all back to work tomorrow."

Tony sighs. "Okay, Jeff. I don't mean to butt in on your job. We are just taking all matters into consideration. That's all. I will talk to you later."

Jeff nods and walks away.

Hans looks around the place and says, "Bullshit. We're not low on supplies. There's stuff stacked all over the place. John is pulling in today; that's true. There's still a lot of stuff here.

"Another thing, getting back to Elmo, I was telling you about. He wasn't wearing a fishing hat. It was a hard hat, and his clothes were dirty. As a matter of fact, they smelled a lot like oil. There's a big difference between a fish smell and an oil smell.

"Tony, I think I will get in my car and go have a look around. You or somebody else want to come along?"

A little puzzled, Tony asks, "Where are you going to look around?"

"At the oil refinery. There's only one on this island, and we all know who owns it."

Quickly Sam says, "Tony, I think Cowboy's on to something there. Let me go with him. We'll take my car."

"Okay," says Tony. "Go ahead but be careful around that place."

Sam and Hans get in Sam's car and leave. Just before they get to the refinery, Hans suggests, "Let's drive through the parking lot if it's not fenced."

"I don't think it's fenced in," replies Sam.

He drives around the corner to the right. Just to the left is the parking lot, and there's no fence. Sam turns into it.

Looking at the cars in the lot, Hans says, "Now let's drive slowly through here and try and spot any cars that look familiar."

Suddenly Sam points and says, "Yep, there are four cars right there."

Hans looks where he's pointing. Then he looks over behind the row of cars that he pointed out.

Hans blurts out, "Just as big as day, there's that shiny, red, beat-up ford pickup.

Starting to feel a little suspicious, Hans says, "I think we better go have another little talk with our friend, Jeff."

Sam remarks, "Oh shit. That damn Lagno and his three bodyguards are coming out of that building over there."

Puzzled, Hans blurts out, "Three bodyguards! That day he came aboard the ship, he had four bodyguards." He looks over at Lagno and his gorillas.

Hans suddenly remembers what the fourth one looks like.

Feeling like a damn fool. He blurts out, "Oh shit, Sam. We've been completely set up. Lagno's fourth bodyguard is Jeff. Dammit, I knew I had seen him before. He completely faked me out. The first time I saw him, he had a thick black beard and wore a suit just like those guys."

As Sam pulls out onto the road. Hans's watching Lagno and his gorillas. One of the gorillas recognizes and points at them. Lagno looks and makes a warning sign with his hand.

Hans shouts out, "Two of his gorillas are running over and getting into a black Cadillac, and now they're coming toward us."

Sam demands, "Climb over the seat and get in the back and get your rifle, Cowboy."

Sam turns left onto a narrow two-lane road, pushes down on the gas pedal, and tries to outrun them.

Hans has the rifle ready.

Sam passes a car and another car. Now cars are coming from the opposite direction. That's keeping the bad guys from passing the cars behind them. The right lane's clear. Sam passes three more cars. No cars are ahead of them. Sam's picking up speed, turns a corner to the right, turns another corner to the left, and catches up to a pickup truck with a trailer full of watermelons and bananas. Cars are coming from the opposite direction.

Sam remarks, "I can't pass him."

Hans looks back behind them through the back window. He blurts out, "Shit, the bad guys are side-swiping and running the cars ahead of them off the road. One car is pushed to the left into a ditch and turns upside down. The other car is pushed off the road the same way. The bad guys are coming and fast."

Sam bluntly says, "Finely, I can pass this guy." He gets around the pickup and trailer and picks up speed.

The bad guys get passed two more cars but side-swipe the last car off the road to get back in the left lane just in time to avoid being hit head-on.

Hans demands, "We better get off this road and onto a road with less, or better yet, no traffic. People might be getting killed because of us."

Sam remarks, "I know where there's an old, abandoned road. After the new freeway was built, they closed the old road. I've been on it. Only part of it is paved. We'll go as fast and far as we can and fight it out with them at the end of the road."

About three more miles up the road, Sam turns off the road to the left. He drives over a big bump and onto an old narrow road. The road has grass and weeds growing through the pavement cracks. On the right side of the road is a sign that reads, "Travel at your own risk."

On the right is green grass, with tall thin pine trees and some hills. On the left is green grass, and to the left of the grass is the ocean.

Sam gives the car the maximum power and hauls ass down the road.

Hans looks out the back window. The bad guys coming onto the old road and picking up speed.

No other cars are on the road. Just the bad guys and them, and they're catching up to them.

The passenger in the bad guy's car rolls his window down, sticks out his right hand with a pistol, and starts shooting at them.

Hans ducks down on the seat. Bullets are coming through the back window. Sam has ducked down low in the front seat. But high enough that he can still see the road. He zigs zags all over the road, making it harder for the shooter to hit them.

Hans rolls down the back left side window of the car, sticks the rifle out the window, points it back at the bad guy's car, and starts shooting. The bullets just glance off their car.

He yells, "That damn car's bulletproof."

They ram the back of Sam's car and cause it to fishtail.

Suddenly, Sam's kicking up a lot of dust. He yells, "We just ran out of pavement. In about a mile, the road will end. There's a wide spot in the road just before we get there."

Hans looks back behind them. The dust is so thick that he can't see the bad guys and hopes they can't see them.

Sam turns off the road onto the wide spot and stops.

The dust is so thick that the bad guys don't stop, drive right past, and go off the road, over a small cliff, and straight down into the ocean.

Hans yells, "Sam, we got them."

They get out of the car, run over to the cliff, and look down at the ocean. The back half of their car's going under the water.

They watch while the car sinks.

Sam says, "Look, there's one of them, and there's the other one."

They both made it out of the car and were alive and swimming back to shore.

Sam asks, "Are you going to shoot them, Cowboy?"

Hans replies, "No, right now they're helpless, and they can't shoot back. Let's get the hell out of here before they get up here. They won't be bothering us anymore today. They have a long walk ahead of them, back to where Lagno is."

They get back to the car. Sam and Hans look at all the bullet holes in his car.

Sam shakes his head and states, "Wow, what a mess. I don't think my insurance will cover this without the cops finding out about it."

Hans claps him on his back.

They get into the car, Sam turns it around, and they head back the way they came.

As they near the building site, Hans looks up ahead and a little to the right of the road. Just above the trees, there's a lot of black smoke.

Right as they get there, the car's rocked by four big explosions. Huge balls of black smoke roll up from the building. The only thing they can do is stop a safe distance away and watch it fall to the ground and burn.

Watching it with despair, Sam blurts out, "Oh my God!"

Hans looks over at the parking lot. It's empty except for his car and Carlos's van. They're far enough away that they weren't hit.

The explosions stop, but the fire keeps burning. They wait and keep looking for Tony and Carlos, hoping they might come walking out of the trees somewhere far away from the fire.

But there's nothing. No sign at all of anything moving except the building caving in. The fire's already starting to die down a bit because they haven't installed a lot of burnable material.

They get out of the car and grab the rifles. Hans can smell the smoke as they slowly walk toward the building and through the nearest open gate, looking all over the place.

Hans blurts out, "Oh shit, something has happened to Carlos and Tony. We got to find them.

As they get closer, Sam turns and walks to the left. Hans turns to the right. Sam and Hans call out as loudly as they can, "Tony! Carlos! Tony! Carlos!" They call every few minutes.

Walking on, Hans notices that a wing of the building isn't burning too severely. He calls out again, "Tony! Carlos! Tony! Carlos!"

Hans hears a voice yell, "Over here!"

Looking to his left, just where the wing starts from the main building, Carlos comes running out.

He yells, "Help me! Tony's in here!"

Hans yells at Sam, and he turns around and looks back. Hans waves for him to come. "Over here, Sam!"

He comes at a run.

Hans runs over to Carlos and asks, "Are you okay?"

"I got bruises all over me from things falling on me," Carlos replies. "Outside of that, I'll live. But come in. Tony needs help."

They run into the building. Tony's caught under a large iron beam, with pieces of smaller wooden beams on top of him. His head's bleeding badly. His chest, shoulder, and one leg are also bleeding.

Scared and excited, Carlos blurts out, "He has broken damn near every bone in his body. He'll die if we don't get him out of here fast and to a hospital."

Sam comes running in. They try to lift the beam off Tony but can't. Hans picks up a smaller beam that's lying loose, and they use it to try to lift the beam that has Tony pinned down. It doesn't work.

Turning and looking out the door, Sam yells, "There's a backhoe tractor outside. I can ram a hole through the wall big enough to get it in here. I'll lift the beam up with the scoop."

He runs out of the building, and Carlos soon follows, saying, "Let's find a heavy chain or something on the tractor."

Hans starts to follow them. Tony calls, "Cowboy."

Hans goes over to him and softly says, "Take it easy, Tony. We'll get you out of here."

"C-Cowboy, I-I am sorry. Pete and I got you into this. It's all over now. C-Cowboy, go home."

This puzzles Hans. He probably doesn't know what he is trying to say. Maybe he is just delirious.

"Come on, now," Hans says. "Let's take it easy. Everything is going to be all right. I wouldn't have missed this for anything. I'm honored that you let me in on this."

Hans stops talking. Tony is no more.

Sam and Carlos find a log chain long enough to reach inside and around the beam. They get the beam off Tony's body with the tractor and chain.

Hans asks, "What are we going to do with Tony's body? Mr. Bacco's in prison. Jennifer's the next of kin. But she's not Tony's real mother. I'll tell Jennifer about him.

Carlos suggests, "Let's take him to a funeral home and find out if they'll take him." They put him in Hans's car and took him to a funeral home.

The funeral director politely says they'll get ahold of Mr. Bacco and take care of everything. Hans's glad about that because he doesn't like funerals.

Once they're outside, Sam asks Carlos, "Do you know anything at all as to what happened to the building?"

Carlos replies, "Tony and I were walking through the building and looking at the work completed. We walked into a room and saw a box of C-4 plastic explosives that someone had carelessly left out. We looked around the room and found a piece of detonator cord sticking out of the wall. Tony took his knife and cut through the sheetrock. They planted C-4 in the walls all throughout the place. There was a cord leading through the wall to someplace else. Before we could get out of there, we heard cars backing out of the parking lot. They were driving away fast. Just like that, the whole place started exploding."

Feeling stupid and ashamed, Hans says, "We thought they were on our side. We were looking for trouble from the outside. We let them sneak in that C-4 right under our noses. We didn't notice a damn thing or suspect anything. They made us all look like asses."

They both nod in agreement.

Sam remarks, "Jeff has the key to the building site. I bet they brought the C-4 over the weekend while we weren't here."

They walk to the car, and once there, they look at each other like, "What's going to happen now?"

Feeling defeated, Hans remarks, "Sam, Carlos, we are done. Lagno has won all the way around, and my obligation's over. I am going to pack up and go home.

"I'm going to find John. He will give me a ride back to the States when he pulls out.

They go back to what's left of the building site and drop Sam and Carlos off at their vehicles.

Sam says, "We will see you before you leave."

After getting to the apartment, Hans gets the envelope Tony gave him out of the glove box. Jennifer isn't here. Hans decides that his going to get his ass home now.

I Hope Jennifer gets here. He has no way to get ahold of her.

Chapter 25

Lagno put's a hit out on Hans

Hans shaves and showers. Almost packed and has a suit on, except the coat and tie, when the phone rings. Hans answers it.

Jennifer's voice softly says, "I'm in my hotel room. I paid off my bodyguard and laid him off. I'm getting the rest of my stuff and checking out. Lagno got Antonio killed."

Hans replies, "I have more bad news. Tony's dead."

Jennifer cries, "Oh, no, Tony too."

"Sam, Carlos, and I took his body over to the funeral home.

Jennifer agrees, "That's good. I'll go over there and make the funeral arrangements for both Antonio and Tony. It may take me a couple of hours to get that done. Thank you.

Hans replies, "Okay, I will be here until around eight p.m. I'm going home."

Jennifer remarks, "I'll be there. Don't you dare leave this island without me? I love you."

Hans replies, "I love you, too.

She hangs up the phone.

Hans gets a beer out of the refrigerator and goes and sits down on the couch. He pops open the beer and takes a big drink.

About two and a half hours later, the door unlocks and opens. Jennifer walks in carrying two suitcases. She sets them down on the floor. She goes back to the door, close's it, and relocks it.

She's dressed in another pair of cutoff blue jeans and a printed yellow blouse.

Hans gets up from the couch.

Not smiling, she runs over to Hans. They throw their arms around each other. She lays her head on Hans's shoulder and sighs, "Oh, what a miserable day this is."

Hans agrees, "But I'm glad it's over with, and we're going home. Did you get the funeral stuff taken care of?"

"Yes, I did. I sent their bodies back to a cemetery near their home in Kentucky. Antonio will be laid by his late wife, and Tony will be right next to them.

This casino idea should never have started in the first place. It has been pure hell for me."

Hans comments, "One good thing about all of this is we don't have to worry about Antonio trying to kill us anymore."

She sighs and nods.

"You still have folks in Kentucky?"

"My Mom and Dad are both dead. I might have a brother someplace. I don't know where or if he's still alive or not. We never got along with each other very well. No, there's nothing there for me anymore.

She opens the refrigerator, looks in, and suggests, "Let's heat up some of the leftovers. I'm hungry."

While they're eating, Hans tells Jennifer about Sam and his car chase with Lagno's two gorillas.

She looks at me and just shakes her head, not saying anything.

"When are we leaving?"

"We better get over to the pier around seven this evening."

"Good, we have time. As soon as we get done eating. Let's go make love."

Hans remarks, "I've got a bad feeling Lagno might try something."

They go into the bedroom. After they make love. Hans kisses her and softly say, "I love you." Then he lies back on the bed for a while.

Suddenly Hans hears something from behind the door. He quickly shoves Jennifer off the bed onto the floor.

He demands in a low voice, "Stay down."

The doorknob's turning. Hans quickly reaches over to the other side of the bed, grabs the rifle, and points it at the door. It swings open wide. Hans starts shooting. One man gets one shot off as he's falling to the floor. Hans's still shooting, and another man falls to the floor.

Jennifer screams.

Hans yells, "Are you all okay?"

She whimpers, "I'm okay."

Hans slowly walks over and peeks his head out to look in the living room. There's nobody there. Steps over the two men and carefully looks in the kitchen. Those two men are the only ones who came in.

How did they get in? Jennifer locked the door when she came in. Looking at the door, it's fine. They must have picked the lock.

Suddenly one of the men groans. He moves his head. Hans leaps over and gets the gun out of his hand.

He looks at Hans and stammers, "Y-your, an h-hard one to hit. H-how did y-you know a-about the b-bomb I-I planted in your c-car?"

"Did Lagno send you to do this?" Hans asks, his voice filled with hate.

He nods. "Someday, L-Lagno will get you. N-no m-matter where you r-run to, h-he will get y-you."

"Where's Lagno now?'

"A-At the c-casino, his main o-office." he gasps, and then he's dead.

Hans says to the dead man, "No matter where I run to, huh? Well, I believe you because I have heard this before. I'm not running. I'm not scared of Lagno. He will have to kill me today. That is, one of his gorillas might kill me. But I will do everything in my power to stay alive long enough to kill Lagno before they kill me."

Hans goes back into the bedroom and looks down at Jennifer, still lying on the floor, crying. There's a bullet hole in the mattress right where Jennifer was lying. Hans leans the rifle next to the bed, reaches down to take Jennifer's hand, and pulls her up on her feet. She puts her arms around Hans and whimpers, "Oh, is this miserable day ever going to end? You saved my life, Hans. I love you so much.

They get dressed, and Hans holds her hand as they step over the two dead bodies and walk into the living room.

Jennifer looks down at the bodies and starts to cry again. She looks scared.

She blurts, "Oh Hans, what are we going to do?"

"I'm going to call Sam and Carlos right now."

Hans goes over to the countertop and gets the phone, and calls. Carlos says, "Hello." Hans asks, "Are you guys okay?"

Carlos replies, "Yes. Why do you ask?"

"Lagno put a hit out on me and tried to kill me. I think he'll try to kill you guys, also. We have some unfinished business to take care of. Can you guys get over here now?"

Carlos replies, "We're on our way." He hangs up the phone.

Hans gets the rifle from the bedroom and leans it next to the front door.

About fifteen minutes later, Sam and Carlos get there and come in. They look over at the dead men.

Hans explains, "Lagno is coming after me with both barrels loaded. He's not going to stop, no matter where I run to. But I'm not running. I'm going to kill him before he kills me. That dead guy talked to me before he died. He's the one who put the bomb in my car. It wasn't Bacco. I thought that Bacco had the bomb put in my car. It must be the way Jesus told me not to get in my car the other night. Miracles do happen."

"You don't have to do this if you don't feel right about it. What you guys need to do is get rid of these bodies. Get John and most of his crew, with guns and ammunition, over to the casino to help me kill Lagno.

"Jennifer, you follow these guys over to the ship in your car and ask John if he'll load it aboard the ship. I think he will.

"We took over one of Lagno's ships. Let's take over his casino. Get everybody out of there and lock it up."

Sam states. "We can't take over the casino because it will go to Lagno's daughter, Lisa. That won't do us any good. I think it would be better if we burn it down."

Hans thinks about that and replies, "You're right, Sam. Let's burn the casino down."

Sam and Carlos grin.

Carlos replies, "Lagno has a hit out on you. That means he has a hit out on all of us. We're in. Let's go."

While Sam and Carlos are getting the bodies out of the apartment, Jennifer and Hans get packed up, take the bags out, and put them in her car.

She remarks, "I have too much stuff. I'm taking just what I need and leaving the rest here. All those fancy long dresses weren't all that comfortable anyway. I'll have no need for them.

She kisses Hans and softly says, I love you."

Hans replies, "I love you."

She gets in her car and follows Sam and Carlos down the road.

Hans goes back up to his place.

He sticks the rifle barrel down through one of his pant legs and wraps one of his shirts around the butt. Grabs the rest of the ammunition magazines that are left. There are only four. Then Hans remembers that there are some in the car. He puts the four in his pants and coat pockets and puts on his western hat.

He picks up the wrapped rifle and goes to the door. He slowly opens it and looks out. There's no one around. He goes down to the car. Just before getting there, Hans looks over at the office. It's open.

Hans opens the car door and lays the rifle across the front seat. Runs over to the office and checks out of the apartment. He runs back to the car. Heads for the casino.

Chapter 26

Trashing Lagno's Casino with the Car

Hans comes to the casino. It's on his right. He drives by slowly, contemplating how to get in with the rifle. There are two big glass doors. Just before them is an archway, and a large lawn is in front of them. Stretching about fifty feet from the road, there's a large, round row of short shrubbery with flowers in the center.

Hans drives on past. If he can turn this car around up here someplace, come back, and turn onto the lawn, with enough speed, he can drive right through the shrubbery, the archway, and smash through the glass doors. Hans finds a place to turn around. He pulls over and stops. He reaches over into the back seat and gets more magazines of ammunition. He puts two magazines in each front pants pocket and two in each coat pocket. He then unwraps the shirt, pulls the rifle from the Levi's, and then lays the rifle back down on the seat.

Well, here goes!

Hans turns around. Starts picking up speed. He's in the left-hand lane of a four-lane highway. The casino is on the left.

The more Hans thinks about getting Lagno, the madder he gets and the faster he drives.

Hans talks out loud, "I'll get you before you kill me, or have anybody else killed, Lagno! Your killing days are over!"

Turning off the road onto the lawn, He makes a wide sweep to keep from turning too sharply at that speed. He drives right through the shrubbery, straightens out, and heads straight toward the archway. Hans holds his breath and just barely makes it, smashing through the glass doors into the casino and sending slot machines flying into pieces.

Hans crashes through four more rows of slots and then stops the car. The front end of the car's smashed in.

A woman screams. Hans slams the car into reverse and backs up. He throws the car into drive, turns right, and pushes down the gas. He crashes through a row of blackjack tables with the right front fender. The first ones he hit are closed. Farther along the row, there are some tables that are open, and people are playing on them. Hans slams on the horn. They look at Hans coming straight at them. They yell, jump up, and run, and so do the dealers. All the tables are smashed to bits, and money and chips are scattered everywhere.

People and dealers jump clear of a craps table, and the car plows through it, busting it all up, and then Hans turns left and smashes into the front of the cashier's cage, which brings him to a stop. He grabs the rifle and leaps out of the car. The front is really smashed up now, but the motor's still running.

Hans points the rifle at the cashiers and demands, "Call Lagno and get him out here. Tell him if he wants to kill the squirrel Edwards, to get his chicken shit son-of-a-bitch ass out here and do it now."

One of the cashiers gets on the phone. There are three more cashiers. Two of them are women.

Oh shit. One of the women is Lisa. She stares straight at Hans.

There's a look of hate in her eyes. She runs to a desk drawer, opens it, pulls out a pistol, and aims it at Hans. Hans shoots her before she shoots him. Lisa screams and falls to the floor. She's lying behind a desk. He doesn't know if she's dead or not.

Motioning, with the rifle, toward a door in the cashier cage, Hans shouts, "I'm only here to kill Lagno. Not you or anyone else, and I'm not going to rob the place. Will you help me get everybody out of here?"

One of the women replies, "Yes, we'll help you. We don't care what you do to Lagno. That son-of-a-bitch. Lisa's just as rotten as her dad. Though, she's only nineteen years old.

"Only Lagno and his daughter can break the rules around here and get away with it."

Hans turns around. Three security guards are running toward him. They catch sight of the rifle and stop.

Hans yells, "Don't go for your guns, or I will kill you."

The women from the cashiers' cage run over to the guards and quickly say, "He's after Mr. Lagno. He doesn't want to hurt anybody. He wants us to get all the people out of here safe."

The guards wave at Hans and give him a thumbs up.

Wow, nobody likes Lagno, and they're all scared to death of him. It's surprising that somebody didn't kill him a long time ago.

Quickly Hans gets back into the car and slams it into reverse. He backs through an empty craps table and smashes through four more rows of slots. He stops on the other side of the casino. The car goes bang! The motor stopped. Hans looks at the hood, and smoke's coming out from under it. He blew up the engine.

Hans grabs the rifle and quickly gets out of the car. Then he runs and crouches down between two rows of slot machines. He's looking to his right, over the top of the row he is in. A blackjack dealer's trying to deal, but he's so scared that he throws down the cards and blurts out, "I'm not getting paid enough money to get me killed for this place. I'm getting the hell out of here. The chips are all yours."

Before the dealer could get out of there, another security guard pulled out his pistol, pointed it at the dealer's head, and demanded, "You get back on that table and guard that money and chips, or I'll kill you."

Hans aims the rifle at the security guard's gun and shoots the gun out of his hand before he kills the dealer. The guard yells in pain. His left hand's all bloody. He runs over to the cashier's cage and bangs on the door. The cashier opens the door and lets him in. The cashier opens a first aid kit and wraps his hand.

With a surprised look, the dealer looks over at Hans and yells, "Thank you."

Hans yells back to him, "Your welcome. Now get all these people and yourself out of here."

Hans waves him on.

He waves back.

The people at that table have a free-for-all.

Hans thinks this place is just like the ship. No one gets fired or quits. They get killed.

At the end of the row, people are grabbing money, and the chips rolling in between the slots all over the place. They're hitting each other and fighting over them. They will not leave, even though shots have been fired, and they're not paying any attention to the security. Before getting to the end of the row, Hans fires the rifle just over the people's heads.

Some people run out of the casino, and some women scream. Most of them are not paying any attention to the shots. They keep right on fighting for the chips on the floor.

They yell at each other: "Those chips are mine!"

"No, they're not! They're mine!"

The women are just as bad as the men.

Hans fires shots again just over their heads. They all stop and look over at him this time. They stare in horror when they spot the rifle. But still, two men reach for a silver dollar.

Hans points the rifle right at them and yells, "Dammit, it's only a dollar. Will you people get the hell out of here?"

The two men gasp, and a woman screams. They all turn and run out the door.

Hans stops at the end of that row and slowly looks over the top and back at the other side.

From straight across the room, Jeff comes running out of a door and into the casino with a pistol in his hand. He stops and looks around. Coming out from behind the slots. Hans yells, "Over here,

Jeff, you son-of-a-bitch!"

He looks over at Hans and yells, "Damn you, I'll kill you." He points his gun at him. Hans shoots first, and Jeff falls to the floor dead.

Hans runs past the front door and comes to some more slot machines. He runs in between two rows and crouches low just in time because bullets are zinging over his head and shattering the tops of the slots.

While running along the row, Hans pulls the empty magazine out of the rifle and throws it down. He takes another one out of his coat pockets and reloads the rifle.

Hans comes to the end of the row, stops, and carefully looks around. To his left is the bar. Straight ahead is the roulette room. To his right are more rows of slots. They stretch back to the other side of the casino.

Hans's surprised when he looks down the rows. People are still gambling. A woman says to the man next to her, "Honey, some lady just came running up to me. She's mad and complaining that somebody ran over her slot machine with a car and then got out of the car and started shooting a gun."

"Oh really?" the man replies. "She must have lost all her money on it. I'm sure winning on this one." He laughs and keeps right on playing.

She shrieks, "Oh, honey, I got a cherry!"

Hans can't believe it. These people are so involved with their gambling that they can't see or hear anything but the sound of those slots.

Right behind them is an old woman, about eighty years old, all by herself, who's playing a machine. She keeps looking over at the guy's quarters in his payout tray.

Going four rows over from them, Hans walks slowly, down low to his right. Getting about even to where those people are playing, he stops and slowly looks over the top, toward them, and a little way past. To his right, a black security guard is running along the same row those people are in.

He yells, "You people have to leave!"

Before he can say more, he sees Hans and stops. He goes for his gun. Hans swings the rifle toward him and fires before he can shoot Hans. Hans shoots him once in the right shoulder and once in the right thigh. He drops his gun and falls to the floor. He's still alive. Hans shoots his gun and pushes it far away from him. He has to crawl to get to it.

The man gasps, and the woman screams. They run out of the casino.

Hans runs down to the end of the roll and to where those people were. The security guard is lying on the floor, trying to get his gun. The couple has left, but the old woman is still there. She isn't playing; she's scooping up all the money out of the tray where the man was and putting it all in her purse. After she gets all the quarters, she slowly walks away with a cane in her hand.

Boy, people are really something else!

Hans looks over at the front door. A whole bunch of men slowly came toward Hans with guns. They're not dressed like security guards.

Oh shit! Hans has got to make every shot count.

He hopes Sam and the others get here soon.

They are all low behind the slot machines. Suddenly, some other men are running through the front door. They all have rifles. They start shooting toward the men coming after Hans.

John and Sam run into the casino. Carlos races in after them. Most of the ship's crew's here.

Hans gets down real low and keeps watching for any sign of Lagno's men.

There's nothing but guns shooting and bullets flying all over the place.

Hans is staying low and working his way around to the door that Jeff came out of. He opens it, goes in, and closes the door behind him.

Hans's in a long hallway and slowly walks down it. There are a lot of offices along the way. Suddenly there's a door with the words "Mr. Lagno's Office" on it.

Walking over to it, the door is open a little. Lagno's loud voice says, "Dammit, can't anybody get that squirrel Edwards, or whatever his real name is. He's just one man. That lucky son of a bitch must have killed Blane and Max because they're not back yet, and he's here in the casino. We'll have to kill him by ourselves.

Lagno's alone with just one of his gorillas. Hans runs on through the hallway. He hears a gunshot and feels a little sting on his left shoulder as he runs into an empty office.

A voice says, "He's in the last office, and I think I hit him."

Hans looks at his left shoulder. There's a tear in his coat. Hans feels the wound with his right hand. He doesn't feel anything wet. Looks at his right hand and doesn't find any blood. The shooter just nicked Hans. Hans waits just inside the door. He sticks the rifle out the doorway and starts shooting back toward Lagno's office. Hans stops shooting. Suddenly, from behind him, Hans hears a side door from another office open. He quickly turns around and dives to the floor behind a desk. Bullets are hitting the desk and all around.

Hans's crawling around to the side of the desk. The gorilla's standing in the doorway, shooting at the desk and all around it.

Laying on his left side up against the desk, Hans points the rifle at him and starts shooting him. He falls to the floor dead.

Hans stops shooting, quickly pulls the empty magazine out, throws it down, reaches into a pocket, gets another one, and loads it into the rifle.

Hans gets up from the floor, walks to the front doorway, and looks out toward Lagno's office in the hallway. He's not there.

Hans steps out into the hallway and cautiously walks to Lagno's office. The door has been left open. Just before he gets to it, Hans looks just inside the door, and a little to the right, there's a picture hanging on the wall and a reflection of Lagno from the picture's glass. He's slowly coming to the door with a pistol in his hand. He stops just inside the door.

Lagno yells, Edwards! You son of a bitch. I'm going to kill you." He starts shooting as he runs out into the doorway.

Just in time, Hans quickly runs back into the office and runs around to an open side door to the other office. He steps over a dead body and runs into the other office to the front door. The shooting stops. Hans slowly looks out the door. Lagno is slowly walking toward the first office. Hans softly walks out into the hallway, with the rifle ready, and yells, "Hey, Shit Head.

As Lagno turns around toward Hans, he starts shooting wild.

Hans quickly starts shooting back at him, about the same time Lagno started shooting. He falls to the floor dead, face down. Hans stops shooting.

Hans walks over to him and looks down at him. He takes his foot and rolls him over on his back. Hans shot him several times in the chest.

Coming from the casino door, a voice shouts, "Cowboy!"

Quickly twirling around, Hans brings the rifle up and then relaxes. It's Sam, John, and Carlos coming through it. They run over and look down at Lagno.

Sam slaps Hans on his shoulder and asks, "Are you all right, Cowboy?"

Hans nods and grins.

John kicks Lagno in the head. "It's about time somebody killed this son-of-a-bitch.

"We got them all back in there. When they saw all of us come in the front door, we fired some shots over their heads, and I yelled, Lagno isn't worth getting killed for. One of them yells back, "You're right." They all put down their guns and walked out the door. We didn't kill anybody. We got all the rest of the people out of here. The casino's all locked up. No one can get in."

Carlos remarks, I saw Lisa's body in the cashier's cage. You still want to burn the casino down, Cowboy?"

Hans replies, "The casino's all yours if you want it. I had to kill a total of eight people. Starting with the ship hijacking, to this. I'm not happy about killing anybody. But it was all in self-defense. They all tried to kill me first. The one that killed Pete, I couldn't kill him fast enough to save Pete. I'm not going to stay here and try to prove it to the law. The main thing is Jesus knows. I don't have to prove anything to him. I'm going home to run the farm. Do what you want. Burn it down, or keep it, and try and make a go of it."

Sam remarks, "Come on, Carlos, let's keep it and try and make a go of it."

Carlos agrees, "Okay, we'll keep it."

There's a door at the other end of the hallway with an exit sign. They all walk out the door into the street.

Looking at the street, Sam quickly says, "Here comes one of your guys in a car, John. Come on, let's get the hell out of here."

The car stops, and they all get in, head for the four-lane highway in front of the casino, and pull up to a stop sign.

Hans's in the backseat on the right side. They have rifles on the floor. All of them are trying to look as cool as they can so no one would notice them because, just to the right, the lawn still has some people on it, and they're still fighting over the chips and money.

Right there on the corner is one of the blackjack dealers. He's laughing and pointing at something. Hans looks over at what he's pointing at. There's a man with a swollen eye, bloody nose, bloody lip, and a cut ear. He looks like he's been in a worse fight than they had. He has the front of his shirt tail out of his pants, with both hands holding the bottom of his shirttail up like a bag. It's overflowing with gambling chips. From their colors, there are five-dollar, twenty-five-dollar, and one-hundred-dollar chips.

With a big grin on his face, he asked the dealer, "What the hell are you laughing at, smart-ass? You don't have any money in your hands."

Still, laughing, the dealer replies with another question, "Where in the hell do you plan to cash in those chips? The only place those chips are any good is in this casino, and it's all closed and locked up, and I don't know if it will ever be open again or not. You can't spend them anyplace else."

The man's mouth drops wide open. He whimpers, "You mean they're no good? I damn near got killed over them."

The dealer shakes his head and remarks, "No, they're not."

The man falls to his knees, drops the chips, and starts crying loudly.

The News media and an ambulance get here, but no cops yet.

Hans remembers the wounded guard and wonders if that is why the ambulance is here.

The driver of their car pulls onto the highway, turns left, and heads straight to the ship.

Just as soon as they get aboard the ship, the crew gets it untied, and they head out to sea.

They all meet up on the bridge. John has a happy grin and says, "I think I will run down to the office and bring us up a bottle of whiskey. We can all use a snort."

Looking out at the open sea sure is a welcome sight, knowing that now Hans's finally on the way back home.

John gets back, and they all have a few drinks.

Hans remarks, "We took Lagno's ship, and we took his casino. It all turned out better than I thought it would. It wasn't all for nothing. I'm going home.

Suddenly, one of John's office workers comes up, opens the side door, and demands, "All of you guys, come down to the office. You've got to see this."

They all follow him down to the office.

The TV is on with a special live breaking newscast, showing a live shot of Lagno's casino.

A lady reporter states, "Mr. Deano Lagno, the casino owner, is dead. He was shot earlier today. I have one of the cashiers here. This is Margie.

Hans remarks, "She's the cashier I talked into helping me get all the people out of the casino.

Margie comments, "Today's a great day. Justice has finally been served. Deano Lagno and his daughter Lisa are the most corrupt and dangerous people I have ever known. He kept a low profile. He wouldn't meet with anyone in person unless he just had to. Most businesses and charities only knew him by his name. He would give a large amount of money to charities for a tax write-off so that people would like him.

"My husband and I went to work here in nineteen sixty-six. A year later, my husband decided to go into real estate. He went to Lagno to give him his two weeks' notice. I never saw my husband alive again. A week later, his body washed up on the beach with three bullets in his head.

"That's when I found out that, through the years, many other former employees that quit or got fired just disappeared, or some of their bodies were found with bullets in their heads. We all suspect Lagno of killing them all! But we can't prove it.

"I knew if I tried to leave, I'd be killed. Against my will, I still work there and raise three kids by myself.

"This is revenge time for me and a lot of the rest of us.

"We all got paid good and got bonuses at Christmas.

Through this news coverage, I would like to show the world the real face of Lagno. It's because many of the Royal Freeport police are corrupt and in Lagno's hip pocket and are paid well to look the other way."

"My three trusted security officers and I are going to take you into the casino and go down into the basement to prove to you and the world that Lagno is human trafficking young teenage girls, along with guns and drug smuggling. The corrupt police would have gotten rid of the proof before you could have seen it.

"I and one of the guards, that's an off-duty cop and isn't corrupt, went to the only Judge on the island we could find that's available to get a search warrant and make this legal. He wasn't going to give it to us at first. I think he's on Lagno's payroll. I told him it would look like you have something to hide if he didn't give it to us. He finally gave it to us. When I closed his door, we heard a bang. I went back into the office to find that the judge shot and killed himself."

Margie unlocks the casino door and states, "This's the only key I have. The off-duty cop got the keys to the other rooms from Lagno's body."

The news crew and one of the ambulance drivers follow Margie and the guards into the casino with the camera on. They come to a freight elevator. They all go in. They go down one floor, and it stops. One of the guards opens a control panel and flips a switch. The elevator goes down one more floor.

Margie states, "I have never been on this floor before."

The elevator door opens. They all go out into a hallway and stop. To the left, there's a door, and it's locked.

One of the guards with the keys opens the door. The room's full of single beds and scared teenage girls.

Margie tells the girls, "You're safe now."

The ambulance driver checks out the girls to ensure they're all okay.

They go across the hall. The guard unlocks and opens the door and goes inside. The room is filled with models of rifles, pistols, ammunition, and grenades.

 In the third room, they find a lot of drugs, mostly cocaine.

Back outside, the news reporter states, "The U.S. F.B.I. is working with the Royal Freeport police to investigate Lagno's death.

"This has been a special breaking news report."

John turns the TV off and remarks, "Well, now the whole world knows what a bastard Lagno was."

Hans says, "Wow, we could have ripped off Lagno's casino for the guns.

"The cops might be all over this ship when we pull into Mami tomorrow. Just because we just came in from the Bahamas.

"We better get rid of everything we got from the National Guard, Amory. There's going to be one hell of an investigation. They already suspect that the Amory, the sheriff's office rip, and the ship hijacking are connected."

Carlos demands, "Cowboy, don't worry about that. We'll take care of it all tonight."

Hans replies, "Okay. Where's Jennifer?"

Sam replies, "Come with me, and I'll take you to her. We have a room for her and you."

They get to the room. Sam knocks on the door and says, "Jennifer, this is Sam and Cowboy. Please open the door."

She opens the door with a big smile on her face.

Sam says, "I'll see you later." He leaves.

Hans steps in and closes the door.

The next morning after shaving and showering, Hans gets dressed.

As Jennifer is getting dressed, Hans looks at her, grinning, and remarks, "We have got some unfinished business to take care of."

Jennifer looks at Hans with a worried look and asks, "What's that?"

"John is the captain of this ship. Let's ask him if he will perform a wedding ceremony for us." Hans's still grinning.

Jennifer's eyes light up, and with a big smile on her face, she throws her arms around Hans and shrieks, "Yes, I will marry you." She kisses him.

They have their bags packed. Hans put his western hat on.

They get up to the main deck and look around. The day is sunny and warm, with a little breeze. Hans discovers that they're docking at Miami, and there aren't any cops aboard the ship looking around. So far, anyway.

They walk over to where they're getting the gangplank set up. John, Sam, Carlos, Mary, and JoAnn are already there.

Jennifer and Hans walk up to them, holding their bags. They set the bags down on the deck.

Jennifer, smiling, asks John, "Would you take the honor of getting us married?"

John looks at them, surprised. He smiles and says, "I sure can and will do that. Let me go get the wedding book." He goes for the book.

Hans looks over at Sam and Carlos. They're standing there with shit-eating grins on their faces.

Hans suggests, "Mary and JoAnn will you be Jennifer's maids of honor?"

They both agree.

Sam and Carlos, "Will you both be my best men?"

Sam laughs and replies. We sure do."

Carlos laughs and remarks, "This wedding isn't very customary, Cowboy."

Hans laughs and replies, "When have you ever known me to be customary about anything?"

Jennifer laughs, "I'm so excited that I forgot all about rings. We don't have any rings."

Hans replies, "Let's not worry about the rings. We can stop someplace on the road and get a couple of rings."

John gets back with the wedding book and a marriage license.

Mary and JoAnn are standing on the left side of Jennifer. Sam and Carlos are standing to the right of Hans.

John starts, "We're gathered here together to unite this young couple in holy matrimony.

"Cowboy, repeat after me. I, Hans Metzger, take thee, Jennifer Bacco, to be my wedded wife,"

Hans repeats, I, Hans Metzger, take thee, Jennifer Bacco, to be my wedded wife."

John continues. "To have and to hold from this day forward."

Hans repeats, "To have and to hold from this day forward."

John continues, "For better, for worse, for richer, for poorer, in sickness and in health."

Hans repeats, "For better, for worse. For richer, for poorer, in sickness and in health."

John continues, "To love and to cherish, till death do us part."

Hans repeats, "To love and to cherish, till death do us part."

John turns to Jennifer and starts, "Jennifer, repeat, after me, I, Jennifer Bacco, take thee, Hans Metzger, to be my wedded husband."

Jennifer Repeats, "I, Jennifer Bacco, take thee, Hans Metzger, to be my wedded husband,

Before John could speak.

Jennifer continues, "To have and to hold from this day forward, for better, for worse, for richer, for poorer, in sickness and in health, to love and to cherish, till death do us part."

Everybody looked surprised, including Hans when Jennifer said the whole vow without John's help.

John contuses, "With no rings, I now pronounce you husband and wife. You may kiss the bride."

Hans kisses the bride.

After the wedding, Hans shakes John's hand and happily says, "Thank you for everything. The M-sixteens and ammunition are all yours. I don't want anything to do with them anymore. Good luck with the ship."

John replies with a smile, "Thanks, Cowboy. If you ever come back this way again, look me up. I will always have a job here aboard the ship if you need one. I have a job for all three of you guys."

"No thanks, John. The sea's not for me."

Jennifer shakes hands with John and gives him a hug. She softly says, "Thank you for the ride and the wedding."

John replies, "Your welcome. Your car is on the pier."

Hans hugs and shakes hands with Sam and Carlos. "Good luck, you guys. If you ever get up to Idaho, look me up. It would be fun to get together and go hunting. From now on, let's kill for food. No more people!"

They all laugh and agree that that's a damn good idea.

Jennifer shakes hands with Sam and Carlos and gives them a hug. She softly says, "Have fun, and good luck with the casino.

They both get a hug from Mary and JoAnn.

The gangplank is set up. They pick up their bags. Hans happily says, "Idaho, here we come." They leave the ship, walk over to Jennifer's car, get in, and Hans puts the car top down and drives away.

As Hans is driving, he says a silent prayer to himself. "Dear Jesus, I want to start over with a clean slate. Allow me to lead a meaningful life and forgive all my misdeeds. I forgive that corrupt sheriff for trying to kill me and Lagno and his gorillas for trying to kill me. That wasn't revenge. It was self-defense, not revenge. Please forgive me for killing Lagno and his two gorillas. Please forgive me for killing the man that killed Pete. I didn't know who he killed until afterward. I forgive Lisa for trying to kill me. Forgive me for killing Lisa and Lagno's hit men and gorillas, including the V. C. I had to kill in Vietnam. Please forgive me. Amen."

www.ingramcontent.com/pod-product-compliance
Ingram Content Group UK Ltd.
Pitfield, Milton Keynes, MK11 3LW, UK
UKHW061222180426
11947UKWH00026B/1971